*I've lived a thousand lives
and traveled to unknown lands
on waves of italic print and ships
made from printed paper.*
~ Aurora Rose Reynolds

Gareth Black is drawn to December Mayson the moment he spots her across the room at her cousin's wedding. When he approaches the beautiful woman, she captivates him with her shyness and wit, making him crave her.

With a pull so strong it's impossible to ignore, December knows there's something between her and Gareth. She just hopes they're capable of jumping the hurdles ahead of them.

Two boys, an ex, a surprise that will change everything, and a disgruntled co-worker, guarantee these two will have their work cut out for them if they are going to find their happily ever after.

PRAISE FOR AURORA ROSE REYNOLDS

"No other author can bring alpha perfection to each page as phenomenally as Aurora Rose Reynolds can. She's the queen of alphas!"

~Author CC Monroe

"Aurora Rose Reynolds makes you wish book boyfriends weren't just between the pages."

~Jenika Snow *USA Today* Bestselling Author

"Aurora Rose Reynolds writes stories that you lose yourself in. Every single one is literary gold."

~Jordan Marie *USA Today* Bestselling Author

"No one does the BOOM like Aurora Rose Reynolds"

~Author Brynne Asher

"With her yummy alphas and amazing heroines, Aurora Rose Reynolds never fails to bring the BOOM."

~Author Layla Frost

"Aurora Rose Reynolds alphas are what woman dream about."

~Author S. Van Horne

"When Aurora Rose Reynolds lowers the BOOM, there isn't a reader alive that can resist diving headfirst into the explosion she creates."

~Author Sarah O'Rourke

"Aurora Rose Reynolds was my introduction into Alpha men and I haven't looked back!"

~Author KL Donn

"Reynolds is a master at writing stories that suck you in and make you block out the world until you're done."

~Susan Stoker *NYT* Bestselling Author

When Aurora Rose Reynolds has a new story out, it's time for me to drop whatever I'm working on and dive into her world of outrageously alpha heroes and happily ever afters.

~Author Rochelle Paige

Aurora Rose leaves you yearning for more. Her characters stick with you long after you've finished the book.

~Author Elle Jefferson

Reynolds books are the perfect way to spend a weekend. Lost in her alpha males and endearing heorines.

~Author CP Smith

OTHER BOOKS BY AURORA ROSE REYNOLDS

The Until Series
Until November
Until Trevor
Until Lilly
Until Nico
Second Chance Holiday

Underground Kings Series
Assumption
Obligation
Distraction

Until Her Series
Until July
Until June
Until Ashlyn
Until Harmony
Until December

Until Him Series
Until Jax
Until Sage
Until Cobi

Shooting Stars Series
Fighting to Breathe
Wide-Open Spaces
One last Wish

Fluke my life series
Running into love
Stumbling into love
Tossed into love
Drawn Into Love

Ruby Falls
Falling Fast

Alpha Law CA ROSE
Justified
Liability
Finders Keepers
One More Time (Coming soon)

How To Catch An Alpha
Catching Him (Coming soon)
Baiting Him (Coming soon)
Hooking Him (Coming soon)

UNTIL HER *BOOK FIVE*

Aurora Rose Reynolds

Acknowledgments

Firstly, I have to give thanks to God, because without him none of this would be possible. Secondly, I want to thank my husband. I love you now and always—thank you for believing in me even when I don't always believe in myself. To my beautiful son, you bring such joy into my life, and I'm so honored to be your mom.

To every blog and reader, thank you for taking the time to read and share my books. There would never be enough ink in the world to acknowledge you all, but I will forever be grateful to each and every one of you.

I started this writing journey after I fell in love with reading, like thousands of authors before me. I wanted to give people a place to escape where the stories were funny, sweet, and hot and left you feeling good. I have loved sharing my stories with you all, loved that I have helped people escape the real world, even for a moment.

I started writing for me and will continue writing for you. XOXO Aurora

This isn't a dedication it's a request.

If you ever have the opportunity to **jump,** *DO IT*!

UNTIL HER *BOOK FIVE*

M A Y

James Trevor

Asher & November

Trevor & Liz

Hanna
Cobi

July
June
May
December
April

James
Dean
Tia
Conner

B E L I E V E   I N

S O N

Susan Elizabeth

Cash & Lilly

Jax
Ashlyn

Hope
Jasper
Edward
Toby
Destiny

Nico & Sophie

Willow
Harmony
Bax
Talon
Sage
Nalia

Ava
Lillian
Alistair
Nash

THE   BOOM!

December

Prologue

$\mathcal{I}$ SIP FROM my fourth—or maybe it's my fifth—glass of wine, not caring one little bit that I'm officially past tipsy or that April and I are both going to have to find rides home tonight. Not that it will take us very long to find people willing to cart us home with our family and friends all here. Most of them are currently out on the dance floor, letting loose to the loud music the DJ is playing. I should be out there with them, but instead, I'm sitting in a dark corner of the room drinking alone.

Okay, I'm actually hiding.

I fan my hand in front of my warm face, unsure if it's hot in here or if the wine is making me feel overheated. I need air, water… and air. I stand, swaying slightly, and catch April looking at me. She's currently pressed tightly to the side of a large man who seems to be enjoying her company, judging by the hand he's had on her bottom for the last twenty minutes. I read her look, the question in her eyes asking if I'm okay, if I need her.

"She really is a good sister, even if she did claim Gareth first," I mutter drunkenly to myself before I give her a dorky thumbs-up and point toward the exit door. She nods one time before focusing once more on the guy she's clinging to. I set down my empty wine glass and pick up an untouched glass of water off one of the tables. I gulp it down before I move toward the bright sign in the back of the room.

When I step outside, I silently congratulate myself for making it without falling on my face in these shoes. The black, clingy dress I have on couldn't be worn with my usual flats, so I'm wearing sandals, high ones, with pointy toes and a slim heel. They look sexy but are sucking the life out of my feet. I lift one foot from the ground to rid myself of the torture devices then giggle as I stumble sideways.

"I got you." Strong arms wrap around me, keeping me from tumbling to the ground, and I shiver from the embrace despite the fact that I feel so overheated.

I glance up and my cheeks grow even hotter than they already are as I look into Gareth's eyes. "Seriously? My luck sucks."

"What?" he asks as he chuckles, the warm sound vibrating against my back and through me.

"Nothing." I turn around to face him, taking a step back. He doesn't let me go completely. His heavy palm is still wrapped around my hip like he doesn't believe I'll be able to hold myself up. "Please ignore anything I say or do from this point on."

His gaze bores into mine before he asks, "So you want me to ignore you like you've been ignoring me all night?"

I have been ignoring him. After April joined us at the bar and told him that I'm always a good girl, I made my escape and have avoided him since then.

I close my eyes and what happened earlier this evening plays through my mind like a movie.

I watch the happy couple enter the ballroom, along with everyone else, and smile when my cousin lifts his new wife's hand in the air, grinning hugely before he spins her around to face him. When he has her where he wants her, he dips her back over his arm and kisses her. Everyone applauds and laughs, including me. I'm happy for him, but happier for Hadley. Over the last few months, we've gotten really close, and I know from her past that she deserves her happily ever after more than most people do.

"I wonder who's next," my sister April says, and I look over at her, feeling myself frown.

2

"What?"

"I wonder who's next. You know—the next person who's going to fall in love. It seems to be happening at an alarming rate." She takes a drink from her beer and glances around. *"I'm saying not it. I have no desire to be shot at or kidnapped just to find love."*

"You're so dramatic." I shake my head at her.

"Am I?"

Okay, she's not. There seems to be a theme when it comes to anyone with the Mayson last name falling in love. But still.

"Are you going to drink?" she asks, changing the subject and studying the glass of water in my hand.

"Probably not." I move to one of the tables set up around the dance floor and take a seat, smiling at a few people I know who are already sitting down.

"Good, you get to be my DD for the night," she says, sitting in the seat next to mine.

"Great," I sigh, not really looking forward to babysitting her all night to make sure she doesn't do anything stupid. I love my sister, but she tends to push the boundaries of stupidity.

"Who's that?"

I look in the direction her eyes are pointed, and the world around me seems to come to a standstill. Across the room, talking to my cousin Sage and Brie's husband Kenyon, is a guy. Not just a guy, but the most gorgeous guy I have ever seen in my life. He's tall, taller than Sage, and almost as tall as Kenyon, who's practically a giant compared to everyone. His dark brown hair is longer on top and clipped short on the sides. He's in profile, so I can't see all of his face, but his jaw, covered in a rough-looking beard, is all sharp edges and straight lines. He has tattoos peeking out from above the edge of his collared shirt, and more on his thick forearms that I can see where his sleeves are rolled up to his elbows. His arms are so huge I doubt I could wrap both my hands around one of his biceps.

When he turns his body in my direction and smiles at something Sage says, my breath catches. I thought he was handsome in profile, but I was wrong. Straight on, his look is captivating and mysterious, with thick brows over his piercing blue eyes and full lips surrounded by his beard.

"Whoever he is, I'm taking him home tonight," my sister says, and my stomach plummets. "God, he's hot. I can't wait."

I swallow the sudden unexpected jealousy I'm feeling and really wish I hadn't agreed to be her DD, because I don't just need a drink, I need a whole bottle of tequila right now.

"Don't do anything stupid," I hiss, cutting her off and catching her gaze.

"Getting laid is not stupid. You'd know that if you ever tried it once in a while."

I bite my tongue to keep myself from saying something mean then look around the room for a place to escape. The sign for the restroom is like a neon flashing light catching my attention. I stand up. "I'll be back," I mumble, before I scurry away with my head down and my heart lodged in my throat.

Since growing up, my sisters and I have had a rule. If one of us likes a guy, he's completely off limits, even if he's not interested in whoever has a crush on him. That rule has saved us on more than one occasion, but now I wish the stupid rule didn't exist. When I get to the restroom, I walk to one of the stalls and stand there trying to get myself under control.

I know April, know she's probably already made a move to talk to whoever he is, and know without a doubt that he will be interested, because I have never met a guy who isn't interested in her. She's beautiful, funny, and outgoing—three things I am not. I'm cute enough, can be funny when I'm with my friends or family, but it takes time for me to warm up to people I don't know. I'm also the opposite of outgoing. I prefer books and laziness to getting out and having adventures. I have always been the same way.

After I know I'm not going to do something crazy, like punch my sister in the face, I leave the bathroom and start to head toward the bar, figuring one glass of wine won't hurt. I place my order with the bartender then lean into the wood bar top with my forearms.

"You're Sage's cousin, right?" a deep voice asks, and my hair stands on end while butterflies take flight in my stomach.

I don't have to look to know it's him speaking. Still, I tip my head *way back to catch his gaze. Lord, save me. He's tall and so beautiful. I thought I got that from across the room, but seeing him up close is something else.*

"I think he told me you were." His brows draw together over his blue eyes surrounded by thick lashes as I stare at him.

I mentally slap myself and force my mouth to start working. "Yes, I'm December."

His brow relaxes and he leans into the bar next to me with his hip, crossing his arms over his chest. "Another month." His eyes twinkle with humor.

"Pardon?"

"Met a July, June, May, and April. Now, December."

At the mention of April, my stomach twists. "Our parents were keeping with a theme." I pick up my wine and take a very unladylike gulp. Why didn't I see him first?

"Gareth." His hand comes my way. I don't want to take it, really don't want to, but my manners force me to place my hand in his. When his rough, warm strength envelops my hand, my breath sticks in my lungs. "It's nice to meet you."

I lick my lips, and whisper, "You too." With my hand still held in his, his gaze searches mine. The intense look in his eyes makes me feel funny, makes me feel like he sees some part of me I don't even know about.

"I thought you weren't drinking." My eyes close, blocking out Gareth, as April suddenly tosses her arm around my shoulders. "You're such a rebel, drinking wine when you're supposed to get me home safely."

"It's just one glass. I'll be fine to drive you home later." I open my eyes and turn my head to look at her.

"I know," she agrees, looking at me, and then she looks at Gareth and smiles. "My sister is a good girl. She always follows the rules."

God, I really wish that weren't true.

"Ember." Warm fingers wrap around my jaw, and I blink away the memory and focus on Gareth's handsome face that is closer than before.

"Did you just call me Ember?" I frown, offended he's forgotten my name already.

"Baby, your name represents the cold, but standing in front of you, I feel nothing but heat."

"It's because I'm drunk."

"What?"

"My body is producing heat in order to burn off the alcohol I've consumed," I tell him matter-of-factly. I leave out that the feel of his hard muscles pressed against my soft body is making me stupid, causing my mouth to form words and speak them without my permission.

"Maybe we should get you somewhere you can cool down."

"I'm outside," I point out while looking around.

"Yeah, but I was thinking more along the lines of a cold shower."

She's always a good girl.

April's words from earlier ring through my mind and my hand balls into a fist. Screw that. For once in my life, I'm going to be bad.

December

Chapter 1

BEFORE I EVEN open my eyes, I know I'm not in my bed. The sheet I'm under isn't soft but rough, and there is bright light pooling in through my normally dark curtains. Still... it's not the sheets nor the bright light seeping through my closed eyelids that leads me to the conclusion that I'm not in my bed. It's the scent of musk and man, and the heavy arm holding me close. I want to relish the feeling of being held like I am. I want to soak up every detail of this moment, but I know... I know the arm holding me so close, so possessively, is the same one that could start a war between me and my sister. Even if April was enjoying the company of another man last night, rules are rules, and my no longer drunken mind reminds me of them loudly in the bright light of day.

With my heart feeling suddenly heavy inside my chest, I carefully and quietly get up. I'm thankfully still fully clothed, wearing my dress from last night, except my shoes. Shoes Gareth rid me of as I lay on his bed. His bed that he curled himself around me in moments later, ordering me gruffly to go to sleep instead of what I really wanted to do and could tell he did too, judging by his hard-on I felt lying heavy between us.

My eyes slide closed. I can't think about his sweet gesture right now. Right now, I need to get out of here before I do something stupid, like climb back into bed with him, or worse, go to his kitchen to make him breakfast. As quietly as I can, I pick up my shoes and purse from the floor and move toward the door. It's only a couple steps, but it feels like it takes forever to finally grasp the silver handle.

After I turn the knob, I look over my shoulder to make sure the man in the bed behind me is still asleep as the door creaks open. Seeing he's just as I left him—his head on his pillow, his strong features relaxed, and his big strong body shut down—I take a second to memorize every detail, hoping it will be enough to get me through the rest of my boring life.

Shutting the door behind me, I walk down a short hallway and stop suddenly just inside the living room that is open to the kitchen. I didn't have time to look around last night. The moment Gareth let us inside, he kissed me and didn't stop until we were in his room. Taking it all in now, I'm surprised. The place looks like a home, not a bachelor pad. It's gorgeous, bright, and updated, with black cabinets in the kitchen and speckled granite on the counters. The furniture in the living room is worn from use, but there are pictures hanging on the walls—some art and some family photos in well-chosen frames. Knickknacks and books are on the built-in shelves, and boy paraphernalia from video games to sports equipment is scattered across the room.

I want to examine the space and photos for clues about Gareth's life, but I don't allow myself the opportunity. I rush to the front door, open it, and step outside. I look around to try to figure out where I am, and my stomach drops to my toes. Across the street is Harmony's car parked in front of her house, with her husband's bike parked next to it. Gareth... My eyes close briefly. I can't believe he is the single dad Harmony mentioned to me and the girls after one of his sons hit a baseball into her car.

Hoping my cousin and her man are still asleep in their bed with no way of seeing me, I put on my shoes and move down the porch to the sidewalk. I hurry to the end of the block and send for an Uber to pick me up. Wrapping my arms around myself, I sigh. I look ridiculous waiting in the chilly morning air, wearing my makeup, dress, and heels from last night. My only saving grace is that it's early and no one seems to be awake yet.

I watch the street for the Nissan that's supposed to pick me up, and frown when it turns the corner with rap music blaring from the interior. When the car stops at the edge of the sidewalk before me, I look through the passenger window at the white kid wearing a backward baseball cap. He looks no older than sixteen, and I wonder if he should even be behind the wheel.

The window goes down but the music doesn't. It just gets louder as it escapes the confines of the car. "December?"

"Yes."

"I'm your ride," he says before rolling up the window without another word.

I check the app on my phone to confirm he is in fact my ride, then open the back door and get in.

"Yo," he greets me over his shoulder, smiling as I put on my seat belt. "Good night?"

"Yeah." I drop my eyes to my phone and ignore the missed calls and texts from April, scanning Instagram so I won't be forced into an awkward conversation. Not that the kid could hear me over the music, even if I wanted to talk. Halfway to my apartment, the battery dies on my phone, but I still keep my eyes on the black screen until I'm home.

Once I'm inside my apartment, I go right to the kitchen and set out food for Melbourne, my invisible cat. He's not really invisible, but he might as well be. I never see him except when he's in need of food or attention—the latter very rare.

After I'm done, I walk to my bedroom and strip out of my dress. I brush my teeth as the shower warms up, then step in and let the hot water run over me. I try not to think about Gareth, but I can't help but wonder if he's realized I'm gone, and then I think about what his reaction might have been when he woke up alone.

Maybe he didn't care that a woman snuck out on him. But in my heart, I want to believe he did.

Once I've washed my hair, conditioned it, and have scrubbed myself from head to toe, I get out and dry off. I wrap myself in my robe then go to the kitchen and make myself a single cup of coffee and some toast. I sit on one of the two barstools at the makeshift island in my kitchen and eat in silence before I go back to my room and put on my favorite sweats and hoodie.

Relaxing on my couch a couple of hours later with a new book, a bag of Cheetos, and a Diet Coke, I groan when my cell phone rings from my bedroom where I plugged it in to charge. I reluctantly get up to answer it then debate taking the call when I see it's April. I must think too long, because the ringing ends, and a notification for a missed call lights up the screen, right before the ringing starts back up again.

Knowing she won't give up, I slide my finger across the screen, and with a sigh, I put the phone to my ear. "Hey."

"Hey? Seriously?" she snaps. "Did you not see I've been calling you since last night, after you disappeared? I swear if Uncle Trevor hadn't told me that you caught a ride home, I was going to call the cops and organize a search party."

Thank goodness I had the sense last night to tell my uncle when I was grabbing my purse that I was catching a ride home and to let everyone know I was okay.

"Sorry, I was tired. All I was thinking about was going to bed and my cell died. I didn't charge it until after I got up." I head back toward the couch and take a seat. "Did you have fun?" I want to... no, *need* to change the subject.

She snorts. "Of course I did. Now, answer your door. I'm outside."

"You're here?" I look toward the door like I can see through it.

"Yeah, now let me in. My hands are full."

I get up, and as soon as I unlock the locks and turn the handle, she pushes her way in. I accept the cup of iced coffee she thrusts at me as she walks by, then shut the door. "It's always too damn quiet in here," she informs me as she plops down on my couch, looking around.

My apartment is small, just one bedroom and one and a half baths. The eat-in kitchen is separated by a wall from the living room, and the living room is just big enough for my fluffy green couch, where I read. I have a TV hooked up on a stand across the room, but I don't normally watch it, since I read so much all the time.

"I was reading. I like it quiet when I read." I do like it quiet when I read, but from time to time, I'll play music, especially if an author I love has a playlist attached to their book.

"You're always reading." She rolls her eyes toward the ceiling then drops them back down to me, getting an odd light in her eyes and a smirk on her lips. "So you left with Gareth last night."

Holy crap, she knows. My fingers clench around the cold cup I'm holding, making the ice clink together. Of course she knows. I told Uncle Trevor who my ride was when he asked, and he obviously told her. "Umm...."

"Seriously, I hope you got his number," she states before taking a long sip from her iced coffee.

I sit there slack-jawed, wondering if she's saying I should have gotten his number for her. What the heck? "Why would I do that?" I try to keep the annoyance out of my tone but know it's there.

"Uh, because he was totally into you."

"What?"

"He didn't take his eyes off you all night. Seriously, the Queen of England could have started doing the hand jive on the dance floor and he still wouldn't have spared her a glance."

"What?" I repeat in utter disbelief. I can't believe Gareth was paying that much attention to me. More so, I can't believe she's telling me I should have went for him after what she said about wanting him.

"He was obviously into you." She shrugs.

My mouth opens and closes before I blurt, "You said you wanted hi—"

She waves her hand out between us, cutting me off. "He's hot. Any woman alive would want him. I might think he's attractive, but he's not my type, and he's definitely not interested in me."

"I—"

"So did you get his number?" she cuts me off once more, and I jerk my head from side to side. I didn't get his number. Not only that, but I snuck out on him just a few hours ago. "Did he offer it to you?" She frowns.

"I thought you wanted him." God, I'm an idiot. I snuck out of his bed, out of his house, thinking I was following some stupid rule me and my sisters made up before we even were allowed to shave our legs.

What the hell was I thinking?

I watch her eyes fill with realization then her lips thin. "You thought I wanted him, so that's why you ignored him."

"Worse," I whisper.

"How could it be worse than you ignoring him because of me?"

"I spent the night with him, and then snuck out of his bed this morning and caught an Uber home."

"You didn't," she cries, sitting toward me. "I can't believe you slept with him."

"I didn't. I mean, we slept together, but we didn't sleep together."

"You really are always a good girl," she sighs like she's disappointed.

"You said...." I close my eyes. It doesn't matter what she said; she's always saying things like that. I should have known. "You saw him first." The words sound stupid, even to my own ears. God, I screwed up, seriously screwed up, and I have no one to blame but myself. I left Gareth without an explanation, without even a note. If I were him, I'd be pissed.

"Hey." April's gentle tone and hand touching mine brings my attention back to her, and I open my eyes. "It's gonna be okay."

"I'm not sure. If he.... If the roles were reversed, I would be mad. I'm not sure if I'd ever talk to him again."

"Blame it on me," she says immediately. "Tell him that I called you and needed your help, so you didn't have time to explain things before you took off on him."

"The only issue with that is I don't know his number. I can't exactly send him an 'I'm sorry I snuck away' text."

"Shit." She looks away, her mind obviously working to try to find a solution. "Sage probably has his number. We can ask him for it."

I don't want to ask Sage for his number. No way do I want to answer any questions, but what choice do I have?

"Okay," I agree.

She pulls her phone out then quickly types a message. I wait then hear her phone ping. When her face lights with a smile, I don't know if I should be nervous or excited.

"I got his number. Get your phone."

I pick up my cell and type in the number she shoots off. When he's added to my list of contacts, a small sense of relief fills me.

"Now text him."

"Right." I nibble the inside of my cheek as I type out a text to him. I read the words three times to make sure everything is spelled correctly and sounds believable before I press Send.

I hope you don't mind I got your number from Sage. I'm sorry I left without a word, but I got a message from my sister this morning and had to take off. Thank you for being so sweet and taking care of me last night.

December

A moment later, a bubble appears and I look at April. "He's typing."

"He's not making you wait a year for a return text. That's a good sign." She smiles.

"Hopefully," I agree with a small smile of my own.

I drop my eyes back to my phone when it dings. My smile slides away and chest gets heavy as I read his reply.

Funny, was awake when you got up and know you didn't even look at your cell. Glad you're good, but don't message again. I don't have time for high school bullshit and games.

"What?" April questions, probably reading the look on my face. I don't answer, so she slides my phone out of my hand and reads the message herself. "Oh shit." She stands, still holding my phone, then she starts to pace. "I can't.... I cannot believe he said that to you." She pauses, looking pissed at the phone then me. "I'm going to message him back."

"What? No!" I shout as I shoot off the couch and launch myself at her over my coffee table. I land against her, and we end up getting into a wrestling match that ends with us both on the floor and me straddling her. When I finally get ahold of my phone and have it above my head, we're both breathing heavily. "He obviously wants nothing to do with me. And I understand why."

"But—" April starts, but I shake my head, my hair flying as I do.

"I should have... I should have...." Really, I don't know what I should have done differently. "It doesn't matter. It's over."

"I'm sorry." She sits up, wrapping her arms around my waist. "I should have kept my mouth closed. I just thought when I saw you looking at him that if I provoked you, you'd make a move on him. I knew you thought he was hot, and I—"

"I'm an idiot." I get up before she can finish, pulling my hair out of my face and holding it back with one hand as she pushes up off the ground to stand before me.

"You're not." She grabs my shoulders, forcing me to really focus on her. "Seriously, if he was awake when you got up, he should have said something. He should have done something to make you stay. If anyone is an idiot, it's him for letting you walk away."

I pull in a breath. Maybe she's right. Maybe he should have said something when he saw I was sneaking out. Then again, I probably would have done the same thing he did if the roles were reversed. With only one long-term relationship in my history that seemed to just happen without much intention on my part, I have no idea how to navigate the whole "getting to know you" side of things. Who am I kidding? I know nothing about men unless it's written in a book. And unfortunately, with time, I have come to find that the guys I read about do not exist in real life. Not only because it's rare to meet a multi-millionaire who will whisk you away on his private jet and confess his undying love, but because men are mostly jerks.

On that thought, I look into April's eyes, and declare, "Whatever. It's done."

We hold each other's stare for a long time before she finally agrees with me, looking disappointed about my statement.

Gareth

Chapter 2

*W*ITH MY HAND around my rock hard cock and my face turned into my pillow, breathing deep, I stroke. Pulling hard at the tip and then back down. The visual in my mind is one that's kept me company for the last few mornings. Blonde hair, gorgeous features, and a body made up of nothing but beautiful curves that seemed never ending. I stroke faster, imagining December whispering my name in her soft, sweet voice. I come, and streams of hot cum shoot against my stomach. My strokes turn lazy until the tension has left my stomach and my cock has gone limp.

Feeling relaxed, I stare at the ceiling, thinking about the woman I just got off on, hating the fact that she wasn't what I thought she was. The morning she took off on me, I watched her walk away, even though everything in me demanded I do something to force her to stay. I just couldn't. As I saw her sneaking out of my room, all I could think about was how many times I witnessed Beth do the same thing.

How many times had I attempted to get her to stick around? How many times had I begged her to stay, not for me but for our boys?

I know the circumstances aren't even close to the same, but that didn't have an effect on the disappointment I felt settling in my gut when the door closed behind December.

"Fuck," I hiss, getting up and heading to my bathroom. I try to block out thoughts of December and how I might have fucked things up between us because of my past, as I shower and then move to get dressed in my walk-in closet. Only when I'm dressed and have my boots on do I come to the conclusion that it doesn't matter; it's done. My message to her after her explanation made it final.

With that thought, I pause at the bedroom door and make a last-second decision. I strip the sheets off the bed along with the cases on the pillows. Maybe... fucking hopefully, if December's scent is gone, I'll finally be able to wake up without a fucking hard-on from her sultry perfume that's clung to my bedding the last few days. Maybe I'll be able to wake up without thinking about her and the ways I might have fucked things up because of my past.

I dump the load in my arms into the washer just off the kitchen and pick up the bottle of soap, dump that in, and then start up the machine. With that done, I start a pot of coffee then go down the hallway.

My boys would sleep all day if I let them—something I'm grateful for on the weekends and in the summer, but something that is a pain in the ass to deal with during the school year. I open my nine-year-old's door first, since it normally takes Max longer to get up. His alarm is going off, but he's pulled his pillow over his head to block out the blaring noise. I flip on the light then walk across the clean space to his bed and tug his foot. "Time to get up, Max."

He groans, pulling his foot away. "Isn't it the weekend yet?"

"Dude, it's Tuesday."

"Ugh, I want to be homeschooled."

"Get up and in the shower," I order, leaving his light on and ignoring his groan of annoyance.

I skip one door, which is to the boys' Jack and Jill bathroom, and open the next. When I flip on the light, my fifteen- going on forty-year-old son, Mitchell, lifts his head off his pillow. "Already?"

I smile. "Sorry, kid."

"You don't look sorry," he mutters before plopping back and covering his face. "Can you shut off the light so I don't go blind?"

"Nope."

I leave him and head back for the kitchen, where I pour myself a cup of coffee and start breakfast. At just thirty-two, I shouldn't have two kids my boys' age. Then again, I shouldn't have been having sex at sixteen and knocking up my high school girlfriend by the age of seventeen. And I really shouldn't have stupidly knocked her up again six years later, long after things ended between us. As stupid as my decisions were, I regret nothing. I love my boys and can't imagine a life without them in it. They are why I work two jobs and have a reason to get out of bed most mornings.

I finish breakfast—scrambled eggs and toast—then wait. Like clockwork, both my boys come into view, each looking almost exactly like me at their age. Tall, and fit without putting work in. Max's hair is a dirty blond and he's a little lankier than his brother, but I have no doubt that will change in a few years. They sit on the barstools across from me and I hand over plates to each of them, watching as they start to devour their food in a few bites. With the way they eat, I might need to get a third job. I swear I cannot keep enough food stocked for the two of them, even with a Sam's Club membership and buying in bulk.

"I'm taking you to school, and Grandma is picking you up. I should be home not long after you get here."

"I have track after school," Mitchell reminds me before shoving the last bite of the toast left on his plate into his mouth. This is the first year Mitchell has been in track, the high school track coach convinced him to try out after seeing him run. And after some debating Mitchell decided to give it a year to see if he liked it. So far so good, who knows what will happen next year.

"She'll pick up Max then wait for you."

"I don't know why I have to hang with Grandma. Especially when I'm old enough to sit home alone for a couple hours. It isn't even like I get to watch him play baseball," Max bickers.

I look at my youngest and pull up patience. Mitchell has always done what's asked without question, when his brother has had a question for everything since he was old enough to form words into a sentence. My boys couldn't be more opposite if they tried. The only thing the two of them have in common is baseball. Where they got the love for the game, I don't know, because I didn't have any interest in the sport growing up and the only reason I do now is because of them.

"When you turn ten, we'll talk about you being here alone for a few hours."

"Flipping great. I only have to wait another freakin year."

"Don't be a dick," Mitchell scolds, and Max turns to glare at him.

Knowing what will happen if I let this shit carry on, I cut in. "Cut it out, Max. You know I cannot leave you home alone, and Mitch, I don't need your help."

Both boys look at me, each with a look of remorse. Fuck, I love my boys. They are good kids, even after dealing with the shit they have in their short lives. Like all kids, they push boundaries, but they tend to listen without too much of a fight.

"Tonight is takeout, so figure out what you want to eat and send me a message. I'll pick it up before I come home."

"Pizza," Max says.

"Chinese," Mitchell puts in.

"All right, change of plans. I'll let you know when I'm off work and you two can call in your orders. I'll pick the shit up."

They both smile at me then go back to eating. When they're done, they drop their dishes in the dishwasher and go to finish getting ready and grab their bags. I sip my coffee as I look out the glass doors in the kitchen. We have a great yard. A large, concrete patio with a table and chairs, the barbeque, and lots of green space—not quite perfect for a game of baseball, but definitely perfect for a dog.

The boys have asked for one in the past, but I never wanted to get one until they were old enough to take on some of the responsibility. They're old enough now, and it's something I should talk to them about.

On that thought, I move to the kitchen, dump the rest of my coffee down the drain, and set my cup in the dishwasher as I hear the boys hit the living room. I meet them at the front door, and they both head down the porch as I lock up. Once we're loaded into my SUV, I take them each to school and go to work. Like every day, I work until I'm exhausted, wishing I were more than just a mechanic and part-time tattooist. I wish I had more, not for myself but for my boys.

Chapter 3

"*A*PRIL FOOLS!" I say loudly, slamming the book I'm holding closed, and the kids sitting in front of me jump then start to laugh. I smile at them, enjoying the way their eyes have lit up.

I love my job as a first grade teacher. There's something so innocent but curious about the way kids at this age view the world around them. And watching them grow mentally and physically each and every day while they're under my care makes my job seem important, vital even.

"Ms. Mayson, will you read another book?" Hanson asks as the other kids around him start to get up off the bright carpet, filled with too much energy to sit any longer.

"Not until Monday, honey."

I touch his soft cheek with the tips of my fingers, and watch his eyes close briefly as he whispers disappointedly, "Okay."

I wonder—not for the first time this year—what his home life is like. His mom and dad are both nice in an uptight way, but neither of them seem to be very affectionate with him, which is sad. He's a great kid, a little shy but so smart it's almost scary. He's already mastered reading at a third grade level and has better penmanship than some adults I know. He's also my favorite, even though I shouldn't have favorites.

"How about you choose which book we read during circle time on Monday?"

"Really?"

"Really." I watch a smile take over his whole face.

"Cool," he says, getting up and heading over to two of his buds.

I look at the clock near the door, and announce as I stand, "All right, kids, time to pack up. It's almost time to go home."

It's Friday, and even at six years old, most of these kids understand the beauty of the weekend. I walk across the room, feeling the excitement in the air as they pick up their things, shoving their work into their backpacks and school stuff into their desks.

When I reach the front of the class, I remind them, "Don't forget to have your parents sign up for what is needed for our class party next week. The list is online." I get a few smiles before a soft chime fills the room, stealing their attention. All the kids grab their bags in a rush to get to the door and line up. When I reach the door and open it, their parents or caregivers who have been waiting out in the hall come in, offering me smiles and hellos before greeting the kids with hugs or soft words.

Like always, the room fills with chatter until one by one the kids leave and silence ensues. The quiet is almost deafening, especially after spending the last several hours answering questions and keeping a bunch of children on task. I go around the room, picking up things left out and straightening up until I know the cleaning crew will be able to do their job over the weekend without the hassle of uncluttering.

Done, I grab my bag and coat then leave, shutting the door behind me. I go to the teachers' parking lot and climb in my car. My Nissan Maxima is old, but it still runs perfectly thanks to my dad and uncles, who've worked on it more times than I can count. I don't go directly home; I stop at the store and pick up a few things then go to the post office to mail a care package to my cousin Hannah. Living in Paris, she misses some of her favorite things from home, so every few months, I send her a package. It's never much—odds and ends, some candy or canned goods she can't find there easily, and a note telling her that if she moved home, she could get everything she loves anytime she wants. Like everyone else, I miss her. I don't see her often enough, but this summer I plan to visit her in Paris for a couple of weeks, something I'm really looking forward to.

After I finish with my errands, I head for my apartment. I started reading a new series a few days ago, and I'm anxious to curl up with my Kindle while eating the store-bought sushi I picked up for dinner. My cell phone buzzes as I pull into my designated parking spot, and I grab it out of my bag then roll my eyes toward the roof of my car.

April has been on me for the last week, demanding I spend time with her, our sisters, and our cousins. It's sweet that she's worried about me after what went down with Gareth, but it's also unnecessary. Yes, I still think about him all the damn time, but no, I do not need the constant pulse-checking. What happened, happened. It's done. I'm fine... *pretty much.*

Okay, so my stupid heart and head haven't gotten with the program, but they will. It's not like I had a relationship with the guy, so I have nothing to really get over.

After an annoyed sigh, I answer my cell with a chirpy "Hey."

"I'm picking you up in a couple hours. We're going to get tattoos."

Wait, what?

"What?"

"You've been saying forever that you want a tattoo. Tonight is the night. I already booked us appointments. I'm picking you up. See you soon."

"April—"

"Later." She hangs up before I can tell her I'm not going with her. Before I can tell her that even though I've talked about getting a tattoo for ages and know exactly what I want, I don't really have it in me to suffer through the pain of actually getting one.

"Crap." I pull the phone from my ear and look out my windshield. No way will April let me out of this. I know I said I need more of a life, but a tattoo? She might as well be forcing me to jump out of a plane with only nylon and a stranger strapped to my back.

With a long groan, I grab my bags and get out of my car then head for my door, giving friendly smiles and finger waves to a couple of my neighbors when I pass them. I step inside and drop my purse on the hook next to the door then slip off my coat, hanging it up. When I turn around to head for the kitchen, I spot Melbourne lounging on the couch. And like always when I see his cute, furry face, I want to go cuddle him, but the minute we make eye contact, he jumps down and runs off.

"Just so you know, I'm going to adopt another cat. One that actually likes me," I call out as his silver tale disappears around the corner. He doesn't even have the decency to acknowledge my threat or me. "I'm not kidding!" I shout as I head for the kitchen to drop my grocery bags on the counter.

After I put out food for Melbourne, I head to my room to change clothes. I switch from slacks to jeans and then from my button-down blouse to a white V-neck tee with a loose, long, black cardigan over it, but I keep on my leopard-print flats, because they're just as comfortable as sneakers.

Sitting in my kitchen, drinking a glass of wine, and eating my sushi, I hold my breath as the hero in the story kidnaps the heroine. I get so caught up in what's happening on my Kindle that I jump when the doorbell rings. I glance at the clock; it's almost seven. I don't know how long it takes to get a tattoo, but with any luck I'll be home before ten so I can get back to the kiss that I'm sure was about to take place. I slam the cover of my Kindle closed then go to answer the door.

As soon as it's open, April eyes me from head to toe. "You're wearing that?"

I look from her outfit of a form-fitting black tank, leather blazer, dark jeans, and black booted heels then down at myself. "Yes." I shrug one shoulder, and she rolls her eyes toward the ceiling before looking back at me.

"Just grab your purse."

I leave her without a word and go back to the kitchen, where I grab my cell along with my Kindle. After I convince April that I'm not getting a tattoo, I'll at least have something to do to kill time. I pick up my bag at the door then follow her out, locking up.

"I can drive," I tell her when we reach the parking lot.

"As if I'd ever let my ass ride bitch in your hooptie." She presses the button on her keys and her car across the lot beeps as the lights turn on.

I don't say a word until after I've slid into the passenger seat of her too small and too fast, silver Corvette and buckled in. "You do know I'm not getting a tattoo tonight, right?" I ask as "Highway to Hell" plays a decibel above normal through the car stereo.

"You are."

"I'm not. I'll watch you, but no way am I willingly going to have a needle plunged into my body over and over."

"Then I'll hold you down while it's done."

"I'm not getting a tattoo."

"You won't regret it or even remember the small amount of pain once it's done," she says before turning up the music, ending our conversation and placing her foot more firmly on the gas.

She drives us through town and pulls in to park in a small strip mall that's mostly dark except for a Chinese restaurant at one end and a tattoo parlor on the other. The Chinese place looks like every other one in town, but the tattoo parlor stands out, even with it being connected to the business beside it. The glass windows are lit up with bright pink and white lights, and there's a hand-drawn painting on the window of cherry blossoms and unique writing announcing the name of the place, Blossom's Tattoos.

"Have you been here before?" I question April as she parks in the mostly empty lot.

"Blossom has done most of my ink," she states before shutting down the engine and opening her door.

I follow her out of the car then into the parlor. The space inside is open and actually really beautiful. Light gray tile flooring that looks like hardwood. Bright lighting, and two glass-enclosed stations are in use with two tattoo-covered men working on their clients. Framed photos cover the walls, and most of the tattoos look like artwork in heavy wooden frames. I stand by the door, taking everything in. In my head, I expected this place to be dark, with books to flip through and hidden rooms down a long, dim hall. This place is nothing like I imagined. I move away from the door and meet April at the curved glass counter on the other side of the room.

The moment I stop next to my sister, a stick-thin woman comes around the corner. She's wearing a ripped up, short-sleeved tee, showing off the colorful tattoos covering both her arms. Her blonde, pink, and lavender hair is braided back on one side of her head, making it look like that side is shaved. She's uniquely beautiful. When she sees April, her face alights with a smile, and she shouts, "Girl! Where the fuck did you get that blazer? I need it."

"Like I'd tell you," April snaps sassily, and I jerk my head back, surprised by her tone.

The woman laughs, obviously not offended. "You're not still mad about us showing up at the same place in the same dress, are you?"

"Mad that you looked better than me and stole the guy I was after right from under my nose? Why would I be mad about that?"

"He was a waste of time. You should be thanking me." She shrugs with a coy smile.

"Like that's ever gonna happen." April rolls her eyes then asks, "Is Blossom set up?"

"She's waiting for you." Her eyes then come to me, and her head tips to the side as she studies me. "You're the sister?"

"This is December. December, this is Lexi," April introduces, waving her hand out.

Lexi's eyes sweep over me again, making me feel awkward. I ignore that feeling and smile, saying, "Nice to meet you."

Ignoring me she looks at April. "This adorable, obviously sweet girl is your sister? She's wearing a cardigan," Lexi states like it's a crime to wear a cardigan. Then she places both her hands on the glass counter, looking over the top and down at my feet. "I knew it. She's also wearing flats. They are leopard print, but they're still flats."

April sighs, and I can't tell if she's actually annoyed or just putting on a front. I'm not annoyed, but I am a little embarrassed and can feel my face getting red. "Can you tell Blossom we're here?" April questions.

"Are you really going to get a tattoo?" Lexi finally acknowledges me, ignoring April's question.

I want to say no, but there is something about this woman that makes me feel like I need to prove a point, that just because I'm dressed like I am doesn't mean she knows me. "Yep." I see April's head swing my way, but I don't look at her.

"Right the fuck on. Let's get you some ink." Lexi laughs then spins around and sashays away.

Crap, what have I done now?

"I don't think you should get a tattoo tonight," April says softly, and I turn my head to look at her. "You can watch as I get mine, and then if you still want, we can come back another time."

"Never put off until tomorrow what you can do today," I mutter, wondering where the books with the tattoos are. Maybe I can get a tiny ladybug or something.

"You don't have to do this."

"You were right. I've always wanted a tattoo. I don't know if I can get the one I always wanted, because I think it will need to be designed, but this can be like a test run."

"A test run?" She raises a brow.

"Yeah. A test run."

"Okay, so what are you thinking of getting?"

"I don't know. Maybe a ladybug."

She snorts. "A ladybug? No fucking way. Tell Blossom what you want; she can draw it up. If you like it, get it. If you don't, then don't get anything. A tattoo is forever, and it should be something that means something to you. I don't want you to get a tattoo just because Lexi is kinda a bitch."

"I heard that," Lexi says, coming around the corner, and my eyes widen slightly. "Don't worry. Your sister and I have a love/hate relationship." She smiles.

"It's more of a hate/hate relationship," April corrects.

Lexi laughs loud as a buzzer sounds, and like magic, a hidden door opens up. Lexi greets us on the opposite side then takes us down a hall. When we enter the large room, a plump, older woman with dark hair and striking blue eyes stands to greet us.

"April." She hugs my sister then turns her attention to me. "You must be December."

"I am." I start to reach out my hand, but she stops me, pulling me in for a hug.

When she lets me go, she keeps a hold of me, and as I look into her eyes, I swear they seem familiar. I just don't know why.

31

"You're very pretty."

"Thanks." I feel my cheeks warm and her expression gentles.

"So what kind of tattoo are you thinking about getting?"

Since it's something I've thought about a lot, even while believing I'd never get one, I give her the details of the design, along with the wording, and explain where I want it. When I'm done, her face is blank but her eyes are bright. "I don't think I can draw that up and do it justice, but if you can wait a few minutes, I'll send my nephew a message and see if he has time to come in and design it for you. He's an amazing artist."

"I don't want to inconvenience anyone."

"You're not," she assures me.

"All right," I agree.

She smiles then grabs her phone and sends a message. When she's done, she goes to a table and picks up a small piece of what looks like white parchment paper and hands it to April. "This is yours."

"It's perfect," April says, and I get close to her side to get a better look at the paper. The drawing is not big, maybe two-by-two inches, but the detail is extraordinary. Straight lines and dots zigzag together, making a starburst that resembles a flower.

"Where are you getting it?" I ask my sister, and she looks over at me.

"The back of my neck." She holds up her hair and points at the spot. "I plan on adding to it over time until it ends at my tailbone. It will be a process."

"That's going to look amazing."

"I think so," she says softly then asks, "Do you see it?"

"See what?" I question.

"Mom and Dad's initials?" She looks back at the paper and I do the same.

I study the details until the N and A finally stand out to me, and then I feel my throat get tight. "Wow, that's... that's amazing," I whisper.

"Blossom is amazing," April whispers back. "I told her that I wanted a tattoo to represent our parents and my siblings, and she came up with the idea. Each one after this will have one initial hidden in the design to represent our sisters."

"I can't wait to see it when it's complete."

"Me neither," she agrees then looks at Blossom. "Thank you, it really is perfect."

"You know I love you, girl." She smiles then picks up her cell when it dings. After she reads the message that pops up, she smiles at me. "My nephew is coming in. He said he'll be here in about twenty minutes. While we wait for him, I'll get started on April's tattoo. By the time I'm done with hers, the design for yours should be complete and we can get to work."

"Sounds good," I tell her as my stomach starts to knot.

Am I really doing this? Crap. I am. I'm actually getting a tattoo. Feeling a little nauseous, I take a seat across the room, watching April take off her jacket and tie up her hair before getting on what looks like a low massage table. She lies like Blossom instructs, with her head down and her chin over the edge, seeming completely relaxed.

Not sure it's wise for me to watch what happens next, I pull out my Kindle and try to read. It's a lost cause when the sound of a soft buzz fills the silence, making me hyperaware of what's going on. Just as I'm about to stand and get closer to watch Blossom work, there's a knock on the door before it opens. Instinctively, I turn toward it, and when I do, my stomach bottoms out.

No.

No way.

The sound of the buzzing ends as Blossom turns to look at the door, but I still hear and feel the vibration of the tattoo gun. "Hey, honey." She smiles widely as Gareth walks across the room toward her, not noticing me sitting a few feet away.

When he's close, he leans down, kissing her cheek and saying "Hey, Auntie."

"Where are my boys?" she asks, and I wonder if April—who is still lying face-down—knows who Blossom's nephew is. If she does and if this was a set up, I'm going to kill her.

"With Mom at a movie."

"Got it," she says, and then she looks at me and I feel myself freeze when he follows her gaze. "That's December. December, this is my nephew Gareth."

"Wait… what?" April's head jerks up quickly.

Okay, seems she didn't know that Gareth is Blossom's nephew. Good to know I don't have to figure out how to hide her body.

"Shit," Gareth hisses.

"Umm...." I look from April, who looks shocked, to Blossom, who looks confused, and then back to Gareth, who looks a mixture of surprised and annoyed.

"Do you two know each other?" Blossom asks, glancing between Gareth and me.

"Umm...." I repeat, my mind so overwhelmed by seeing him again that I can't seem to form a thought, let alone words.

"You could say that," Gareth answers in a low voice that sends a chill across my skin and through me.

"Well." Blossom frowns. "She has a tattoo she needs designed. Are you cool if she explains it to you?"

I watch him closely and can see his mind working. I can tell by his expression and body language that he doesn't want to talk to me about a tattoo, or about anything at all.

"It's okay. Maybe I'll—"

"No problem," he cuts me off before I can get us both out of this awkward situation. "Let's go to the drawing room."

"I don't think that's a good idea," April snaps, and my gaze goes to her. I can see she's still pissed about his text and is getting ready to pick a fight.

"It's fine. I'll be back." I stand, trying to give her a reassuring look, which she doesn't catch because she never pulls her eyes off Gareth, even as he turns his back to her to open the door.

With a deep breath, I follow him into another room, watching him flip on the lights and then the computer. I wrap my arms around my middle and wait, not sure what I'm supposed to do or say.

"You can sit over here." He doesn't look at me; he just motions with his hand to an empty chair cattycorner to his.

I don't want to sit. I want to find a bathroom and throw up. My stomach is turning with a mixture of nerves and anxiety as I stare at the side of his face. Lord, he's still gorgeous, and seeing he's still mad at me about what happened doesn't sit well.

When I don't move, he turns his head and our eyes lock. "Come sit down."

My stomach knots at his rude order, and my mouth opens without my mind telling it to. "Please."

"What?"

"Come sit down, *please*. Is the polite way to ask someone to sit."

"Come sit down, please," he repeats with his jaw clenched. I move then and take a seat, twisting my hands in my lap. "My aunt said you want a tattoo designed and that it's detailed. Tell me about it."

God, I wish things between us weren't like they are. I wish I would've never snuck out on him. I wish he could understand why I did and forgive me. "I'm sorry," I blurt, and his head jerks back in surprise. "About what happened... I'm sorry about what happened."

"I'm over it." His jaw ticks. "Now tell me about your tattoo."

Obviously, he's not over it. Actually, I wonder if like me he's been dwelling on it for days. "You might be over it, but I'm not," I say quietly. "I hate that you're mad at me. I wish I could change things, but I can't. All I can say is I'm sorry for leaving like I did. You were right that it was immature, and—"

"Stop," he grounds out, and I snap my mouth shut then bite my bottom lip. What the hell am I doing? "Why did you leave?" At his question, my body jerks and my muscles lock. I can't possibly tell him why I left. "Tell me."

"Why? It doesn't even matter." My heart starts to pound in my chest as he stares at me.

"I think you and I both know it does," he says softly while his eyes scan my face. "Tell me." Why did I open my mouth? "Tell me," he repeats, and I pull in a breath, figuring it doesn't matter if he knows now.

"My sister said she wanted you," I admit, dropping my eyes from his to look at my hands still clasped in my lap. "She doesn't. She just—"

"I don't care about that. I care about why you snuck out of my bed without a word."

"Can we not do this?" I question, peeking at him through my lashes.

35

My heart is not just pounding against my rib cage anymore; it's now thundering away while embarrassment creeps up my chest and neck, flooding my cheeks making them hot.

"I think you owe me some kind of explanation, since every fucking day for the last week I've woken up with you on my mind, a hard-on I can't seem to get rid of, and your scent still clinging to my bed, even though I've washed my sheets three fucking times since you were in it."

Is he serious? I lift my head to search his gaze.

"Why did you sneak out?"

God, I don't want to tell him, but I need to. I need to get this over with so I can move on. So *we* can move on. "When my sisters and I were younger, we had a rule," I start, and he cuts me off.

"Fuck me, let me guess." He shakes his head. "If one of you was interested in a guy, none of you could approach him."

"Basically," I agree. I know if I caught a glimpse of myself right now, my chest and face would be bright red.

"You came home with me," he states.

"I know."

"So you coming home with me was about what? About you rebelling against your sister?"

"No!" I almost shout. No way do I want him to think I went home with him just because of April.

"Then why?"

"When I first saw you—" I stop and press my lips together, and then close my eyes and finish. "—there was something about you, and when April said she wanted you, I got mad. I was mad that she saw you first. Mad that I was going to miss out on something, even if I didn't know what that something was."My throat gets tight.

"You snuck out."

"I know."

"Look at me, babe," he orders, and my eyes open. "I should not have said what I said to you over text." My lips part at his admission. "I've wanted to call you every fucking day to apologize. I didn't, but I should have. If you can forgive me for that, I can forgive you for what happened."

"You were right to be mad. I would have been too," I say softly, and his eyes flash with some kind of emotion that is there and gone way too quickly for me to read. "But I am really sorry."

"It's all good."

"Are you sure?"

"Yeah, babe." He leans back. "Now, tell me about your tattoo."

I study him for a moment, trying to understand why I still feel this heavy weight in my stomach, the one that's been there since I read his text. It should be gone now that we talked and after he accepted my apology, but it isn't.

Figuring the best course of action is to get this over with so we can both go our separate ways, I explain the tattoo then sit back and watch him create magic with a pencil. Forty minutes later, we say goodbye, and a part of me knows it will be the last time I see him. That hurts more than it should, but as I lie on the tattoo table with Blossom embedding my tattoo into my skin, I know that a part of him will always be with me.

"Now that you're officially a badass, let's go get a drink," April says with a grin while grabbing my hand and leading me toward her car.

I do kinda feel like a badass. I now have a tattoo, a fricking beautiful tattoo I know I'll never regret getting, and not just because Gareth designed it, but because it's beautiful and exactly what I always wanted. "Where are we going?"

April stops as soon as the question leaves my mouth, and her head swings down toward me. "What?"

"What?" I repeat, frowning at her.

"*You* want to go get a drink?"

"Isn't that what you normally do after you get a tattoo?"

"Yeah."

"Okay... so like I said, where are we going?"

She studies me for a moment, and then her lips tip up into a smile and she mumbles, "Apparently to the bar."

Beeping the car alarm, she lets go of my hand and I get in, feeling a slight twinge of pain hit my side as I twist to slide into the low seat. Once I'm settled and we're buckled in, she starts the engine. Until that moment, I never understood the appeal of the loud rumble of her car, but apparently being a newborn badass, I'm able to appreciate it now. And I appreciate it more when she switches the song playing from the speakers from one I don't know to "Welcome to the Jungle," turning the volume all the way up and rolling down the windows. Even though it's cold out, I relish the moment, and knowing the lyrics, I sing along at the top of my lungs.

We pull into the parking lot for one of the local bars, and April waits until the song comes to an end before she rolls up the windows and shuts down the engine. The smile on my face is huge as I get out, slamming my door. When we meet at the hood, she tosses her arm around my shoulders then leads me inside.

The place is packed. There are a few college kids, but most of the people are our age or older. We go right to the bar, and as soon as we reach the edge, April lets me go and leans over the top of the counter. I look around; the music and chatter is deafening, but every person seems to be smiling and enjoying their night out. Before I even have a chance to glance back at my sister, she's shoving a glass into my hand. I take it then follow her across the room to a table that has free chairs but is covered with beer bottles and empty glasses.

Suddenly feeling out of place, I take a sip from my drink and start to cough. It's vodka, and if I'm not wrong, nothing else besides ice. "Vodka?"

"You're a badass, and badasses drink vodka straight." She grins, finishing her drink in one gulp.

"Screw it." I down the rest of the drink in one large gulp then slam it on the table.

"Total badass." My sister grins, and I laugh.

Gareth

Chapter 5

"*I* TALKED TO your aunt last night," Mom says casually as she wipes down the counters in my kitchen like I haven't done it in ages, when I just did it this morning after cooking the boys breakfast.

"And?"

"She mentioned a girl who came in last night to get a tattoo. Who was she?"

"No one."

"Seriously, Gareth?" She shakes her head, looking frustrated, and I glance over my shoulder at my sons to make sure they're still preoccupied with the video game they're playing. I should have planned for this. I knew when my aunt witnessed my reaction to seeing December again that she would be all too happy to tell my mom about that interaction and that my mom would be curious.

"Mom." I sigh.

"Honey, you haven't dated since—"

"Don't. Do not bring her up," I growl. I don't even like thinking that woman's name, let alone hearing it. "I have two boys to raise and two jobs. I don't exactly have a lot of free time for dating anyone."

"Blossom said she's really pretty and sweet. She also said you seemed a little annoyed seeing her but could tell there was something between you two."

Fuck, my aunt is observant, and she has a big mouth. I jerk my fingers through my hair. If I'm honest, I was completely thrown off guard when I saw December, and struck stupid by just how beautiful she looked without even trying.

"So who is she?" Mom questions again quietly this time.

Who is she?

The woman who's taken over my every thought, the woman who rocked my world with an apology she didn't really owe me but still gave me anyway, in which she sounded sincere and like she really hoped I got that she regretted leaving. The woman who would probably want nothing to do with me if she knew I had two boys I'm raising on my own, and a crazy ex who shows up out of the blue from time to time just to fuck with me and my kids.

"So?"

I look at my mom, the woman who gave birth to me, the woman who raised me and my sisters on her own, doing it and never once complaining. Just like she's never complained when I've needed her to help with her grandsons. I wish I could give her something, something to make her stop worrying about me, but I can't. Even if I want to be the asshole who storms into December's life and forces her to take a chance on me.

"It doesn't matter," I tell her, and her eyes narrow. "She's a nice woman, but she's not for me." Why the fuck does my chest suddenly hurt at that bit of self-truth?

Mom studies me for a moment then her eyes fill with a disappointed light. "All right, honey."

Thank fuck. I know my mom can be persistent when she gets something in her head, and if she thinks for one second I'm missing out on something, she will make it her mission to get me what she thinks I need.

"You staying for dinner?" I ask, needing to change the subject.

"It depends. What are you making?"

"The boys want lasagna, so I picked up the stuff yesterday."

"Are you making your cheesy garlic bread?"

"What do you think?" I raise one brow.

She grins. "Right. Then I'm definitely staying."

I grin back before looking toward the couch, where both Max and Mitchell are sprawled out. "Boys, I'm gonna start dinner soon and Grandma is staying." I get a "Cool" and a "Right on" before I continue. "I hope you both got your homework done, because it's your turn to do dishes and it's Yahtzee night." I listen to both of them groan and turn off the game along with the TV before heading for their rooms without a word. When I look back at my mom, she's got an odd look on her face. "What?"

"Nothing." She shakes her head, still watching me closely.

"What?" I repeat, curious now.

"You," she whispers.

"What about me?"

"You're an amazing dad. Those boys are lucky."

My throat gets tight, but I swallow through it. "I learned from the best."

"I might have had a hand in you becoming the type of parent you are, but the hardworking, loyal, loving, and protective man you've grown into is all you. You're stronger and more determined than anyone I know. Hell, most people given the hand you were dealt as a kid then as an adult would have given up, but not you. You keep going, keep fighting to have better and do better, for you and your boys."

The tightness in my throat grows and my chest constricts, which means I wheeze out, holding her stare. "You're the best mom a kid could ask for, and regardless of what you think, I'm the man I am today because you showed me how to be everything that is good."

"Oh, God, I'm gonna cry." She starts to sniffle and I laugh. "It's not funny." She swipes her cheeks, glaring at me.

I move off the stool I'm sitting on and go around the edge of the counter. "Come here, Mom." I hold open my arms and she gives me one last annoyed look before wrapping her arms around me. "I love you."

"To the moon and beyond, baby boy," she whispers before tightening her hold. We stay like that until we hear one of the boys' doors open and shut then she looks up at me, giving me a shaky smile and letting me go. "I'm just gonna fix my mascara."

I lift my chin and she smiles then disappears right as Mitchell comes around the corner.

"Dad, I can't find my backpack."

"Did you check your room?"

"Yeah it's not there."

"You sure? I know you think you know where everything is in that mess, but I guarantee you don't."

He smiles crookedly. "I looked through everything."

"Did you leave it in the truck?"

"Maybe." He shrugs.

"You know where the keys are. Go on out and check."

Without a word, he takes off. I hear the rattling of my keys then the sound of the door opening and closing. Not even two minutes later, he comes back in, shouting, "Found it."

"Good," I reply, and then I listen to him go into his room and close the door. Mom comes back when I'm already at the stove cooking the ground beef for the sauce, and I look at her when she gets close.

"I'm just going to say one more thing."

I let out a frustrated breath. "Mom—"

"No, you need to hear this." I watch her head jerk from side to side. "If you think for one minute you're not good enough for that girl, you're wrong. You deserve everything, honey, everything good in life. And if this girl doesn't see the amazing man you are, she's not worth your time." She looks away then continues. "Now, I'm gonna go check on the boys to make sure they don't need help."

She knows they don't need help; if they did, they'd ask for it. She just wants to leave me to think about what she said. And it works, because once again December is at the forefront of my thoughts as I make dinner for my mom and boys, and still long after I get to bed.

Which means I don't fall asleep until I lose myself with my hand wrapped around my cock, thinking of December.

"I don't know why we have to go to some fancy dinner. It's not like

44

Aunt Selma or Sejla even care if we're there," Max grumbles from the back seat as I pull into one of the empty parking spaces at the restaurant.

"You think they don't care, but they do. Otherwise, they wouldn't have asked us to come," Mitchell snaps from the passenger seat at his brother in the back, sounding annoyed. It's something that's becoming more frequent whenever he deals with his little brother.

"I know they care about us, but they never care about these events. They don't even wanna go most of the time, so I don't see why we have to."

He's not wrong. My twin sisters, who are both in banking, couldn't care less about these events, but each and every time they're given something in their honor, they invite us. They are considered rock stars in the banking world, and the company they work for appreciates the amount of clients they're able to secure, and also the big names attached to them and only them, from country singers to corporate clients. People trust them, because they are trustworthy and honest. They never let their clients make financial decisions without knowing exactly what they will be getting into, even if that means they have to hold off on a loan until they're more financially secure.

"Hold on, you two," I say, hearing both boys' seat belts unlatch as I'm shutting down the engine. Once I have my belt unhooked, I turn in my seat to look at Max in the back. "How would you feel if we didn't show up to one of the dinners the baseball team holds for you, your teammates, and their parents every year?" At my question, his lips press together and his eyes fill with understanding. "You'd be disappointed, even if you didn't really want to be there. Am I right?"

"Yeah," he mutters then looks at his brother, and his eyes narrow.

I glance to Mitchell and see he's smirking. His eyes come to me, and the smirk slowly slides away as I shake my head. "Your brother is younger than you. He's still learning. If I remember correctly, when you were his age, you had the same outlook on life that he does now. It's your job as his big brother to show patience and to lead him down the right path. What you don't do is act smug when you're right about something."

His eyes drop from mine as he says, "Sorry."

"You don't gotta be sorry." I wrap my hand around the back of his neck and wait for him to look at me, and when he does, I continue gently, "This is just one more lesson you'll learn in life, kid. A man never pretends he knows everything, and even if he happens to know something someone else doesn't, he never acts smug about it. Instead, he appreciates the fact he's able to help them learn something new." When he nods, I tighten my fingers affectionately then let him go and look between both my boys. "I don't like getting dressed up or going to these events any more than either of you do, but this is what family does. We show up when someone we love is celebrating, or even when they just need a shoulder to cry on."

"You're right," Mitchell says, and I see Max nod out the corner of my eye.

"Now let's go inside and help your aunts celebrate, with hopefully really great food. And if the food sucks, let's pretend like we enjoy it while looking forward to the pizza we'll pick up on the way home," I tell them, getting two smiles before I open my door and get out.

I meet the boys near the trunk and we go inside. Once we tell the hostess who we're meeting, she begins to usher us toward a private room in the back. Halfway across the crowded restaurant, I almost come to a complete stop when I recognize December, looking as beautiful as always, sitting at a table with a man I don't recognize, along with her cousin Sage and his wife Kim.

"Dad," Mitchell calls, obviously sensing my distraction, but I can't seem to pull my eyes off December when she starts to laugh along with the man sitting way too fucking close to her.

"Dad, are you okay?" Max grabs my hand and attention, and I attempt to ignore the knife that suddenly seems to be jammed into my gut as I look at him.

"I'm good." I force my feet to move while giving both my kids reassuring looks.

I can't say I ever saw December before her cousin's wedding, but I swear she's everywhere I am now, haunting me like a bad dream. Fuck. I should have taken the shot she gave me with one look after our talk, when she'd been obviously open to us getting to know each other without the other bullshit in the way. I should have fucking put my stupid inhibitions aside and asked her if she wanted to get together for dinner or a drink.

Fuck. I'm an idiot, and now she's out with another guy, her cousin, and his wife, obviously enjoying herself enough to laugh freely.

When we finally enter the private room, the boys and I greet my sisters with hugs then settle into our seats at the table. The fancy salad that is served to us first tastes like shit, but I force myself to eat, wanting my boys to follow my lead. When the main course comes out—steak, fancy mashed potatoes, and asparagus—I don't enjoy a single bite, even though it looks delicious. My mind is on the woman in the other room, and the jealousy that is still twisting my insides.

Halfway through the main course, with people chatting around me and the boys entertained by their aunts, I tell them quietly that I'll be back then get up from the table. I leave the room and head toward the bar to get a beer but stop midway when I spot December heading toward the bathrooms at the back of the restaurant. I glance at the table she was at earlier and note that Sage, his wife, and the man who December was sitting next to are all still eating, so I change direction and follow her.

Not sure what the fuck it is I'm doing, I try to talk myself into leaving her be as she's in the bathroom, but the image of her laughing with the man has consumed my thoughts. And the idea of her going home with him has filled me with jealousy. When she comes out of the restroom with her head down, I don't even think about what I'm doing. Honestly, I don't even know if I have control over myself at this point. I block her path, and as she looks up, her eyes meet mine and widen. I bore down on her with my stare then grab hold of her hips and start walking her backward toward the end of the hall where it's dark.

"Gareth," she whispers, and I drop my head forward to look her in the eye. Fuck, she's tiny, so fucking short and so damn innocent-looking, even wearing the somewhat revealing, black, clingy-as-fuck dress she has on. "What are you doing?" Her voice is breathless.

"Who are you here with?" Fuck. Why the fuck did I ask her that question? I don't want to know who that fucking guy is or if she's dating someone, and really I have no fucking right to ask her that question when she isn't even mine.

"What?" Her hands move to my chest to hold me back as I press her more firmly against the wall. "Sage?"

"Not Sage," I growl, and her eyes widen.

"My cousin."

"I know Sage is your cousin." I dip my face closer to hers, smelling the sweet, sultry scent of her perfume. "The other guy, who the fuck is he to you?"

"Talon."

The way she says his name sets my teeth on edge. "Are you seeing him now?"

"No." Her face twist. "He's Sage's brother and my cousin." My jaw clenches tight. Why the fuck didn't I think about that guy being her cousin? Shit, I should have fucking known, should have remembered the Mayson family is huge. "Can you let me go now?" she asks.

"No," I say without thinking.

Her mouth opens and shuts before she asks, "No?"

"Um, Dad?" At the sound of Mitchell's voice, I swing my head around and find my son standing close but not too close, with his eyes bouncing between December and me.

"Dad?" December whispers, sounding surprised.

I let her go and take a step back while I turn to face Mitch, whose eyes are on her, and he looks confused. Not confused because he just found his old man holding a woman against a wall, but like he's confused as to *why* I'm holding December against a wall.

"Hey, Mitch," December says softly, and I tip my head down toward her, wondering how she knows my boy. "Your dad and I were just—"

"How do you know Ms. Mayson?" Mitch asks me before December can finish speaking, and I wonder how the hell he knows her. And then I remember her telling me she's a teacher, but I thought for sure she said she taught kindergarten or first grade.

"We're friends," she tells him, coming to stand at my side.

"You are?" He looks to me for confirmation.

"We are," I agree, then ask, "Is everything okay?"

"Yeah, Aunt Selma said I had to come ask you if Max and I can have another Coke, since we already had one."

"Are you two going to be bouncing off the walls all night?"

"Probably." He smiles and I sigh, which makes him grin. "Tell your aunt I said it's cool."

"Cool," he says, and then he looks at December. "See you Wednesday, Ms. Mayson."

"See you Wednesday," she returns with a smile in her voice, and I wait until he disappears around the corner then look down at her and raise a brow. "What?"

"Wednesday?"

"Wednesdays, I take my class to the high school for a mentoring program. It's kinda like Big Brothers Big Sisters, but during school hours. My kids love it."

"Mitch is a mentor?"

"Yeah, he and a few other kids from his grade."

"How long has he been doing that?"

"Since the school year started," she says, and I look toward the end of the hall, wondering why he never mentioned it to me. Then I wonder if he has but I don't remember because I didn't really pay attention when he brought it up.

Fuck, I need to pay more attention to my boys. Especially Mitchell, seeing how I was about his age when I started getting really interested in girls. Shit. With a short shake of my head, I look at December. "You should get back to your family."

"What?" she breathes.

"You should get back to your family before they start to worry," I say then start to walk away, my mind filling with unhappy thoughts about my boys growing up and exactly what that could mean for our futures. Futures I pray are centered around sports and colleges, not picking out cribs and trying to find money to pay for diapers.

"Hold on." She steps in front of me with her head shaking and her blonde hair flying over her shoulders as her palms come up to rest against my chest to push me back. "What just happened back there?" She waves one hand toward the wall she was up against not even five minutes ago.

"Nothing happened."

Her eyes narrow. "Did you just say nothing happened?"

"Go back to your family, December."

"You're unbelievable," she hisses loudly, shoving my shoulder.

I look to where her hand is still resting against my chest then to her eyes, and order, "Calm down."

"Don't tell me to calm down." Her hair flies again as she jerks her head from left to right. "You... you... jerk." She points at me. "I didn't corner you outside the bathroom, force you down the hall, or trap you against a wall, demanding to know who you're out with."

"I gotta get back to my boys," I say, fighting the urge to touch her, to kiss her, do something, anything to quench the need growing inside me that has everything to do with the insane pull I feel toward her.

"You are really something else." She lifts up on her tiptoes, bringing her gorgeous mouth closer to mine. "You said you didn't have time for games. Obviously, that was a lie, because you seem like you're a pro at playing with my fricking emotions." She falls to her flat feet then shoves both her hands against my chest with more force than before, making me take a step back. "Now that I know exactly the kind of jerk you are, I'm going back to have dinner with my family, and seriously, I hope I never see you again."

"Ember." I grab hold of her before she can walk away, and her eyes narrow on my fingers wrapped around her wrist.

"Do not call me that."

"There are things about me, things about my life that you don't know."

"Yeah." She shoves the fingers of her free hand into my chest, and snaps, "You know what? There are things about my life that you don't know either, because we don't fricking know each other. Now let me go." She tugs to get free.

I keep my hold tight and counter her pull, forcing her a step closer to me. A move that makes her eyes flare and pupils dilate. "I have two boys."

"Yeah, I know that. Remember my cousin lives across the street from you? She told me about them. I just didn't know that you were you or that Mitch was one of your sons."

Why the fuck didn't I think of that? I should have known Harmony would have told her about me, Mitchell, and Max. Shit. "I also have an ex."

"Yeah, that kinda goes with the territory of having kids. I'm not a flipping idiot, jerk," she seethes, tugging her hand and trying to break free.

"Don't be ugly."

"Don't tell me what to do," she counters, still struggling with the hold I have on her.

"Jesus, I had no fucking idea you were this big of a pain in the ass."

"Newsflash, buddy: we don't know each other."

I scan her face, taking in the pink of her cheeks, her eyes flashing with anger, and her lips that are full, even pressed tightly together, and I fight the urge to go hard. "Why the fuck do I want to kiss you right now?" I ask out loud, and her expression gets tight.

"Do it, Gareth, and I swear to God I will bite your face off," she says, sounding breathless and furious.

Looking into her gorgeous eyes full of rage mixed with sparks of desire, I'm torn between laughing and roaring my frustration. I don't think I've ever been turned on and pissed at the same time, but I'm definitely turned on and pissed right now. I drop my eyes to her mouth and watch her tongue slip out to wet her bottom lip, right before she whispers, "Gareth, don't."

A rumble of frustration slides up my throat, vibrating my chest, right before I drop my head. And without another word, she lifts up to meet me halfway, our mouths lock, our tongues tangle, and her soft body presses against mine. I wrap one arm around her waist and tangle my fingers into her unbelievably soft hair, keeping her close while I devour her mouth and soak up her taste.

"Oh shit," I hear, and December does too, judging by the way her body goes rigid against mine and her fingers against my chest dig in. I jerk my head back and lock eyes with Kim, Sage's wife, over the top of her head. "I... I'm just going to the bathroom," Kim stutters before she opens the door to the restroom quickly and disappears behind it.

"Oh, God," December whispers, jerking away before I have a chance to get ahold of her. Then she takes a step back out of reach, holding her hands up between us. "I don't...." She shakes her head with her eyes looking wild. "I'm sorry. I..." Her tongue once more touches her bottom lip. "I don't know what happened. I'm sorry," she says, right before she turns on her heel and takes off. I watch her go with my gut tight. The only thing that brings me relief is knowing without a doubt that this is the last time I'll ever let her walk away without a fight.

December

Chapter 5

"*WH*AT THE HELL?" I groan as the doorbell rings for the third time in a row. "Seriously," I shout, stumbling through my mostly dark living room, pretty sure I'm still drunk, really sure I haven't even been asleep for more than an hour. "I'm here," I call when the bell goes off again. "You can stop pressing the stupid button." I fumble with the locks then swing the door open and stare in disbelief at Gareth. "This is not happening."

"Do you sleep in that every night?" he asks, referring to my blue Supergirl nightgown that has a red cape attached at the shoulders, and my eyes narrow on his.

"How did you find me?" I bite out while I grab a jacket off one of the hooks near the door and put it on as he walks past me into my living room.

"The same way you got my number—your cousin hooked me up."

"Sage gave you my address?" I ask, not believing him for one second.

"He did." He shrugs. "Or I should say Kim talked him into giving it to me after I told them what happened earlier at the restaurant and explained I wanted to talk to you in person and apologize."

"Great," I mutter, because that I do believe. Women always think crap like that is romantic, and I'm sure Kim was swooning all over the damn place when she heard it from a guy who looks like Gareth.

"Where are your kids?" I ask, stopping in the middle of my living room and watching him as he walks around, looking at the photos and things I have on the walls and shelves.

"I tried to call you, and I sent you a few texts," he says, ignoring my question. I know he tried to call and sent me a few texts. I read each one at least a dozen times while I drank a bottle of wine all alone, trying to forget the kiss he gave me and remind myself why he's bad news.

"Where are your boys?" I ask again, glancing at the clock. It's not exactly late; it's only a little after eleven, but I'm not sure two kids should be home alone at this time of night.

"They both decided to go home with my sisters after dinner," he says, studying a photo of my sisters and me. My mom took the picture without us knowing last summer, when we were all at the lake. It's one of my favorite photos of my sisters and me. We're all standing in a row with our arms wrapped around each other's shoulders, laughing at something. I don't remember what we were laughing at, but I do remember feeling happy and thankful, and I get that same feeling every time I look at it.

"Did you want something?" I ask, fighting back a shiver as his attention moves to my bookshelf and his fingers skim down the spine of one of my books.

"You read a lot." His eyes meet mine. "Do you read anything besides romance?"

"I read a lot of different genres. My favorite books usually have a little romance mixed into the stories, but I read a lot of mysteries and I love paranormal. The series I'm reading right now is actually fantasy, and it's amazing. It's about a girl who's grown up as a servant, and she doesn't know she carries royal blood that has magic in it…" My words taper off when I notice he's smiling.

"And what happens with her?" he asks, and I can't tell if he's really curious or just messing with me. Either way, I need to get this done and get him out of here. I don't like that he seems to have some kind of power over me, even after experiencing his dismissal a couple of times.

"Can you just tell me why you're here?"

"You know why I'm here."

Yeah, I do. Unfortunately, the chemistry we have is something I've only read about in books and he'd have to be a dunce not to recognize it for what it was. That said, I don't want to play the game he seems to be interested in playing. "In that case, you can go." I wave my hand toward the door. "Because like you once said, I don't have time for games or high school bull manure, so we have nothing to talk about and you have no reason to be here."

"Bull manure?"

My cheeks warm with embarrassment. "You know what I mean."

"Yeah, and it's adorable that you can't say the word *shit*."

"I'm glad you think so. Now please go," I say once more, wondering how many times I'm going to have to ask him to leave before he actually does.

"I think you know I'm not going anywhere." He takes a seat on my sofa making himself comfortable with his long legs spread wide and his arms engulfing the back of it, making my couch that's much too large for my apartment look minuscule.

I stare at him in disbelief, wondering exactly how unhappy my neighbors will be if I start screaming at the top of my lungs.

"We need to talk."

"We don't need to talk," I deny, shaking my head, feeling like an idiot standing in my own damn house wearing a jacket over my nightgown with him sitting a few feet away like he has the right to be here. "You need to leave."

"I've been single a long fucking time."

"I'd like to say that's shocking, but it isn't," I say, expecting him to react, but instead he continues speaking.

"There aren't many women I'd trust around my boys, or trust to stick with me if shit got hard, but I swear to God the moment I saw you I thought, *She's the type of woman you should take a chance on.*"

Why the hell is he telling me this, and why is my stomach all of a sudden starting to hurt?

"Then I spoke to you and got a dose of your funny and sweet, and I thought for sure I was right about taking that chance. But then I watched you sneak out of my room and out of my house without a word," he tells me, and I wrap my arms around my stomach, trying to control the pain there as he continues. "I know it was unfair of me to paint you with the same brush as my ex, but I can't even begin to tell you the number of times I watched her sneak out. I can't count how many times I watched her walk away from my boys, or how I had to try to explain to them why their mom took off after she was there for a few days then suddenly gone."

"You don't have to tell me this," I say, thinking I might get sick.

"I do. I fucked up. I've fucked up a couple of times since we met, and I hate that you've been the one who's taken the brunt of that shit. I hate that my reservations about starting something up with a gorgeous, smart woman have nothing to do with her but with my own personal baggage."

"Gareth," I whisper, fighting back tears.

"I want to get to know you, Ember," he says solemnly. "I want to spend time with you. I want to take you out to dinner and listen to you talk about weird scientific facts and the books you're reading. I want to kiss you, and fuck you, and understand that tattoo you now carry around, after you tell me your reason for getting it."

"I... I don't know what to say," I confess, because I don't.

"Say you'll give me a shot." He sits forward, placing his elbows to his knees and looking me in the eye. "Tell me you're willing to get to know me. Tell me I'm not the only one who feels this fucking"—he shakes his head—"whatever the fuck this is between us."

"I feel it," I admit without thinking, and he sits forward.

"That's good." He pushes up off the couch and walks toward me. No, scratch that; he prowls like a predator who's zeroed in on its prey. "I just need a shot. I just need you to tell me you're open to the idea of getting to know me."

God, can I do this? Can I put myself out there with him? A guy with two kids—one of whom I already know—and as he put it, an ex who likes to mess with him. I stare into his eyes as he comes closer, and that pull in my belly that exists when he's around comes to life. My pulse starts to pound so hard I hear it in my ears, giving me my answer.

"One date," I say, sounding breathless, and his hand comes up like he's going to touch me.

Before he makes contact, he drops it to his side. "Do you have plans tomorrow evening?"

I never have plans unless one of my family members drags me away from my Kindle and out of the house, so I shake my head then say, "No."

"I'll pick you up tomorrow at 5:30 and take you to dinner."

"I can meet you."

His eyes light with humor at my offer and he takes another step closer to me, so close my chest meets his each and every time I take a breath. "It wouldn't be a date if I didn't pick you up, so after dinner I can walk you to the door and kiss you good night." Before I can respond to his statement, he leans in and places his lips to my cheek then leans back to catch my eye. "I'll see you tomorrow evening, Ember."

I swear I hear a hint of warning in his tone as I feel the phantom trace of his fingers brush against mine while he steps around me.

I stand in the middle of my living room with my head turned over my shoulder, wearing my goofy nightgown under my coat and watch the door open then shut behind him. "Well." I let out the breath I was holding. "It seems I'm going on a date tomorrow night," I mumble to myself while I take off my jacket and walk toward the door.

I start to hang my coat on its hook, when the door opens and Gareth pokes his head inside, ordering "Make sure you lock this."

Panting with my hand against my chest, I glare at him and hiss, "You just scared me to death."

He grins then sweeps his eyes over me. "Seriously, that shit is too fucking cute for words."

"Go home, Gareth." I walk to the door, putting pressure on it as I place myself behind it, and I hear him laugh as I push it closed and hit the three locks.

With my mind filled with fear and excitement, I head for my bedroom. I don't know why I do it, but I call April and tell her what happened. I tell her about Gareth cornering me at the restaurant, our argument, him kissing me, and me running off. Then I tell her about him showing up and laying things out about his ex—something that makes my stomach turn even just thinking about.

"So what are you going to wear on your date?" she asks when I finish talking, and I almost laugh. It's so April to completely forget that she was mad at Gareth not long ago and be concerned about what I'm going to wear on my date.

"I have no idea."

"I'll come over tomorrow morning and help you go through your shit. If we don't find the perfect outfit for you, we have time to hit the mall before and find something there."

"Have I told you that I love you?"

"Not lately, but I know you do, so it's all good," she says, and I know she's smiling.

"Well, I do. So thanks for listening to me."

"I'm here anytime you want to talk. You know that," she adds, and I do know that; it's just one of the many things I'm thankful for. "Try to get some sleep. I'll see you tomorrow."

"Bring coffee," I say before she can hang up, then add, "And breakfast sandwiches from Marco's."

"Got it." She laughs, saying, "Later."

I start to drop my cell to my bedside table but stop when it buzzes in my hand with an incoming text. I smile when I see *hot jerk do not answer* on the screen.

I'm looking forward to tomorrow. Sleep well.

My fingers hover over the keyboard of my phone before I finally decide exactly what to say in reply.

Me too, good night.

I turn my ringer on silent so I'm not tempted to look at it then drop my cell to the table by the bed and turn out the light. I pull my covers up to my shoulder, and Melbourne jumps up on the bed, curls into the crook of my stomach, and starts to purr. I reach my hand out from under the blanket and run my fingers over the top of his head, listening to the sound grow louder.

"I wish you were this sweet all the time," I tell him, and he responds by turning to nip my fingers hard enough to sting. "Jerk." I tuck my hand back under my covers. "You are so getting a furry friend who actually likes my attention." With a loud meow, he gets up, walks the length of my body, and then presses his face to mine like he's silently threatening me before he curls up on my shoulder. "I'm not kidding. First chance I get, I'm talking to July about my options," I warn, and he rubs his head against my jaw. "It's too late to be sweet now," I mutter, closing my eyes, and surprisingly, even with my impending date on my mind and my cat who doesn't really like me lying on my shoulder, I fall asleep quickly.

"Finally." April sighs dramatically as I walk out of the dressing room and stop in front of the three-way mirror.

"You think so?" I run my hands down the soft, black material and take in the cut of the sleeveless, tight dress that looks simple from the front, with a high neckline and a hem that hits me midcalf. Then I turn to look over my shoulder at the racer back that shows a good amount of skin.

"It's perfect. Casual and sexy. It doesn't matter if he takes you to McDonald's or Frank's Steakhouse." I grin at my sister. "Though, if he takes you to McDonald's, I don't think you should give him a second date, or the vagina."

I laugh and shake my head at her, knowing for sure Gareth isn't taking me to McDonald's, even if I don't know exactly where he's taking me to dinner. When April came over this morning, she asked if I knew where we were going so she could help me find the perfect outfit, and when I told her no, she handed me my cell. I called him to ask, and he teased me, asking if my nightgown was an option. After I threatened to hang up and listened to him laugh, he told me that I should wear a dress.

"I'm pretty sure he wouldn't tell me to wear a dress if he planned on taking me through the drive-thru line at Mickey D's."

"I don't know. A dress is easy access, and fast food is... well, fast. Get it, go back to his place, and—"

"You can stop." I laugh, cutting her off, and she smiles and stands up, coming up behind me.

"Seriously though, this is the dress. You look sexy, and I have no doubt he's going to be wondering how he got so lucky when he sees you in it."

I turn to face the mirror once more and examine myself before I meet her gaze. "So now what shoes do I wear?"

"Heels, the ones you have with the thin black heel, the bow on the back, and the ankle strap. Those are perfect."

"So flats aren't an option?" I ask half joking, because even thinking about those heels makes my feet hurt.

"You can handle heels for a few hours, Grandma." She rolls her eyes. "Now, go change, pay for this dress, and let's hit the food court for some grub and a coffee."

"Sounds like a plan." I head into the dressing room and change out of the dress and back into my jeans and tee. Then I take the dress up to the register, where I pick up some cute stack bracelets with multicolored beads and a pair of hoop earrings that April tells me will be perfect with the dress. I pay for my stuff, and after that, we go eat lunch then grab coffee before we leave the mall and go back to my place. April takes off after she talks me through how I should style my hair and do my makeup, and I promise I'll call her when I get home to tell her how the date went.

With her gone and a few hours to spare before I have to start getting ready, I find my Kindle and make myself comfortable on my couch. I settle in, and just as I start to lose myself in a completely different world, my phone rings. The first call is not surprisingly from my sister May, who lives with April. She informs me that April told her I was going out on a date, and then she tells me I should ignore any advice April might have given me about sleeping with Gareth tonight—something that makes me laugh.

While she and I are still on the phone, June and July three-way call me, saying they talked to April. I tell both of them what they heard is true, and they make plans to meet me for breakfast tomorrow morning. Not even a minute after I get off the phone with them, my phone rings once more, and I sigh when I see my mom's name. And I swear that if April ever meets someone she's even a little serious about, I will pay her back tenfold for opening her big mouth.

"Hey, Mom," I say as I put my cell to my ear.

"I just got off the phone with April," she tells me, something I already figured out. "I just want to tell you that your dad and I spent a little time with Gareth at Cobi's wedding, and we were both seriously impressed with him."

"Mom," I start, but she cuts me off.

"I know you don't need our approval, but I want to let you know we approve. He seems like a good guy, and from what Sage and Cobi said, he's a hard worker and he loves his family."

"He has two kids," I insert, thinking that's a deal breaker, if not for her then definitely for my dad.

"I thought you wanted kids?" she prompts quietly.

My eyes slide closed. "I do, but there is a difference between having kids of my own and dating someone who already has kids," I say, feeling a little guilty for admitting the truth. If I'm honest, the idea of Gareth having kids his boys' ages kind of freaks me out. Okay, it *really* freaks me out. I know Mitch from spending time with him at school, and he's a great kid, but that doesn't mean he'd be okay with me dating his dad. And what if his brother hates me? What if things between Gareth and me get serious, and his boys end up resenting me? Or what if—

"Honey," she cuts off my rampant thoughts. "You love kids; you always have. And kids love you," she says softly. "I'm sure you're freaked. Honestly, I'd be worried if you weren't." I listen to her pull in a deep breath. "I don't know what will happen between you two, but I wanted you to know we like him."

"Mom." I sigh, worried she is mentally planning a wedding and preparing for more grandkids, even older ones she can spoil rotten—

"I liked him, honey," she says, and my chest gets tight, because she's using the tone she always uses when she really wants me to hear her. "Honest to God, it was a little scary how much he reminded me of your dad when we first got together."

"What do you mean?"

"At Cobi's wedding, I saw the way he was looking at you before he approached you at the bar. I saw the look on his face when he finally got your attention, and then—" She pauses. "—I ummm... saw you two together outside."

"What?" I squeak.

"I promise I wasn't spying," she says quickly. "I just noticed you were a little off balance when you snuck out the back exit, so I followed you just to make sure you were okay. By the time I got out there, you were with him, and… well, I could tell you'd be okay, so I left."

"Oh my God," I whisper, now completely humiliated.

"It was sweet the way he was holding you," she says dreamily.

"April was cozied up to a guy all night. Did you think that was sweet?" I ask, wanting to change the subject.

"Your sister is a different breed of woman, honey, and your father and I have come to terms with that. I don't know what kind of man she's going to end up with, but we're praying he'll be the kind of man who knows how to deal with her."

"She needs *someone* to deal with her," I mumble, still annoyed she called not only our sisters but our mom to let them all know I was going on a date. I wouldn't be surprised if she's on the phone right now with our cousins, aunts, uncles, and grandparents, letting them know the news.

"Don't be mad at her. She's relieved that things are working out after what happened."

Oh my Lord, I thought this couldn't get worse, but I was wrong. "She told you?"

"She was upset."

"I cannot believe she told you what happened," I hiss. I didn't mind her sharing with our sisters, or even our cousins who have the same X chromosomes, but our mom?

"She felt like it was her fault."

It was her fault. Okay, it wasn't, but still, in my head it kinda was.

"It doesn't even matter, since you're going on a date with Gareth tonight," Mom reminds me, sounding happy once more.

As much as I want to argue, I know it will be pointless. And really, I just want to get off the phone and try to relax before I have to start getting ready. "You're right, it doesn't matter."

"Exactly," she says, and then adds, "Have a great time tonight."

"I will." *Hopefully*.

"See you at breakfast."

Wait… what? "What?"

"We're all meeting you for breakfast in the morning," she says, and I blink at the ceiling, wondering how it would feel to be in a family that didn't care at all about what I was doing or who I was going out with.

With a short shake of my head, I realize I probably wouldn't like it much. My family might be insane and a whole lot in my business, but I wouldn't trade them for the world.

"I guess I'll see you in the morning." I sigh.

She laughs then says what she always says when we're hanging up. "Love you beyond each and every galaxy, beautiful girl."

"Love you more than that, Mom, and tell Dad I love him just as much."

"He knows, but I'll tell him anyway," she promises, and I know she's grinning, because I can hear it in her voice. "Have fun tonight, and be safe."

"I will."

"Until later, honey."

"Until then." I pull my cell from my ear and glance at the clock. I see I still have an hour to read before I need to start getting ready, so I turn my phone on silent so I won't be interrupted, pick up my Kindle that's resting on my lap, and flip it on. I proceed to get lost in a story that's filled with adventure, magic, and romance, and while I read, I try not to think about my boring life. I try not to wonder what would happen if I had an adventure of my own.

Still, I think and wonder until I look at the clock and realize that Gareth is going to be here in less than a half an hour and I'm going to be late for our first date.

Gareth

Chapter 6

I SIT UP on my weight bench then lean forward, placing each of the fifty-pound weights in my hands on the ground at my feet, when I hear Max shout, "Dad, we're home!" over the music I have playing.

I get up, turn down the radio, and shout back, "I'm in the garage!" listening to the sound of footsteps on the hardwood floors get closer. "Did you guys have fun?" I ask Max as he jumps through the open doorway with his brother, my twin sisters following close behind.

"Of course, they had fun," Sejla says as I pick up my weights and place them on the rack where they belong.

"What is that smell?" Selma asks.

"It's called sweat." Max laughs.

"It's gross. You need a candle or something in here," Selma waves her hand in front of her face.

"It's a gym. It's not really supposed to smell good," Mitchell informs his aunt with a smile, and I chuckle.

"Well, boys are gross," she says with a disgusted expression.

"What are we doing tonight, Dad?" Mitch steps up onto the treadmill and turns it on before proceeding to walk backward.

"You boys are hanging with Grandma for a few hours tonight."

"Are you working with Grandma B? Can I come to watch?" Max asks, and I shake my head.

"Where are you going then?" Mitchell asks, studying me.

Fuck, it shouldn't be so fucking hard to say I'm going on a date, but it is, since it's not something I've ever had to tell them before. "I have a date."

"A date? Like... with a girl?" Max asks, and I hear either Selma or Sejla laugh, but I'm not sure which one, since their laughs are almost as identical as they are.

"Yeah."

"With who?" Mitch questions, and I look at him.

"December."

"Miss Mayson?" His brows knit together over his eyes.

"Yeah, you okay with that?" Shit, I don't even know what I'd do if he says no.

"That's cool." He shrugs.

"You're going out on a date with December Mayson?" Selma asks, and I look at her.

"Yeah."

"Wow." She looks at Sejla, and they share a look that I've learned over the years is actually a full-blown conversation.

"Who's December?" Max asks, glancing at everyone in the room with a look that states he's feeling left out.

"She's cool," Mitchell tells his brother. "She's a teacher."

"At the high school?" Max clarifies.

"No, she teaches first graders."

Max frowns. "Then how do you know her?"

"She and a few other first grade teachers bring their classes to the high school once a week. Me and a bunch of the kids in my class play games with them, shoot hoops, or read books. It's fun, and plus we get to skip study hall," he says like that is the best part. "Miss Mayson is one of the coolest teachers who comes. Most of the other teachers are stuck up, but she's always laughing and joking with us when she's there."

"Cool," Max says, and Mitchell grins.

"About that, kid. I don't remember you ever mentioning it to me," I say, watching my oldest closely.

"It's not a big deal." He shrugs casually before he turns to press the up arrow and increase his speed on the treadmill.

"You're right," I agree when he looks at me, continuing to walk backward just faster now. "It's not a big deal, but it's still something I'd like to know you're doing. It's also something I'm proud of you for doing."

"It's awesome you're doing that," Selma inserts, and I see Sejla nod in agreement. "I'm sure the kids love it and really look up to you."

"I guess," Mitchell murmurs, looking a little embarrassed.

"I'm proud of you, kid," I say, and his eyes meet mine. "Your aunt's right. Those kids probably look up to you and look forward to the time you spend with them each week."

"Thanks, Dad," he mumbles, and I lift my chin, not wanting to make him feel any more awkward than he already does.

"So where are you taking December?" Sejla asks, and I look to where she's standing with her arms crossed over her chest as she studies me. "Please tell me it's some place nice and not out for pizza or a burger."

"I'm taking her to Flame," I reply, and her eyes grow wide. I'm not surprised by her expression. Flame opened three months ago, and the waitlist for a table has been a month out since opening. "I know the owner. I've done quite a bit of work on his cars, and he told me awhile back that if I wanted a table, it was mine. So I pulled a favor."

"Well, color me impressed."

"Glad you approve," I mutter sarcastically, and she grins.

"What time is Grandma coming over?" Max asks behind me, and I turn to find him on the treadmill with his brother.

"Around 4:30."

"Can we go to the movies tonight?"

"If your grandma is up to taking you, sure," I answer, and the two of them smile, since they know from experience that all they have to do is ask and their grandma will jump at the chance to make them happy. "That said, you two should get a head start on whatever homework you've got before she gets here. That way, tomorrow, you're not complaining when I'm watching the game and eating junk food without you."

"Homework sucks," Max states as Mitchell turns to power down the treadmill.

"Look at the bright side; you two only have a few more months of school before summer is here," Sejla tells him, and his eyes go to her as he jumps away from his brother, who playfully pushes him off the now still treadmill.

"I guess you're right," he agrees with his aunt then peers up at me. "If I'm gonna do homework, I need brain food."

"You just ate an entire meal from McDonald's in the car on the way here. How are you even hungry right now?" Selma asks, sounding astonished.

"That was like forever ago," he says with a straight face, and she shakes her head in disbelief.

I curl my boy into my side and tip my head down toward him. "Turn on the oven and I'll put in a pizza for you before I hop in the shower."

"Cool." He grins, and I ruffle his hair then let him go to watch him hug his aunts before he disappears through the doorway into the house.

"I need brain food too, Dad," Mitchell tells me with a grin as Selma and Sejla start muttering back and forth under their breath about how much my boys eat.

"I'm sure one pizza will be enough to hold you and your brother over until dinner."

"I guess so," he grumbles before he starts for the door.

"Umm... are you forgetting something?" Sejla asks his back, and his shoulders sag as he turns to face both his aunts, who are looking at him expectantly.

"Sorry." He holds up his hand for a high five, and my sisters take that as a challenge and rush him at the same time. Once he's stuck between them, they begin to hug and kiss him.

"Dad!" he yells, looking at me for help, and I hold up both my hands and laugh while he groans and grumbles, trying unsuccessfully to dodge them.

"Now, you can go." Selma laughs, releasing him at the same time as Sejla. I hear him growl under his breath as he adjusts his clothes and fixes his hair, and I smile as he glares at me before stomping away, disappearing back into the house.

"He's growing up too fast," Sejla says, and I feel pain slice through my chest. She's right. I try not to think about it, but I know it's only going to be a few years before we're searching for colleges. And on the heels of that, he'll move out, eventually find someone to spend his life with, and start a family of his own. And not long after he's gone, Max will do the same and begin his own life. It feels like it was just minutes ago that I was holding each of them against my chest, marveling at the fact that I created them. And now they are on the cusp of becoming men of their own.

"Both my boys are growing up too quickly," I reply, watching my sisters' faces soften in understanding. "I've loved watching them grow and become their own men, but—"

"You miss your babies," Sejla says quiet, cutting me off.

"Yeah." I rub the tension from the back of my neck.

"Maybe you'll have another baby one day," Selma says, and I shake my head in denial.

"No sleep, bottles, and endless amounts of diapers? No thanks. I did that twice, and I'm not going back."

"You're still young," Sejla points out, like that's reason enough to have another kid.

"I have my boys. I've done the baby thing and enjoyed every second of it, but I'm not interested in going through that again," I say, then watch my sisters share a look of disappointment. "What?" I ask, looking between the two of them.

"You're young," Sejla repeats, then holds up her hand when I start to open my mouth to reiterate my earlier statement. "Whoever you end up with will most likely be young too, so what will happen if they don't have kids and want to start a family with you?"

My chest tightens as I fully comprehend the point she's trying to make. Still, I say, "Whoever I end up with will have my boys and me."

"Okay, I get that, but maybe you shouldn't completely close the door on the idea of having more children," she tells me, then continues with her voice dipping to a solemn tone. "With both Mitchell and Max, you were a single dad doing all the heavy lifting alone. It would be different if you found the right woman, someone who wanted to be a mom. Someone to share things with, who'd stick around even when things got hard."

I want to tell her I'd be open to the idea of more kids with the right woman, but in all honesty, I don't know if I would be.

"Please, please don't shut that door," she pleas, reading my expression.

"I won't shut that door," I agree just to get the look of concern out of her eyes, and she lets out a deep breath before she looks at Selma then back to me.

"We've both met December. She's sweet, and her family is awesome, and I think I speak for the two of us when I say we're happy you're finally dating."

Shit.

"You deserve someone like her," Selma adds, and I realize at that moment exactly why Sejla was so adamant about me being open to the idea of having more kids.

December is young, she doesn't have children, and if she's like most women, she's probably thought about having kids of her own. It's not a subject I'd broach tonight, but it's definitely something we will have to talk about if things between us progress.

"Just have fun tonight." Her lips tip up into a smile then she looks at Sejla. "We need to go if we're going to make it to Nashville in time."

"Nashville?" I ask, wondering why they're heading into the city.

"One of our favorite authors is signing at the bookstore downtown," Selma says, and I roll my eyes. My sisters are both avid readers. If they aren't working, they're traveling to reader events all over the world to meet their favorite authors and hang out with their book friends.

"You can bore me with the nerdy details later," I tell them, and they both laugh as I walk the two of them into the house. I stop in the kitchen to take a frozen pizza out of the freezer, and while I put it on a pan and place it in the oven, they go to say goodbye to their nephews. I meet them at the front door a few minutes later and hug each of them before they leave. Once they're gone, I knock on Mitchell's door then Max's, telling them to keep an ear out for the timer I set for the pizza, hoping one or both of them will hear it.

Getting grumbled agreements from both boys, I go to my room and hop in the shower. Forty minutes later, dressed in dark gray slacks and a burgundy button-down shirt, I head toward the sound of voices in the living room. I find both boys on the couch and the pizza I placed in the oven earlier between them on the coffee table. I start to open my mouth to ask how their homework is coming along, but I freeze when I hear Max ask, "But what if Mom comes back?"

"Dude, seriously?" Mitchell responds instantly, sounding annoyed. "Mom and Dad aren't together, and they haven't been together in like... years."

"I guess you're right." Max's voice is barely above a whisper. "It's just... when Mom comes around, Dad always seems like he wants her to stay."

"Dad wants us to have Mom, but that doesn't mean *he* wants her," Mitchell tells his little brother matter-of-factly, and my chest gets tight. "We haven't seen Mom in months, and Dad should find someone who makes him happy."

"Do you think..." Max pauses and seems to ponder what he's going to ask. "Do you think December will make him happy?"

"I don't know, but I saw them together and—" He cuts off his own words, and I watch as he shakes his head. "She's nice. Dad deserves someone nice."

"Mom is nice," Max says, sounding defensive. Him defending his mom isn't surprising. Beth has been in and out of his life since he was born, but anytime she's come around, she has made it a point to bring gifts and make it seem like she'd been on an adventure she couldn't wait to come back from, just so she could share all her stories with him.

I see an irritated look fill Mitchell's eyes, and when he sits up straight and starts to open his mouth, I know it's time to step in. I force my feet to move and my mouth to open before Mitchell has a chance to respond. "I see you two managed to share a pizza. Now, tell me. How's your homework going?"

"I'm just about done," Mitchell tells me, and my eyes go to Max.

"I don't have much left either."

"If you guys get everything done today, we'll go to the batting cage tomorrow before the game."

"We'll have it done," Max assures with excitement, and Mitchell nods in agreement with his brother.

"Good," I say, turning toward the door when it's shoved open and my mom walks in.

"I brought chocolate chip cookies," she says in the form of a greeting, holding a Tupperware container in the air.

"Right on!" Max exclaims, jumping off the couch to greet her with a hug before taking the container from her. Mitchell isn't far behind him in greeting his grandma, but I notice he doesn't hug her. He just smiles and allows her to kiss his cheek.

When both boys are settled back on the couch with their pizza and the tub of cookies, I glance at the clock to check the time then go to the front door and shrug on my jacket.

"You're leaving already?" Mom asks.

"Yeah, I want to stop and pick up flowers, and I know traffic will be crazy with all the construction happening around town."

"Flowers," she murmurs, looking proud, and then she eyes me from head to toe. "You look handsome. Burgundy looks good on you."

"Thanks," I mutter, and she grins. "The boys asked about seeing a movie. I left a hundred dollars on the kitchen counter for you, if you feel up to taking them."

"I can pay for my grandbabies to see a movie," she snaps, sounding as annoyed as she always does when I leave money with her for the boys.

"It's not for the movie. It's for the forty dollars' worth of junk food they will want, along with whatever you guys decide to pick up for dinner."

"We'll go to Walmart before and get stuff to take in with us." She waves me off.

"They'll still want frozen drinks at the movie, along with popcorn, and food afterward."

"Yeah, and I can afford that stuff too. I'm not broke."

She's not; she's always been careful with money. Still, I always leave money, even if I know it will be right where I left it when I get home. "Use it or don't, but it's there if you need it," I say, and she gives me a look full of annoyance. I glance at the couch, where the boys are now eating chocolate chip cookies and watching some show on TV, and then look at my mom. "After they eat, urge them to finish their homework before you go to the movies."

"It's Saturday. They have tomorrow to do homework."

"Yeah, but I told them I'd take them to the batting cages tomorrow before the game comes on. If they have homework, they will have to miss out on one or the other."

"Oh, right."

"I'll be back before eleven," I tell her, then add, "If I'm running later than that, I'll call."

"Eleven, midnight, tomorrow morning—we'll be good." She smiles, back to being happy, and I shake my head at her.

"Boys, be good for your grandma!" I shout as I grab my keys.

"We will!" Max shouts back.

"Have fun, Dad," Mitch says.

"Thanks, bud." I lift my chin.

"Have fun tonight." Mom winks.

"Thanks," I shake my head.

After fighting traffic and picking up flowers from the florist in town, I head to December's apartment building and get there ten minutes before I'm supposed to arrive. I climb out, taking the bouquet of pink peonies with me, and move to her door. I knock and get no reply, so I knock again and ring the bell, hearing a muttered curse right before the door is yanked open.

"You're early," she says with her fingers wrapped around the robe at her waist, her hair still up in curlers and one eye darker than the other with makeup.

"Eight minutes."

"What?" She shakes her head, taking a step back as I walk into her apartment.

"I'm early by eight minutes." I glance at the clock on her wall. "Actually, seven." I look around and see her e-reader on the couch, along with an open bag of Cheetos and a Diet Coke on her coffee table. "Did you forget about our date?"

"What? Of course not. I just—"

"Let me guess," I cut her off. "You were reading and lost track of time."

"Something like that." She looks away as her cheeks grow pink with embarrassment.

"You'll have to tell me about the book at dinner."

She looks at the clock and her eyes widen. "Crap." She spins around, "I'll be back in ten minutes, make yourself at home," she calls as she runs off.

Figuring it will take her longer than ten minutes to finish getting ready, I place the flowers in my hand next to her Coke on the coffee table then take a moment to look around. Her living room is small, but it's also bright and filled with color. There are photos on the walls, along with framed pieces of floral art and quotes from various people, all artfully arranged. There isn't an empty space to be seen, and even though it's chaotic, it's still somehow her.

I walk to her bookshelves, pick up the top book from a stack all from the same author, and flip open the cover. Just like my sisters' prized books, it is signed to her. I smile then place it back where it belongs before examining the rest of her book collection.

Minutes later, I start to move to look at some of her photos, when I hear a door open. I turn and freeze as I soak in every single detail. From her smoky eyes, the fall of her hair around her shoulders, and the black material contouring to every single inch of her voluptuous body.

"I'm really sorry about being late," she tells me, turning away to bend and pick up her purse off the couch.

Jesus Christ. My hands itch to touch her. The dress is simple; she's not showing a lot of skin, but with the way it molds to her tits and ass, she might as well be naked. Then, there are the heels she's wearing, heels I can imagine sinking into my flesh while I fuck her. Without a doubt, every man who sees her tonight is going to be thinking the same dirty things I am right now. Lucky for me, she'll be on my arm.

"I'm ready when you are." She ducks her head to avoid looking at me.

I walk across the room and stop just long enough to pick up the flowers, and her gaze finally meets mine when I hold them out to her.

I watch her lick her lips as she tips her head down toward the bouquet while lifting them to her nose.

"Peonies are my favorite."

"I know," I admit, and her startled gaze comes up, locking with mine. "I asked Sage, who asked Kim, who eventually got back to me after calling your sisters."

Her lips part in surprise, making it really fucking hard not to kiss her. "I... I don't know what to say except thank you," she says shyly.

"You're welcome." I reach out, touching my fingers to hers holding the flowers, and her pupils dilate. "You wanna put them in something?"

"I'll do it when I get home. I know you made reservations, and we're already running late because of me." She turns, taking the bouquet through the open archway into her kitchen, and I follow, watching her place a stopper in the drain then turn on the water. Once the sink has a couple of inches of water in the bottom, she rests the flowers against the edge, shuts off the pipe, and turns toward me. "I really am ready now." She smiles, and I chuckle, placing my hand against her lower back to lead her outside, hoping like fuck this woman isn't too good to be true.

Chapter 7

$\mathcal{B}$REATHE, JUST BREATHE, I repeat over and over in my head as Gareth opens the passenger door to his SUV. I swallow, looking up at the seat that is chest high on me. wondering nervously how I'm going to get up there without looking like an idiot. My dress is too tight for me to pull myself up gracefully, and I still have yet to master the art of doing anything more than walking or standing in heels.

"Let me help you." His warm hand comes to rest on my lower back, and heat seers through the thin material of my dress, making me shiver.

I look up at him and shake my head. "I can manage." Or I hope I can. He grins then suddenly his hand on my back slides around to my hip. He turns me to face him, and when the opposite hand curls around my waist, I start to ask what he's doing. Before I get my mouth to form actual words, my feet are no longer on the ground and my bottom is on the leather seat.

"You..." I start to accuse him of picking me up, but his fingers curl around my calf, making it tingle, and I lose my train of thought.

"Tuck your feet in and buckle up, Ember."

With my heart pounding, I quickly tuck in my feet, but when the door slams closed, I don't buckle up. I watch him through the windshield as he prowls around the hood, pondering how I feel about what he just did. I realize, as he opens his door, I liked it. Not sure how I feel about *that*, I grasp my belt as he settles behind the wheel and lock it in place. "I could have gotten into your vehicle on my own."

"Yeah." He puts the key in the ignition and starts the engine, looking over at me. "But you contemplating how you'd do that gave me an excuse to touch you, and since you walked out of your room in that dress, my hands have been itchy."

"What does that mean?" I ask, even though I'm pretty sure I already know the answer.

He turns fully to face me, and the heat I see in his gaze causes tingles of desire to light me up from the roots of my hair down to the tips of my toes. "Means I'm gonna find any reason I can to touch you tonight."

Breathe! my mind screams as my lips part to form a soft O.

His eyes, now on my mouth, lift to meet mine, and he whispers, "Yeah." With no response from me, he places his hand on the headrest of my seat and carefully backs out of his parking spot then puts the engine in drive.

I clutch my purse in my lap with both hands as he drives out of my apartment complex, willing my heart to slow down. "Where are we going?"

"Dinner," he answers simply, and I want to roll my eyes.

"I know that, but where?"

"It's a surprise."

I don't know if I can handle any more surprises from him tonight. The flowers he brought me were a shock, especially after admitting he didn't just bring me a store bought bouquet of flowers he picked at random. No, instead, he went out of his way to find out my favorite. Then his compliments and admitting he wanted to touch me have pushed me over my limit.

"Can I have a hint?"

"It's hot."

"Do you mean spicy?" I ask, and I see his lips twitch like something is funny. "What?"

"Do you not like surprises?"

I think about it for a second, then answer honestly, "Not really."

"That's a surprise."

"Why do you say that?" I ask, adjusting in the seat.

"You read, and judging by the number of books you own, it's a lot. I doubt you go into each book wanting to read it because you know how it's going to end."

Darn, he has a point. Still, he's also kinda wrong. "When I'm reading and get to a point in a book that makes me nervous about how things will turn out, I skip to the end just to make sure everything ends up okay."

"Really?" He glances at me.

"Really. In my mind, I can't move on with the book if I don't know there is a happily ever after coming."

"That doesn't ruin the story for you?"

"No, it's kind of like biting into a sandwich. The bread tastes good, but the meat, cheese, mayo, and mustard is what make it delicious. I never read much of the ending, just enough to feel good about what I'm going to get before I continue on."

"Oddly, I get that."

"You do?" I ask, knowing I sound as surprised as I am.

"I do, but still, I like being surprised." He stops at a red light and turns to smile at me. "Imagine thinking you grabbed the same sandwich you've eaten every day, but then you bite into it and realize it's actually something you've never had and better than anything you've ever tasted."

"But what if it's not?" I ask, holding his stare. "What if it's gross and you have to toss it in the garbage and feel hungry for the rest of the day, because you didn't stick to what you know?"

"That's life." He looks away when the light turns green. "We can plan all we want, but at the end of the day, some things are out of our hands. One day, you might feel like you've got it all figured out, and then the next day comes and something unexpected happens, knocking you down or shoving you forward."

"That's kind of deep for sandwich talk," I say, half joking and half serious, his words resonating with a part of me I'm still trying to figure out. A part of me that wants to be brave and take chances.

"You're right, so we should go eat," he replies, and I notice then that we're pulling into a parking lot that is packed full of cars.

It takes me a couple of seconds to figure out where we are, and when I do, I shake my head. "It's hot," I repeat his earlier clue, and he grins as he rolls into an empty space and shuts down the engine.

"Surprised?" He turns toward me after putting the engine in Park and shutting it off.

"Very." Flame has been the talk of the town since it opened, and everything said about it has been good, which is why you need to call months ahead for a reservation. Or at least that's what my dad said when he mentioned wanting to bring my mom. *How did he get us a table?*

"I know the owner," he answers my unspoken question, and I raise one brow. "I've done some work for him."

"Tattoos?" I ask, and he shakes his head.

"No. Besides Flame, Mack, the owner of this place, has an online luxury car dealership. He made his money by purchasing vehicles from auctions for less than market value and then fixing them up and selling them online for less than what they are worth but more than what he paid. I'm one of the mechanics he uses to make whatever repairs are needed on his vehicles before they go up for sale."

"That's smart."

"Yeah," he agrees then asks, "Are you ready to go inside?"

"Yes." I unhook my belt as he opens his door and hops out, and when I open my door to do the same, I pause. Logically, I know the distance to the ground isn't that far. Still, I'm not sure I'll be able to make it without spraining my ankle or worse.

"I got you." He appears in my open door, holding out his hands.

I don't think about what I'm doing. I lean toward him and wrap my palms around his shoulders, feeling his muscles bunch under my fingers. His hands curve around my waist and he carefully lifts me from the seat. When my feet touch the gravel, I tip my head back toward him, feeling off balance by our closeness. "Thanks."

"Anytime." He doesn't step back. Instead, he lifts his hand and touches my temple with a finger before slowly sliding my hair away from my face and tucking it behind my ear. I hold my breath as I stare into his eyes and fight the urge to use my hold on him to lift myself up and press my lips to his. "We should go in before they give away our table."

He takes a step back, leaving me off balance once more, even with his hand on the curve of my hip still holding me steady. With no other response, I nod as he lets me go and lift my purse over my shoulder, stepping away from the door so he can shut it. I take his hand when he offers it, and try to ignore the zap of electricity that zings through our connected palms as our skin makes contact. There is no denying there is some serious chemistry between us; I just hope we have something deeper than sexual attraction. Otherwise, this thing between us will burn out quickly. When we finally make our way through the crowd that is gathered around the front door, Gareth stops at a podium where three women, all dressed in black, are gathered around the tablet in the middle one's hands. It doesn't take long for them to look up, and when they do, I recognize one of them immediately as the mother of one my students from last year.

"Miss Mayson." She smiles at me.

"Hi, Lina. Please, call me December," I return, and she nods then looks at Gareth. Her eyes fill with appreciation before meeting mine once more. "This is Gareth," I introduce, then ask, "How has Tiffany been?"

Her face softens at my question and my heart warms. Lina is a single mom, and the relationship I witnessed between her and her daughter was something special. "Good. She loves her new school and her teachers. Though, she still talks about you all the time."

"I think about her often." It's not a lie. I think about all my kids when they are no longer under my care. Normally when they graduate from my class, they stay in the building I work in, so I'm able to check up on them from time to time. But Lina was forced to transfer Tiffany to a different school when the zones were changed. "I'm glad she's doing good. You should bring her by the school sometime. I'd love to see her."

"I'll have to do that. She'd enjoy that," she says, and then glances at Gareth quickly. I notice he hasn't said anything, but his fingers around mine have gotten tighter. "Sorry." She shakes her head, looking a little embarrassed. "We're not here to catch up. Do you two have a reservation?"

"We do," Gareth puts in, letting my hand go to wrap his arm around my waist. "Under Black."

Lina looks at the two women still standing next to her listening to our exchange, and the one in the middle types quickly on the tablet then looks up at us with wide eyes. I don't know what to make of her expression, or have time to ask about it, before Lina is grabbing long sheets of paper out of a holder at the side of the podium. "Your table is ready." She starts to walk away then looks at us over her shoulder. "Sorry." She smiles. "Please, come with me."

We follow her through the packed restaurant, and I notice that every single table is taken up with people either enjoying their food or chatting with smiles on their faces as they wait for their meals to arrive. I feel Gareth close on my heels as we walk through a doorway behind Leah and up a set of stairs. When I crest the top of the stairs and see the view before me, my breath catches. Through the glass-enclosed space, there is nothing to see at this vantage point but twinkling stars and city lights. And with only four tables within the space and only one of them taken up with an older couple, it feels private.

"This is beautiful," I murmur as Lina stops at a table near the edge of the building, and Gareth pulls out my chair for me to sit.

"Mack just finished this two days ago. You two and that couple over there, who are his parents, are the first to eat up here." She looks at Gareth. "You must be good friends with Mack."

"You could say that," he responds casually, and she eyes him for a moment then looks between the two of us.

"Your waiter Simon will be with you shortly to go over the menu with you, but I have to tell you my favorite thing here to eat is the ginger, garlic, and honey baby back ribs, the house mac and cheese, with a side of greens."

My mouth waters. "That sounds good," I say, because everything she mentions does. Still, I know I will never, not ever, order ribs to eat on a first date.

"Trust me, everything on the menu is delicious," she replies, looking pleased, before she bows slightly. "I hope you two have a great dinner."

"Thanks," I tell her, and she smiles at me. I watch her walk away then look at Gareth, who touches his fingers to mine on top of the table.

"You getting the ribs?" he asks with a small twitch of his lips.

I shake my head then answer, "No. I mean, they sound good, but I don't trust myself to eat them without making a mess of myself."

"You want them though, don't you?"

"Was I drooling when she was talking about them?" I ask.

"A little." He laughs. "I'll order them and you can have one of mine."

"Just one?" I frown.

"Don't be greedy."

"Just one of anything is never enough," I inform him straight-faced.

He laughs again and I enjoy the deep sound. "Okay, two, but only if you promise to share whatever you order."

"I think you should know now that I'm greedy when it comes to my food." I pick up my napkin and place it over my lap.

"Does that mean you won't share with me?"

"I grew up with sisters who had no problem taking the last piece of pizza or the last scoop of ice cream. I learned early on to get as much food as possible before it was all gone. If you give me three of your ribs and a scoop of your mac and cheese, I'll give you the scraps off my plate, but I can't promise there will be much left."

He shakes his head. "I think I need to see what you order before I take that offer," he responds, as a thin older man with no hair on his head approaches our table.

"Good evening. My name is Simon, and I will be your server this evening." The older gentleman inclines his head before he quickly rattles off the wine list and tells us about the house specials for the evening. I order a glass of wine, and Gareth orders a beer. We both agree on an order of fried green tomatoes as an appetizer, which means my stomach is growling in anticipation when Simon walks away.

"Do you know what you're going to order?" Gareth asks.

I don't even look at the menu. "The house special of fried hot honeyed chicken, mashed potatoes, and bacon green beans."

"Have you had hot chicken before?" he asks, looking concerned.

"Have you ever been to Hattie B's?" I answer his question with a question. Hattie B's is famous for their hot chicken, and it's one of my favorite chicken spots in Nashville.

"I know it."

"I go there once a month. I would go more often, but I'm not normally in the mood to stand in line to eat."

"Seriously?" He looks surprised.

"Seriously." I nod, and he shakes his head in disbelief. "I would eat there every night if I could. I love it."

"I went once and never went back."

"Some people can handle the heat, and others can't." I smirk. "One thing I also learned growing up—the spicier the food, the better my chance of getting more of it for myself."

"You probably have a point, because if the chicken you get tonight is even close to the heat of Hattie's, I'll keep my hands on my own plate."

"That's fine, but just remember you already promised me a rib."

"I won't forget," he says as Simon comes back to drop off our drinks and take our orders.

When he leaves once more, I lean back in my seat and take a sip of wine as Gareth takes a pull from his beer. "Where are your boys tonight?" I ask, not wanting to pretend like they don't exist when they most definitely do.

"With my mom. She's taking the two of them to the movies and filling them up with junk food."

"What are they seeing?" I ask, setting my glass back on the table but keeping my fingers wrapped around the stem.

"The new Marvel one that just came out."

"I want to see that," I say, and he tips his head to the side. "What?" I ask when I see the look of disbelief in his eyes.

"You like action movies?"

"My list for movies goes: comedy, action, mystery."

"What about romance?"

"It depends. Only if it's a romantic comedy. If it is, it's up there with my love of comedies, but if it's just a romance, it's normally a hard pass."

"That's surprising."

"Why?"

"You read romance."

"I do, but reading a romance book and watching a romance play out on screen are completely different. When you read about a couple, it's like you are there with them, falling in love at the same time they are. You feel, smell, and see what they do. It's difficult to portray that into actions and looks in a movie, which makes things awkward for me when I watch a romance unfold on screen."

"So your favorite movies are comedies?"

"Yes, and I'm that person who is laughing the loudest in the theater, annoying everyone sitting around me."

He smiles. "What are your favorite types of books to read?"

"It would be a tossup between fantasy and rom-coms. I love disappearing into a new world and experiencing things that don't exist. I also love romantic comedies, where funny things happen to bring a couple closer together." I ask, "What are your favorite types of movies?"

"Comedies first then action movies, and occasionally I like to watch sci-fi, depending on what the movie is about."

"What is your favorite movie of all time?'

"*Die Hard.*"

"Such a guy." I roll my eyes, and he chuckles, taking a sip of his beer while leaning back in his seat. I take a sip of wine, amazed at how relaxed I feel. This morning, I was a nervous wreck even thinking about going out with him. But now, I feel surprisingly at ease, even with the constant flutter of butterflies in the pit of my stomach.

"What are you thinking about?"

"This is easier than I thought it would be," I say truthfully, and he tips his head to the side questioningly. "It probably hasn't slipped your notice that you make me nervous, but I'm not tempted to run away, or fumbling around knocking over glasses and tripping over my own feet."

"If you run or if you fall, I'd catch you," he says, holding my gaze, and my heart begins to pound while my blood warms, making my cheeks hot. "I love it when you blush," he adds quietly.

"It's annoying." I duck my head and fiddle with my napkin on my lap.

Warm fingers touch my cheek and I look up. "It's adorable and refreshing."

"Why?"

"It shows that you're worried about what I might think and are interested in me enough to care. Most people try to hide how they feel; that way, if things don't work out like they want, the person responsible for hurting them doesn't know they ever had the power to hurt them. You can't hide how you feel. Your emotions are written on your skin."

"I think you just proved why my blushing is annoying," I say, and he smiles.

"You can think that, but just know I feel differently about the cute way your cheeks get pink," he tells me, smoothing his thumb over my warm skin, and I lean into his touch. "You should know I'm just as interested as you are."

"Ahem." Simon clears his throat, and Gareth's eyes locked on mine fill with frustration before he looks up at him standing at edge of our table. "Sorry to interrupt." He places a plate of fried tomatoes between us then bows and backs away quickly, looking nervously at Gareth, and I almost laugh.

"I wonder if that's what it's like for royalty?" I muse, spearing one of the fried green tomatoes and placing it on my plate.

"If it is, that's probably why they always look so pissed," he answers, and I giggle.

We talk about random things as we devour our appetizer, and when our meals arrive, we pick food off each other's plate without permission. Once we finish, we agree to share the chocolate molten lava cake and vanilla bean ice cream for dessert.

"Oh my God," I whisper as warm chocolate and cold ice cream meet my tongue.

"That good?" Gareth asks, and I look up at him, about to make a joke, but the look in his eyes is so hot I feel it sizzle against my skin, making my toes curl.

"It's good," I whisper with nothing else to say. He nods, not even lifting his spoon to take a bite. Instead, he lifts his chin to someone over my shoulder, and a moment later, Simon appears.

"Can we get the check?"

"Mack insisted your meal be on the house this evening," Simon replies, and Gareth's jaw ticks.

Reading his expression, I reach for his hand and he looks at me. "You can always leave a tip."

"Are you finished?" he asks. Even though I wouldn't mind having another bite of cake, the shortness of his tone tells me I shouldn't, so I nod. "Let's go." He stands then offers me his hand to help me from my seat, and I take it. I turn to grab my bag from the table as he tosses two hundred-dollar bills down, and my eyes widen.

Feeling a little awkward about what's happened the last couple of minutes, I look at Simon and smile. "Thank you."

The older man pulls his eyes off the money waiting for him and grins at me. "Come back soon."

I make a non-committal sound as warmth and pressure are applied to my lower back to lead me away. When we reach the parking lot and stop at the passenger door of his SUV, I look up at Gareth and break the silence. "I think a two-hundred-dollar tip was overkill."

"That was our first date. If I couldn't afford to take you there, I wouldn't have." The angry tone in his voice surprises me.

"Okay." My brows draw together in confusion.

"I have two boys I'm raising on my own, and everyone who knows me knows that my ex walked out and left me with bills, a mortgage, and two boys to take care of."

I shake my head, unsure of the point he's trying to make. "And?"

"And I don't like people feeling sorry for me," he growls.

Realization slams against me, making my temper flare, and I turn to face him fully. "You think your friend Mack offered dinner on the house because he felt sorry for you?" I know my voice is full of disbelief. He doesn't respond with more than a twitch of his jaw. "My dad owns a construction business; he's always getting free stuff from the people he works for. It's the way of the world. When you help someone, they want you to know they appreciate you, and if they are able to give you something to show it, they do."

"That's different."

"Is it? Why? Because you're a single father whose ex left him?" I laugh without humor. "Maybe instead of feeling thankful the next time I get a gift card from one of my students' parents, I should be offended that they think I'm a poor teacher who can't get a cup of coffee from Starbucks without their help."

"Again, that's different."

"Is it, or is your ego so big that you can't accept a gesture of gratitude without thinking someone is doing something for you, not out of kindness but pity?"

He looks away.

I sigh, wondering how we got to this point, when tonight was going so well. Feeling disappointed and frustrated, I turn to open the door.

"You're right," he says, surprising me, and I stop to look at him over my shoulder.

"About which part?"

"All of it. When my ex left, I had to depend on people to help me out, and it ate at me every time I had to ask someone for a favor."

"You're lucky you even had people you could lean on," I reply quietly.

"You're right."

"I know I am."

"Fuck," he clips, tipping his head back toward the sky. "I shouldn't have given that guy two hundred dollars."

"You really shouldn't have," I agree, turning to face him.

"Especially after he kept fucking interrupting us."

The statement erases the tension between us, and I throw my head back and laugh. Once I have myself under control, I wipe the tears from my face.

"He was our waiter. It was his job to deliver food and check on us."

"He was annoying." His fingers curl around the side of my neck and he dips his head toward mine. "Are we good?"

"I think so. Are you over being angry?"

"Yeah." He brushes his lips across mine then uses his hold on me to tip my head farther to the side and deepens the kiss. When he pulls back, I'm panting for breath. "You ready to get home?"

I force my eyes open as my mind screams no.

"Yes."

"Come on." He keeps his hold on me and uses his free hand to open the door then, just like earlier, he lifts me off the ground with ease and places me on the seat. I smile down at him, tucking in my feet, and he smiles back before slamming the door closed. When he gets in behind the wheel, I buckle up, hating that our date is over but loving that it went as good as it did, even with the bit of drama.

"In case I forget, you should know I had a great time," I tell him as he backs out of the parking space, and looks over at me.

"Me too." He reaches for my hand, and once he has it in his grasp, he kisses my fingertips then locks our hands together. He rests them on his hard thigh, keeping hold of me as he drives us across town.

When we reach my place, my nervousness once again kicks in as the energy between us zaps with an undercurrent of heat, making my skin tingle and my heart pound. Without a word, he gets out and comes around to help me down, and after my feet are firmly on solid ground, we walk hand in hand to my apartment. As soon as I have the door open, the heat between us is ignited, and whatever has been keeping us both in check is forgotten.

I'm not sure who kisses who first, but I memorize his taste as his tongue thrusts between my lips and moan as he slides his hands down my body then back up to slowly peel my dress off over my head. I help him out of his shirt with fumbling fingers, and when he's free of the garment and it's discarded on the floor with my dress, my palms skate across his warm, muscular skin. We stumble toward my bedroom, devouring each other at a frenzied pace, touching, nipping, gripping anything we can get our hands or mouths on.

When my back hits my bed and his warm body settles over mine, I whisper his name, and he kisses me before moving his warm mouth down the column of my throat to my breast. I arch into him and whimper when I feel the fabric of my lace bra between his warm, wet mouth and my skin. Reading my distress, he slides the material down then captures my nipple between his teeth, flicking it with the tip of his tongue. I almost come from the contact and dig my nails into his back.

When he pulls away, we're both panting with need and the desire between us is saturating the air. "Ember." The look in his gaze is questioning.

"Gareth." I raise my hips and wrap my legs around his waist in answer.

"Jesus." He grinds his cock against my still covered pussy, and I shiver in need.

"Please don't make me beg." I dig my nails into his skin, and he slides his hands down my hips, dragging my panties off. The moment the material is gone his fingers slide over my clit, my inner muscles spasm.

"You never have to beg with me." He kisses me once more then the sound of a condom being torn open rips through the silence, and seconds later, he fills me in one smooth stroke. I cry out in pain and pleasure. He's huge, wide and long, and I feel every single inch of him branding my insides, making them his own. When he pulls back with just the tip of his cock resting against me, I lift my head and capture his lips while using the heels of my feet to bring him back into me. Every part of us is in sync as he fucks me into oblivion, and when I start to come, I know he's capable of touching a piece of me I didn't even know existed until him. "Oh, God."

"Jesus. Give it to me. Let go," he growls, thrusting harder and faster.

"Gareth," I hiss his name, not sure I'm capable of handling what I feel coming.

"Let go, Ember. I've got you." He moves his thumb to my clit, and that's all it takes. My mind blanks and I feel nothing but the piercing pleasure of my orgasm as it radiates from my inner core outward to each cell in my body, lighting me up. As I let go, I disappear over the edge, panting for breath with my eyes closed, not wanting to miss out on one second of what I'm experiencing. "Fucking Christ, you're perfection," he rumbles, smoothing my hair away from my damp face. "I'm close, baby."

I force my eyes open and stare up at him, mesmerized by how feral he looks with his head back and jaw tight. I lift my fingers to the side of his neck and his eyes open. The moment his focus is on me, I lift my head. "You're beautiful."

"Fuck," he groans, tipping his head down to take my mouth in a kiss that leaves me shattered. His muscles bunch under my hands, his fingers dig into my flesh in a way that I know I'll have bruises, and he growls down my throat as he comes. When he drags his mouth from mine, I gasp for air, and he tucks his face into the crook of my neck then rolls to his back, keeping me wrapped in his arms and holding our connection.

Exhausted, I rest my cheek against his chest and listen to the sound of his heart beating hard against my ear as his fingers begin to slide up and down my back.

"You going to sleep?" I hear and feel him ask, and I nod my cheek up and down against his skin. "Fuck, I hate that I can't stay and sleep with you just like this."

My stomach rolls as real life pops my euphoric bubble. How could I forget? How did I forget he's not just a normal guy who can stay out all night without having plans in place to do so? How did I not remember he has two boys at home that he needs to get back to?

"It's okay." I start to lift up to move off him, but his arms tighten around me, holding me prisoner.

"I didn't say I gotta go right now. I just hate I gotta go at all," he says gently, gripping my chin to get my attention.

But I keep my eyes averted, not wanting him to see exactly how I feel about him having to leave. "I understand."

"Yeah, then look at me." I do, and when I see the torn look in his gaze, my chest grows tight. "I wouldn't leave if I didn't have to." He slides a piece of hair behind my ear and shakes his head. "I'm a package deal, baby. If you get into this with me, you gotta know I come with two boys who are a priority."

"I know you come with kids," I whisper. "If I wasn't okay with that, I wouldn't have gone out with you tonight. I know you can't sleep over and that you need to get home to them."

"Yeah, but we have time before I gotta do that." He lifts his head and looks around then frowns. "Where is your clock?"

"On my phone?"

"You don't have an alarm clock?"

"I do; it's also on my phone." I smile.

"Smart ass." He rolls me to my back and I lose my connection with him, which makes me mewl in disappointment. "You'll get me back." He smiles smugly, touching his mouth to mine. "Do you know where my pants are?"

"On the floor somewhere."

He smiles then leans over me, crushing me to the mattress with his weight as he reaches down over the side of my bed. A moment later, he comes up with his pants and reaches into the pocket. Once he retrieves his phone, he clicks on the screen and I see it's just after nine.

"Two hours."

"What?" I struggle for breath, and he leans back, grinning at me, and then gathers me against his chest. He rolls us once more so I'm straddling his hips.

"After I get rid of this condom we have about two hours to do that again."

"Oh," I whisper, enchanted by his words, our new position, and the feel of him under me.

"Oh yeah." He tangles his hand in my hair at the nape of my neck and drags my mouth down to his. For the next two hours, we don't waste a moment talking. We spend each second exploring each other in the best possible ways, and when he kisses me goodnight at my door, I'm pretty sure I just had the best first date in the history of first dates.

Chapter 8

$\mathcal{I}$ PULL OPEN the door to Jones's, a small restaurant that is nestled between other businesses on Main Street, and am immediately bombarded by the chatter of talking patrons and the scent of breakfast foods coming from the open kitchen. I scan the small space and find my sisters along with my mom all seated in a booth near the window, drinking coffee and waiting for me to arrive.

I force my feet to take me forward, hoping no one can tell what happened last night just by looking at me. When I reach the table, Mom gets up to hug me, and when she lets me go, April nudges her elbow into May's side, forcing her over so I can sit next to her.

"Sooo, how did it go?" April lets the first word drag on, and I tangle my fingers in my lap.

"Good." I accept the cup of coffee my mom slides toward me and she winks. Crap, she totally knows what I did last night, the same way she knew everything I did when I was growing up.

"You didn't call me until almost midnight, and then all you said was you were going to bed and would talk to me in the morning. So I'm guessing the date went better than good," April states as I take a sip of coffee.

"Okay, it went better than good." I sigh, wishing I woke up in time to get some caffeine into my system before I had to leave my place.

Unfortunately, I slept through the three alarms I set in fifteen-minute increments and still pressed Snooze on the last one, which left me only minutes to get showered, dressed, and in my car to make it here.

"So," June cuts in. "Did he bring you peonies?"

"I think you all already know he did," I say, looking around the table and feeling overwhelmed when I see everyone waiting for me to elaborate.

"We knew he asked for your favorite flower, but we didn't know if he'd actually buy them for you, since they aren't exactly easy to come by," July pipes up, looking happy.

"Where did he take you for dinner?" Mom asks, and I pull my eyes off my sister's smiling face to look at her.

"Flame," I reply, and Mom's eyes widen with awe. "He knows the owner. We had dinner on the rooftop, which has been enclosed with glass, and were the only people there after the owner's parents left."

"Was the food good?" May asks, and I look around April at her.

"It was one of the best meals I've ever had."

"Peonies and dinner at Flame," Mom says, and I find her shaking her head. "He's not messing around."

"Can we please cut all this crap and get to the good stuff? What happened when he brought you home?" April asks, raising one brow.

My chest gets tight and my face warms. It's one thing talking with my sisters about sex. It's completely different with our mom present.

"April," Mom scolds.

"What?"

"You know what. We talked about this." Mom narrows her eyes in disapproval, and April shifts uncomfortably next to me.

"I see the last of you has arrived," a waitress says, appearing suddenly at the side of our booth, and I couldn't be more thankful for her interruption. "What can I get you ladies to eat?"

We give her our orders, food enough to sustain six grown men, and she looks impressed by the time she walks away. Once she's gone, I focus all my attention on the cup of coffee in front of me, waiting for April to continue with her interrogation, unsure how I will handle it if she does.

"Do you like him?" At my mom's quiet question, I lift my eyes to hers and nod. "Good," she whispers, and I bite the inside of my cheek.

"At least tell us the good night kiss was mind-blowing." April, never one to give up, prompts and I hear my mom huff in frustration. Still, I turn my head to look at my sister.

"The kiss good night was everything I hoped it would be." I watch her expression fill with relief. Seeing that look, I realize she hasn't stopped worrying about her role in the way things played out between me and Gareth and has still been feeling guilty about it. "We're good." I reach under the table to squeeze her hand, and her fingers lock around mine tightly before they let go.

"So, when are you seeing him again?" June asks as I pick up my coffee.

I hold my cup inches from my lips and shrug. "I'm not sure. We didn't make plans."

"Oh." She looks forlorn by my answer, and I wonder if I should be worried that we didn't agree on a time to see each other again.

Did he just tell me what I wanted to hear so he didn't have to deal with things being awkward? I mean, I did sleep with him on our first date; maybe he thinks I'm easy now and wants nothing to do with me. My stomach turns at the thought.

"He'll call," April says, and I glance at her. "He'll call. Just give him time."

"Sure," I agree, not feeling sure at all. Actually, now I'm wondering what the heck I was thinking, sleeping with him last night. I should've had better control. I should have.... "Oh no." My heart pounds, remembering him telling me that the condom broke the last time we had sex. How did I forget about that until now?

"What?" Mom asks worriedly, and I shake my head.

"Nothing. I... I thought I saw that crazy-haired guy walk by, from the alien show July watches."

"What? Where?" July looks behind her out the window to the sidewalk.

"It wasn't him. It just looked like him," I say, because I know she will get up and go search him out if she thinks he's out there.

99

"Bummer." She turns back toward the table. "I'm trying to convince Wes to take me to Alien Con in Arizona next year, but so far it's a no-go." Her nose scrunches up in annoyance. "Do you guys want to go with me? We could make it a girls' trip."

"I'm not going to an alien convention," April refuses immediately.

"I'll go," June says, and we all look at her doubtfully, knowing there is no way her husband would let her go to another state without him. "I mean, I'll come and bring my husband and baby."

"Maybe if Evan goes, Wes will agree to come with me," July plots, sounding hopeful.

"If you really want to go, I think you should buy your tickets and tell Wes you're going with or without him," Mom says with an evil smile before she continues. "I bet he'll change his mind about going then."

"That's actually genius." July nudges Mom's shoulder with her own. "You really are the master Alpha tamer."

Mom laughs at the newly bestowed title and looks around the table at each of us. "I've had a whole lot of years dealing with you girls' father, so take it from me when I say sometimes you just have to play dirty to get what you want."

"I'm sure Dad loves it when you play dirty," April says, and I giggle in spite of the unease building in my chest.

"You're not wrong." Mom grins.

"Gross," May mumbles.

I have to agree; it is gross to think about what our parents do behind closed doors, but they have never been a couple to shy away from PDA. Since I was little, I have found them making out more than once. Thankfully though, it's always been when they were fully clothed. If I ever did walk in on them doing the dirty, I would have to go in search of someone capable of erasing my memory.

"Anyway, what's everyone doing today?" June asks, looking at each of us. "I was thinking of hitting up the mall after breakfast, since I have some time to kill while Evan and Tia are in Chattanooga visiting Colton and his wife."

"I need to go to the drugstore," I blurt without thinking, and everyone looks at me. *Crap*. "I need to pick up shampoo and body wash."

"We can do both," June suggests, and everyone agrees, making me wish I hadn't opened my big mouth. There is no way I can get what I actually need from the drugstore with my sisters and mom present.

"We haven't had a girls' shopping day in forever. I love that idea. After we finish breakfast, we can walk to the drugstore down the block, then since I drove your dad's SUV and we can all fit, I'll drive us to the mall," Mom says excitedly, and my stomach sinks as I listen to them all talk about what stores they want to go to. I cringe when they start talking about having lunch and seeing a movie after shopping.

While they are distracted, I pull out my cell phone and don't even look at the few texts I have, since I'm sure they're all from my sisters and mom asking where I was this morning. I go to my search link and google information about the morning after pill, feeling relief when I read that I have to take it within seventy-two hours after unprotected sex for it to be effective.

"Did he text?"

At April's question I quickly exit the page I was looking at and glance at her. "Umm." I click on my messages, and my heart beats harder when I see he did—not once but twice. The first message from him came in late last night when I was already in bed asleep.

Home in bed, thinking about you.

The second message is from early this morning.

What are your plans today? I'm taking the boys to the batting cages this afternoon then coming home to watch the Mets on TV and eat junk food.

"He did," I whisper in disbelief.

"What did he say?" April asks, keeping her voice surprisingly quiet.

"He asked what I was doing today."

"Did you message him back?"

"Not yet." I shake my head, looking back at my cell phone and wondering exactly what I should say.

"Tell him you're spending the day with your sisters but you're free tonight if he wants to do something."

"It's Sunday." I sigh, knowing how crazy Sundays are for me and I don't have kids. I need to get ready to face another week of school.

"So?" April prompts, and I look over to find her frowning.

"He has kids," I remind her, and understanding fills her features. "He can't exactly come see me without having someone to look after them, and I don't know if we are at a place where he'd feel comfortable having me around his boys."

"You're right. Still, you can let him know you do want to see him. Unless…" She pauses, studying me. "Do you want to see him again?"

"Absolutely," I say, knowing without a doubt that there is something between us worth exploring, even with all the hurdles we might have to face along the way.

"Then you should tell him that. I know we think men should be able to read our minds, but they can't. They only understand directness."

"How do you know that?" I raise a brow.

"Because unlike you, my sweet, rule-following sister, I have had to experience falling for a guy, thinking he could read between the lines, and the unfortunate luck of finding out he couldn't."

My heart aches and a lump forms in my throat when I see the deep hurt she always tries to hide. I know she's speaking from experience and talking about her ex, Cohen Abbott—the only guy she's ever really loved, and the one that got away.

"I…." I don't even know what to say to make her feel better. I can't imagine having the image of the man I once loved forced down my throat each time I turned on the TV or looked at the magazine rack at the store. Or worse, having to hear his voice every time I turned on the radio, singing a song about lost love that I know is directed at me. "Maybe—"

"Please don't," she whispers tightly, cutting me off, and I swallow hard. "Just text Gareth and let him know you'd like to see him."

"Okay."

She looks away, and I pull in a breath, look down at my phone, and start to type.

I just saw your messages. I overslept this morning and had to rush to meet my sisters and my mom for breakfast, AKA an interrogation session regarding you and our date last night. Somehow, in the last few minutes, I've ended up agreeing to go to the mall and maybe a

movie. **I should be home by five. I don't know if you'll be free this evening, but if you are, I wouldn't hate seeing you.**

I press Send before I can talk myself out of it then hold my breath when a bubble appears under my sent text.

Interrogation? Should I come rescue you? I'm not sure I can get away this evening, but if you feel like eating pizza and wings for dinner, you can join me and my boys in front of the TV at my place.

I read his text and breathe, "Holy cow."

"What?" April asks.

I lift my eyes off my phone to look at my sister. "He said I could join him and his boys for pizza and wings tonight."

"Awesome, are you going?"

"I don't know." I look back at my cell and type quickly.

Do you think that's a good idea? Is it too soon for me to meet your boys?

My phone rings in my hand and his name flashes on the screen, making me feel elated and freaked. "I'll be right back." I don't even lift my head, even though I feel everyone's eyes on me. I slide out of the booth then step out of the restaurant, putting my phone to my ear. "Hey."

"I want you to hear my voice when I say what I'm gonna say."

"Okay." I wrap my arm around my middle, not sure by his tone if I'm going to like what he has to say.

"You already know Mitchell."

"I know, but that's—"

"And," he cuts me off before I can explain how me knowing Mitchell at school is completely different from me seeing his dad and going to his house. "I wouldn't have you over if I didn't know it was inevitable that you'd be spending time with my boys. I already wasted weeks trying to deny the way I feel and am pissed at myself that I lost time I could have spent getting to know you because I'm an idiot."

"You're not an idiot," I whisper, feeling lightheaded by his words.

"Not anymore, which is why I'm not going to play this cool and see you when I see you, which, baby—" His tone softens. "—it wouldn't be often. I work two jobs and have two boys. I don't have a lot of free time to take you out, so if we're going to do this, we need to jump in and figure it out along the way."

"Three jobs," I state.

"Pardon?"

"You work as a mechanic, a tattooist, and you're a dad. So, really, you have three jobs," I say, studying the sidewalk under my flats and wondering how he's able to do everything he does. I have one job and myself to look after, and some days that seems like a lot of responsibility.

"I guess you're right," he agrees quietly then asks, "So what's it gonna be Ember are you gonna run or jump?"

I think about every moment I've spent with him and all the things he's made me feel since the we met, and ask, "What will you do if I run?"

"Chase." The one word is spoken roughly, making me shiver and smile at the same time.

"I guess I don't have a choice but to jump then."

"I'm glad you're seeing things my way." He sounds like he's trying not to laugh, and I hold myself a little tighter, not wanting to lose the feeling in my belly. "I already talked to the boys about you."

"What?" I squawk.

"When I got home last night, they were up and wanted to know if I'd be seeing you again. I told them yes." *He told them yes!* I want to dance around or do a cartwheel. "They were cool with it, so while I'm out with them today, I'll let them know you'll be over for pizza tonight."

"Okay," I say, sure that the happiness I'm feeling is leaking into my voice.

"I'll order dinner around 5:30. Is there anything you want, hate, or are allergic to?"

I giggle. "I love food. All food."

"Anchovies?"

"Would you be repulsed if I told you I love them?"

"Seriously?"

I smile. "My dad always got a can of them whenever we were going to order pizza. I always thought they were gross, but then one day curiosity got the better of me and I found out the salted fish add something unexpected to each bite. After that, I kind of fell in love."

"Your taste buds are adventurous."

"Yeah," I agree, knowing that's the only part of me that is adventurous. "The rest of me is kind of lame." *Why did I say that, even if I was thinking it?*

"You're perfect."

"I—"

"Honey, breakfast is here." I lift my eyes at the sound of my mom's voice and find her standing in the open door to the restaurant. I nod then hold up one finger, letting her know I'll be a minute.

"Go eat, baby," Gareth says in my ear, having heard my mom as well. "I'll see you this evening. Have fun with your family."

"Have fun with your boys."

"Always do," he says then murmurs, "Later, Ember."

"Later, Gareth," I whisper then look around to make sure no one is watching and do a little dance in the middle of the sidewalk. When I get back to the table, I notice each of them are fighting laughter. "What?"

"Cute dance." Mom grins and I groan. "We're just glad you're happy, honey." She reaches across the table to grasp my hand and gives it a squeeze, saying "Now, let's eat. We have a busy day ahead of us." Without another word, we all dig into our food, and like always when I'm with my family, I spend the day with a smile on my face.

I pull into Gareth's driveway more nervous than I was last night before our date. Even after talking to him before I left my apartment and his reassurance that the boys were okay with me joining them tonight, I still feel uncertain about his decision.

I take a deep breath as I park then lean over to grab my purse from the passenger seat, along with a shopping bag containing a gallon of ice cream and the store-bought cupcakes I picked up on my way here. If I hadn't been out all day, I would have put more effort into winning over Gareth's boys through their stomachs with my favorite chocolate cherry brownies. A recipe that calls for hunks of chocolate in the brownie mix and maraschino cherries and mini chocolate chips swirled into the vanilla icing. Unfortunately, there wasn't time for me to bake or do anything more than change and feed Melbourne before I had to get back in my car to make it here for dinner.

With my hands shaking, I start to open my door then squeak when it's suddenly tugged from the tips of my fingers. I look up at Gareth with wide eyes then sigh when he bends to brush his lips over mine, causing a little of the nervousness I'm feeling to melt away.

"Hey," I greet when he leans back and smiles, taking my bags from me.

"You looked like you were about ready to bolt when I saw you pull in to park."

"I was," I admit, biting the inside of my cheek as his eyes scan mine.

"Did you forget I'd chase you?" he asks quietly, taking hold of my hip then using it to force me a step closer causing a small gasp to pass between my lips.

I lift my hands and place them against his warm chest to catch myself and feel his muscles bunch under his shirt, reminding me exactly how it felt last night to have his strength pressed against me. "No," I say, and his eyes grow darker while his lips twist into a smirk. My toes curl and my heart pounds as his fingers dig into my skin through my light jacket and T-shirt.

"Fuck. I hate I can't kiss you the way I want to with my boys watching us."

Feeling like a bucket of ice water has been dumped on my head, I immediately withdraw my hands from his chest like it's on fire and drop them to my sides. "They're watching?" I whisper like they might be able to hear then try to step around him. When he blocks my way, I tip my chin back toward him. "We need to go in."

"We will after you tell me you're okay."

"I'm okay," I say instantly.

He shakes his head, not releasing the hold he has on me. If anything, his grip gets tighter as he dips his head toward mine. "Trust me." Those two words wrap around my insides as he stares into my eyes, imploring me to believe that everything will be alright. "My boys are good with you being here. I just need *you* to be good with it."

"He knows his boys better than you do." My mom's words from earlier today when I admitted my doubts about tonight fill my mind, and I know I need to trust him to know what's best for his kids.

"A lot has happened in the last twenty-four hours," I say, and he lifts his chin slightly in agreement but doesn't comment. Resting one hand on his large bicep, I squeeze. "I trust you. If you say everything will be alright, then I believe you."

I watch his expression gentle and the unease slide out of his features, but then lose the look when he bends to touch his lips to my forehead. "Come meet my boys."

His breath warms my skin before he pulls away, and I force my eyes open then take his hand and walk at his side toward his front porch, noticing the blinds snap back into place as we head up the steps. My fingers flex around his and my step falters.

"Jump," he whispers.

I fight against the fear making me want to run, and tighten my hold on his hand and whisper back, "Jump." The moment the word passes my lips, he turns the handle, and as soon as the door opens, I know my life will never be the same.

Two smiling faces greet us as soon as we step into the house, and I notice both Gareth's boys are already as handsome as he is.

"Hey, Miss Mayson." Mitchell's smile turns into a grin as he hauls his blond-headed brother against his side roughly with his arm around his neck. "This is my brother Max."

"You can call me December," I tell Mitchell then look at Max, whose face has become red. "Hey, Max. Nice to meet you."

"You too," Max grunts, trying to get away from his brother, who's now holding him captive just because he's bigger and sibling law written thousands of years ago requires him to do so.

"Boys," Gareth warns, sounding like the dad he is, and Mitchell reluctantly releases his brother, who takes full advantage of being free. He elbows Mitchell in the ribs, making him grunt, and then when Mitchell lunges for him, he rushes across the room to hide safely behind his father's back, making me laugh.

"Welcome to the crazy house." Gareth shakes his head at both boys before looking at me.

I smile up at him. "I grew up with four sisters, so this was my normal until I moved out to go to college."

"You have four sisters?" Max asks, peering at me from around his father's side.

"I do."

"Are they all as pretty as you are?" he asks, and I notice a hint of pink hit his cheeks.

Okay, I think I just fell in love.

"Prettier," I say quietly, and he eyes me doubtfully.

"I always wanted a sister," Mitchell pipes in, and I glance at Gareth, noticing he's frowning at his oldest. "Well... I did." Mitchell shrugs his already broad shoulders, tucking his hands in his pockets.

"Sorry, kid. That's not gonna happen," Gareth says, and my insides twist, reminding me that I didn't get what I need to get from the drug store today, which means the seventy-two hours I have are quickly ticking away.

"Pizza's here!" Max shouts, making me jump, then I watch him rush to the door and pull it open before the doorbell even rings.

"Finally," Mitchell says, sounding a lot like his dad as he walks past me toward the door to help his brother.

"Baby." Gareth's fingers capture my chin, gaining my attention, and I focus on the man standing above me. "What's in your head?" he asks quietly.

Oh nothing, except I'm not on birth control, the condom broke last night and I haven't gone to get the morning after pill which means there is a chance Mitchell could get his wish. "Nothing's in my head," I lie, and his eyes search mine then move over my face narrowing slightly.

"You're lying."

"I'm not."

"Dinner is served!" Max shouts, and I pull in a relieved breath when Gareth releases the hold he has on me.

"We'll talk later," he states, and I nod even though the thought of what we need to talk about makes me uneasy. Giving me a contemplative look, he takes my hand and we go to the open kitchen, where both Max and Mitchell are placing pieces of pizza onto their plates along with wings slathered in BBQ sauce.

"Do you really like these things?" Max asks, holding up a tin of sardines, and I laugh.

"Yes." I take the tin from him and pull back the tab.

He eyes the tiny fish then mutters, "Gross."

"You can't say they're gross unless you've tried one," I tell him, accepting a plate with two slices of pizza from Gareth.

"What do they taste like?" Mitchell asks.

"Salty?" I shrug.

"I'll try it." He holds out his plate, takes a small piece of fish, and places it on the end of his slice.

"I'll try it too." Max pushes his plate toward me, and I hear Gareth laugh as I place another small piece on the end of his slice.

"On three," Mitchell says, and after they count, I watch both boys take a bite, and the two of them have completely different facial expressions as they chew. Mitchell looks like he is trying to figure out if he enjoys the new taste, while Max just looks like he wants to be sick.

"I can't." Max gags, running to the sink, and I start to laugh.

"It's actually not bad." Mitchell shrugs, taking another slice of fish from the tin and placing it on his pizza.

"Do you want to try?" I look up at Gareth, who's grinning and shaking his head.

"You have to try it, Dad," Max urges while washing out his mouth.

"I think I'll stick to what I know," he tells his son then asks, "What are we watching tonight?"

"Not some girl movie," Max says then looks at me sheepishly. "No offense."

"None taken." I smile. "I don't really like girl movies either."

"What's your favorite movie?" Mitchell asks.

I don't even have to think about the answer. "*The Goonies*. It was one of my mom's favorites, so we used to watch it a lot when I was a kid. Anytime it's on TV now, I have to stop to watch it, even if it's almost ending."

"I've never seen it. What's it about?" Max asks.

"It's funny. It's about a group of friends who go in search of pirate treasure so they can save their families' homes, only they end up running into some bad guys and they have to outsmart them." When I notice both boys are looking at me like I've grown a third head, I shrug. "It's hard to explain. You have to watch it."

"I haven't seen that movie in years." Gareth rests his hand against my back then looks at the boys. "Change of plans. I'm renting *The Goonies* tonight; you guys can pick the movie next weekend."

"Cool," they both agree without a fight.

"Get drinks," Gareth orders them then looks down at me. "What do you want? We've got Coke, tea, and water."

"Coke please."

"Grab two Cokes," he says toward the fridge, where Max is standing with the door open.

"Got it, Dad."

"Come on." Gareth urges me toward the living room, where we settle on the couch side by side. Once we are seated, the boys come in and Max hands me and his dad each a Coke before taking a seat on the floor in front of the coffee table, while Mitchell lounges at the end of the couch opposite us. Gareth starts up the movie, and I dig into my pizza, listening to the boys laugh at one of my favorite scenes.

Hearing that and replaying the last half hour, I know Gareth was right. I just hope we can handle some of the hoops we might have to jump through.

Gareth

Chapter 9

"SO, WHAT DID you two think?" December asks as soon as *The Goonies* comes to an end, and both boys, who are now lounging on the opposite end of the couch from where I have December tucked against my side, turn to look at her.

"It was awesome." Max smiles. "And the Baby Ruth guy was totally cool."

"The kid with all the gadgets was my favorite." Mitchell grins. "But my favorite part was when they sent that girl's jacket up to those jerks."

"I like that part too," December agrees. "But I love when Chunk gets caught by the Fratellis and they interrogate him, and he tells them about puking at the movies."

"Yeah, that was funny," Max says, and Mitchell and I both laugh. "Do you know any other old movies like that one?"

"Have you seen *Don't Tell Mom the Babysitter's Dead*?" she asks, and the boys shake their heads. "What about *Adventures in Babysitting*?" They shake their heads again. "Okay, what about *Back to the Future*, *The Gremlins*, or *Beetlejuice*?"

"We might be here all night if you keep naming movies, babe," I say, and she turns to frown at me, making me want to kiss the adorable annoyed look off her face.

"Those are some of the best movies of all time. How have they not seen them?"

My lips twitch. "The best movies of all time?"

"Uh… yeah. *Back to the Future* is iconic."

"Can we watch that one now?" Max asks, and I look at the clock then him.

"Sorry, kid. It's time for you and your brother to get showered and into bed."

"Ugh," he groans, flopping back against the couch. "I wish I could do homeschool."

"You'd still have to go to bed at nine and be up early."

"Okay then, I wish I was an adult," he counters, and December laughs softly.

"Come on, dude." Mitchell gets up off the couch and tugs Max up with him. "Night, Dad. Night, December."

"Yeah… night." Max pouts.

"Good night, guys," December says, laughing.

"I'll be in to check on you in a few," I tell them, and they both nod before heading down the hall.

Once they are gone, December turns to look at me. "You have great kids."

"Yeah." I touch the side of her face and her eyes warm. "Tonight, wasn't so bad, was it?"

"No, it was actually really nice. Thank you for inviting me over." She starts to get up.

Not wanting her to leave, I capture her thigh with my hand to keep her in place. "Stay the night with me," I say quietly, and her eyes widen.

"What?"

"Stay the night," I repeat then lean forward, brushing my lips across hers.

She shakes her head then looks past my shoulder and down the hall. "I can't. We…. The boys—"

I cut her off, "They're going to bed. They won't even know you're here."

"I have work tomorrow," she whispers, and I can tell by the look in her eyes she's torn.

"I'll wake you up early so you can go home in time to get ready for work," I assure her.

"I don't think.... I mean, I don't even have pajamas or my toothbrush."

"You can borrow a T-shirt from me, and I'm sure I have an extra toothbrush. If not, you can use mine."

"Use your toothbrush?" Her nose scrunches.

"I've had my tongue in your mouth," I remind her with a grin. "I'm not going to take no for an answer. You might as well just agree to stay."

"You're very persistent," she murmurs, and I squeeze her thigh, which causes her pupils to dilate. "Okay."

"Okay? You'll stay?"

"Yes, but I... I don't want the boys to know. I don't want them to get the wrong idea."

"What idea would that be?"

"I don't know, but it's not seemly for me to be staying the night with you, especially with your boys here."

"Seemly?" I chuckle, and her eyes narrow. "Don't be pissed that I'm laughing, babe. No one uses the word seemly."

"Obviously, they do, since it's included in the dictionary, honey."

Fuck, but I kinda like her calling me honey. "Okay, no one under the age of ninety uses the word then."

"You're very annoying."

"Yeah, and you're seriously fucking adorable." I lean in and kiss the tip of her nose then move back. "I'm gonna get the kitchen cleaned up. Feel free to watch what you want." I pick up the remote and hand it to her.

"I can help." She starts to stand when I do.

"You can." I hold her back with my hand on her shoulder. "But you're not going to. Hang here and watch TV. After the boys go to bed, we'll do the same."

"If you're forcing me to sit here, can I at least get my Kindle from my purse so I can read?"

"I'll get it for you." I go to the kitchen and grab her bag.

After I take it to her, I go back to the kitchen and put away the leftover pizza then shove the plates and bowls we used for the cupcakes and ice cream into the dishwasher. I start to wipe down the counters and glance into the living room, feeling the space where my heart is twitch. Seeing her comfortable, tucked into the corner of the couch with her shoes off, her feet on the cushion, and her legs tucked close to her chest, while her Kindle propped up on her knees.

I don't know what it is about seeing her like that, but I do know I like it a whole fuck of a lot. If I'm honest, I just fucking like *her*. There is something about her that puts me at ease, and not surprisingly, she has the same effect on my boys. From the time she walked into the house, there was no nervousness from either of them. If anything, they acted as if they had known her for years. Mitchell might have had something to do with his brother's easy acceptance of December, but I have a feeling she just has that kind of effect on people.

With a deep breath, I finish wiping down the counters and cleaning up the kitchen then go down the hall and knock on Max's door.

"Yeah," he calls.

I push the door open, finding him lying on his bed with his Switch. "You good, kid?"

"Yep." He glances at me quickly before going back to his game.

"Twenty minutes and lights out."

"I know."

"Love you," I say, and he finally stops what he's doing to look at me. "Always."

"Love you too, Dad," he replies quietly.

I lift my chin, back out of the room, and close the door, then head down to Mitchell's room and knock. "Come in," he grunts, and I frown as I push the door in.

"What are you doing?"

"Rearranging my room."

"I see that. Can I ask why?"

"In *feng shui*, it says your bed shouldn't be under the window."

"*Feng shui?*"

"Yeah, my friend Kim's family is big into it, and she told me about the whole window thing."

"Kim's a girl?" I question, and he looks at me and shrugs. I smile.

116

"Do you need my help?"

"Nope."

"All right, yell out if you do."

"I will," he says then asks, "Is December still here?"

"She is."

"Cool." His smirk makes him look older than he is.

"Don't forget about bedtime."

"I know." He rolls his eyes.

I leave him to finish moving his bed then go back to the living room. As soon as I take a seat on the couch and pull December's feet onto my lap, she asks, "Are the boys okay?"

Fuck but that question shouldn't make my chest warm, but it does. "They're good. Mitchell's rearranging his bed, and Max is playing a video game."

"Rearranging his bed?"

"*Feng shui.*"

"Awww." She nods. "Kim."

"You know her?"

"She's one of the kids who comes every week to help mentor, and I've overheard her talking about *feng shui* a few times. I think Mitch has a crush on her. Most of the boys do." She presses her lips together for a moment. "Not that she seems to notice. She's a little bit of a nerd."

"I see," I mutter then dip my head toward her book. "Are you still reading or do you want to watch something?"

"I'll watch something." She sets her Kindle on the coffee table and moves her feet off my lap, turning so we're sitting much like we were earlier, with her resting against my side. "Wait, go back one channel," she says as I'm flipping through the stations. "I've been waiting for the new season of this to start. Do you mind if we watch this?"

"What's it about?" I ask her as I slouch back in the couch with her in my arms.

"That guy—" She points at the guy on the screen. "—helps solve murders that have gone cold. It's kind of interesting how he goes about things, and a little scary the amount of evidence it takes to convict someone of a crime, even if it's clear they are the one who committed it." She lays her head on my chest. "I really liked last season."

"You're such a nerd."

"Whatever." She sighs, and I capture her hand and hold it over my heart as we watch a real-life murder mystery unfold. The show isn't something I'd normally watch, but I have to admit it's good. When it comes to an end, I go check on the boys one last time. I find Max asleep holding his Switch, so I take it from him then tuck his blankets up around his shoulders and kiss his head. When I open Mitchell's door, I find him asleep with his window open a crack and a slight breeze blowing his curtains. Smiling, I walk across the room and touch my fingers to his dark hair before leaving him to sleep.

"The boys are both out," I tell December as soon as I hit the living room, and she looks at me over her shoulder. The moment her eyes meet mine, I see nervousness enter her gaze. I don't say a word about it; I turn off the TV and then hold out my hand for her to take. She doesn't hesitate, placing her hand in mine, and I use it to help her up off the couch then lead her toward my bedroom, which is just off the kitchen and living room on the opposite end of the house from the boys.

Once we're in my room, I close the door then take her to the bathroom. I dig through one of the drawers to see if I have a spare toothbrush for her to use, and when I find one, I turn holding it out and see she hasn't moved from the doorway.

"Come here." I drop the toothbrush then lean back against the counter, half expecting her to ignore my request. But surprisingly, she walks toward me and settles her weight against my body. Grabbing hold of her hip, I dip my head and touch my lips to hers before asking, "What's on your mind?"

"Nothing." She shakes her head. "Everything." She bites her bottom lip. "Can I tell you something?"

"Anything." I give her hip a squeeze.

"You know when the condom broke?"

"Yeah."

"I…. Well, I'm not on birth control. I don't know why I didn't think about that when we were talking about it, but I want you to know now." My heart starts to pound as I study her face. "I'm going to get the Plan

B pill. I was going to do it today, but I didn't. But I'll get it tomorrow."

Why the fuck do I feel disappointed? I told my sisters I didn't want more kids and told Mitchell he won't be getting a sister. Still, there is a strange feeling of excitement at the idea of getting this beautiful woman pregnant.

"I'm sorry. I should have told you." She drops her eyes, and I feel like an ass. She thinks I'm pissed she didn't tell me she's not on birth control. She has no idea that I'm thinking about all the ways I could knock her up, something I really do not need to be thinking about doing.

"I'll be more careful," I grunt, wrapping my hand around her jaw and forcing her to meet my gaze. "You have nothing to apologize for, nothing to feel bad about. All right?"

"All right," she whispers.

"Is there a reason you're not on birth control?" I ask gently, and her cheeks fill with color. "You don't have to be embarrassed with me."

"When I was on the pill, it made me feel wonky." She shrugs. "I mean, I haven't tried any of the new forms of birth control in the last few years, since there was no reason to, but that's what the pill made me feel like, so I stopped taking it."

"No reason?"

"Umm… I wasn't having sex." The pink at her cheeks spreads down her neck.

"Right," I mutter, happy it's been years since she's been with anyone, but annoyed someone else touched her at all.

"Why do you look annoyed?" she asks, studying me, and my fingers flex around her hip.

"I have never been the type of man to be jealous or possessive, but there is no denying I'm both of those things when it comes to you."

"Oh," she says breathily, like she likes the idea of causing those feelings in me.

"You like that?" I hold her more firmly against me, and my cock twitches behind my zipper.

"Like what?"

"That I'm feeling crazy when it comes to you?"

"Kind of," she admits.

119

I tangle my fingers in her hair and position her just like I want her then lick across her full lips. Her mouth opens, and when her tongue touches mine, I lose control and turn her ass toward the counter, lifting her up and settling her on the edge. Her legs wrap around my hips, and when she pulls me against her, I groan and lean back to rip her shirt off over her head, doing the same with my own. Once I have her bra off, I cup her breasts and bend over her, taking one pink nipple into my mouth.

"Gareth."

"You gotta be quiet," I order, moving to her neglected breast, and her hands tangle in my hair, tugging hard. Wanting to feel how wet she is for me, I snap the button to her jeans open, tug down the zipper, and slip my hand into her panties. "You're soaked, baby, and so fucking warm." I slide two fingers inside her and she clenches around me. "You gonna come on my fingers?"

"No," she denies, shaking her head, and I pull back to look into her eyes.

"It feels like you're about to come."

"I need you."

"You want my cock?" I ask, thrusting harder and using my thumb to rub her clit.

"Yes!" She starts to cry out, but I cut off the sound, covering her mouth with my own as she orgasms. While she's still panting, I pull her off the counter and help her out of her jeans then turn her to face the vanity, leaning her over the cold surface. Once I have her positioned, I kick off my jeans and step up behind her.

"Gareth," she whispers as I take hold of her hip with one hand and use the other to wrap around my cock.

I slide the head up and down her wet slit then freeze. Gritting my teeth, I grab my jeans then dig a condom out of my wallet. After putting it on, I don't waste another second. I sink into her from behind, holding her eyes in the bathroom mirror.

"Oh, God," she cries, tossing her head back.

"Shhh." I trace her plump bottom lip with my thumb. "Don't forget you gotta be quiet, baby."

"I don't know if I can," she whimpers.

"You can." I slide out of her an inch then thrust my hips forward. When she looks at me in the mirror once more, my breath catches. *Christ,* I don't know if I have ever seen anything more beautiful than her face when she's on the verge of coming. "Spread your legs, tip your ass, and let me in deeper," I order quietly, placing a kiss against her neck while sliding my hand down to her chest, cupping one breast while palming the cheek of her ass with my other hand.

"Oh, God, don't stop."

Her needy whimper just about pushes me over the edge. Knowing I'm about to lose it, I slide my hand from her ass to cup her between her legs. As soon as my fingers make contact with her clit, her back arches, sending me deeper. Her pussy begins to ripple around my cock as she comes, and I wish we were in my bed, where I could flip her to her back and plunge into her.

"Christ." I lean her farther over the counter, and she moans loudly as I grind hard, going as deep as I can. I move my hand from her breast to cover her mouth and feel her teeth sink into my palm, seeing stars as I follow her over the edge.

Completely spent, I drop my forehead to her shoulder and try to catch my breath as she attempts to do the same. Once my legs don't feel so weak, I slide out of her warmth, turn her to face me, and gather her against my chest. "You okay?" I use my fingers under her chin to force her gaze up to me and study her.

"Yeah." She gives me a small, tired smile.

"How about a shower?"

"A shower sounds good," she says, resting her body against mine while wrapping her arms around my waist. I hold her against me and walk to the shower, turning it on. Once the water is warm, I help her inside.

"Are you asleep?" I ask, looking down at the top of her head, and she tips her head back toward me.

"Maybe." She smiles sleepily.

"Let me get you washed up and into bed," I say quietly, kissing her before grabbing the bar of soap from the cutout in the wall. Being quick,

I wash her and me then shut off the water and get out.

Still dripping wet, I grab a clean towel and hold it out for her, and she steps toward me. "Thanks," she whispers as I wrap it around her.

"Let me get you a shirt." I reach for a towel for myself and place it around my hips. Going to my closet, I grab her a shirt and find a pair of boxers then help her into both. When she's dressed, I lead her to my bed, and she doesn't make a peep as I tuck her in. "What time do you need to be up?"

"Normally, I get up at six, so probably five." She yawns.

"I'll set my alarm." I touch my lips to hers, and when I pull away, her eyes are closed. Shaking my head, I go back to my closet and drop the towel around my hips then slip on a pair of boxers before going out to check on the boys once more. Seeing they are still asleep, I set the house alarm, turn out the lights, and then head back to my room. When I open the door, I find December has moved to the middle of the bed and is now wrapped around my pillow. Smiling, I set an alarm on my phone, shut off the side lamp, and get into bed with her.

"Gareth," she calls as I tug my pillow from her hold and get into bed, dragging her closer.

"Sleep, baby," I order.

"Okay," she agrees, curling herself into a ball under my arm and falling back asleep. And with her in my arms, in my bed, under my roof, I sleep easy.

I stand on the opposite side of the island from the boys, watching the two of them scarf down the breakfast I made them like it's a race to see who can finish first.

"Done!" Mitchell proclaims himself the winner while chewing the sausage patty he shoved into his mouth whole.

"Should I get you a trophy for your accomplishment?" I ask, and he grins at me as he slides off his stool with his plate to take it to the sink.

"Dad," Max calls, and the tone of his voice has me focusing on him. "I..." He presses his lips together then looks past me toward his brother, and I look over my shoulder at my oldest.

"What is it?"

"Max was wondering when we'd have another movie night with December," Mitchell says, and I turn back to Max.

"You want to hang with her again?" I question, setting my cup down. I didn't ask him last night if he liked December. I didn't want to make him feel like he had to say he did by questioning him.

"She's nice," he says, ripping his toast into tiny bits, not looking at me. "I guess it would be cool to hang out with her again."

"I'm sure we can set something up. Maybe not a movie night, since you boys have school this week, but we can have dinner with her," I tell him.

He looks up and gives me a half smile. "Right on."

Feeling relief, I dip my chin toward his plate. "If you're finished, dump your plate in the dishwasher and get packed up. I'll meet you and your brother in the driveway."

He gets up, taking his plate with him, and after he rinses it and drops it in the dishwasher, he leaves the kitchen, heading around the island and down the hall toward his bedroom.

"He liked her a lot," Mitchell says as I'm taking a sip of coffee, and I turn toward him, resting my hip on the counter, and lift my chin for him to continue. "He didn't think he would, but he does, and now he's worried about what will happen if you and her keep seeing each other and Mom shows up."

Shit. Their mom can be a handful on a good day, so I know his concern is valid. I also know I've been done with taking her shit for years, so if she shows and tries to stir up trouble, I won't let it happen. "That's not something you or your brother need to worry about."

"I know, but Max still thinks Mom is cool," he says softly. "He doesn't get that she's nuts and that she's only around when it's good for her."

I study my boy, wondering when he started to see things as they are. There was a time he saw his mom the same way Max sees her now, and a part of me wishes he still viewed her in that same light, that he didn't know how selfish his mother is.

"He doesn't get it," he adds.

"Get what?"

He shrugs. "Get that Mom doesn't really care about us."

My throat gets tight, and I fight against the anger I feel threatening to take over. I never want my boys to feel unloved, and I have tried to make it so they never will, by giving them good people who they can count on. Unfortunately, I have never been able to control the impact their mother has on their lives any more than I can direct the sun from setting each evening. "Your mom is—"

"A bitch."

My spine stiffens. "Language. I get that you're upset with her, but do not ever disrespect her. She's your mother. She loves you boys."

"If she did, she would be around." His jaw ticks. "She's not around unless it's convenient, and when she *is* here, she's always talking about where she's going or what she plans on doing next. I'm not stupid; I know she only shows up to make sure we haven't forgotten her. The thing is… I always forget her the moment she walks out the door, because she doesn't matter."

Fuck, my throat gets tight. "I hate you feel that way."

"I hate that Max thinks she's perfect, but I also know I won't be able to change his mind about her. He has to learn that for himself." He pulls in a breath. "I just…." He pauses to shake his head. "I was just thinking that if you and December did get together and Mom did come around, he'd see the difference, and maybe it wouldn't be so hard on him."

"What do you mean?"

"Like… he could see what a mom is supposed to be like."

"Mitch—"

"I know you're going to say it's too soon for that," he cuts me off, holding up his hand toward me. "I just know that it would have been nice when I was his age to have a mom type person around, and maybe if December is that, it would be good for him."

I stare at my son, not sure I'm able to stomach what he's saying. I have tried to keep what happened between his mom and me away from him, but nonetheless, it's obviously seeped through. I hate that he's had to witness it; worse, I hate that he's now trying to protect his little brother from experiencing the same thing.

"I'm sorry."

"For what?" he asks, looking older than he is. "I know you've put up with Mom for years because you wanted us to have her in our lives."

"You're right. I want you boys to have your mom. Still, I'm sorry that you feel the way you do, and I don't like that you've had to deal with things you shouldn't have." I close the distance between us and rest my hand around the side of his neck, giving it a gentle squeeze to get his attention. "I'm glad you're trying to look out for your little brother, but this is something you don't need to worry about."

"Okay." He dips his chin.

"Love you, kid." I rest my forehead against the top of his head.

"Love you too, Dad," he whispers back, and even though I've heard that from him time and time again, I know it will never get old.

"I'm proud of you." I lower my voice. "I got this. Trust me to look out for you and your brother," I say, and he nods.

"Ready!" Max shouts, cutting into the moment, and I lean back grinning, wanting to ease the tension in the air.

"You better go get packed up before your brother beats you to shotgun."

"Yeah," he agrees, but he doesn't move. Instead, he wraps his arms around my waist suddenly, stunning me. And then before I can hug him back, he lets me go and rushes out of the kitchen, shouting "Shotgun!" as he rounds the island.

"No fair!" Max yells.

"Totally fair," he counters, and even though I can't see either of them from my vantage point, I know they're in a scuffle, because I hear their grunts along with their shoes skidding on the hardwood.

I think about stepping in but decide to let them fight it out, since neither of them are crying or yelling for me. I pick up my cup of coffee and down the rest of it in one gulp then take the empty mug to the dishwasher and drop it inside. I continue to listen to them as I shrug on my jacket, and when I round the island, I find Max with his arms spread wide, blocking the hall. "Can I have shotgun?" he pants, giving me a pleading look.

125

"Your brother called it first, bud."

"He doesn't even have his bag," he points out.

I glance at Mitchell. "Get your stuff."

"I would have already if he let me down the hall."

"Let your brother by," I tell Max, surprised he was able to keep his brother back, when Mitchell has at least five inches and thirty pounds on him.

"Fine." Max steps aside, glaring at his brother before transferring the look to me and heading outside in a huff.

With a short shake of my head, I grab my keys then walk out to the driveway, beeping the locks, and get in behind the wheel. Max gets into the back seat, grumbling about how unfair things are, and then as soon as Mitchell gets in, he announces that he's calling shotgun for the ride home after school.

I fight back laughter, wondering how December would hold up in this situation. She'd probably think it was as hilarious as I do and wouldn't even bat a lash at the boys arguing. That thought gives me pause. Like Mitchell pointed out, it's too soon to be thinking of December's reaction to my boys' everyday antics, but still, there's no denying I want to see her reaction and intertwine her in our lives in all the ways she can be.

Shit.

December ▬ Gareth

Chapter 10

𝓗EARING SOMEONE SHOUTING, I pull my eyes off my students, who are all turned to face the door, and frown as I walk across the classroom. Not sure what is happening, I turn the handle and peek out into the hall, seeing Jetson—one of the fifth grade teachers—arguing loudly with the assistant principal, Gladys.

"Lower your voice, Mr. Jetson, and please go to the principal's office," Gladys says, and he glares at her then storms off.

"What was that about?" I look across the hallway at Tasha, another first grade teacher, and shrug. "Hopefully, he's getting fired. He's such a jerk," she whispers, and I don't agree even though she's right. Mr. Jetson is not a teacher I would consider friendly, and I've overheard his students complaining more than once about how hard he is on them.

When Gladys goes into his classroom, I step back, shutting the door and turning to face my kids, who all look nervous. "Everything is fine," I assure them then look at the clock, seeing we have twenty minutes before the day will come to an end. "Since we don't have much time left, how about we play Heads Up Seven Up until the bell rings?"

At my suggestion, the tension in the room eases immediately and each and every one of their faces lights up with smiles. I pick seven kids at random then call out "Heads down, thumbs up." All the kids still sitting in their desk lower their heads and close their eyes while the kids standing walk around, tapping thumbs at random. When the seven kids I chose go to the front of the class, I call, "Heads Up Seven Up," and the kids all lift their heads. One by one, they try to guess who tapped them, and if they guess correctly, they trade places with that student.

Five rounds later, the bell rings, and the kids quickly pack up, get in line at the door, and then greet their parents when they come in. Once they are all gone, I pick up the classroom and wipe things down with disinfectant. I gather my stuff from my desk, along with my planner and a stack of spelling tests I need to grade tonight. Normally, I set my weekly lesson plan on Sunday, but staying at Gareth's last night threw me off my schedule, so I need to get it done this evening. I leave the school and start through the teacher's parking lot toward my car. Digging through my bag for my keys, I don't see the car racing toward me until a loud horn honks and tires skid across the gravel lot.

"Watch where the fuck you're going!" Jetson yells, rolling down his window, and I start to open my mouth to tell him to slow down, but before I can he peels off, causing dust to fill the air and tiny rocks to fly out around me.

With my hands trembling and my heart beating wildly, I shake my head then glance both ways to make sure there aren't any more cars coming before I rush to mine and get in. Once I have the door closed, I pull out my cell phone, and even though I don't like being the kind of person to tell on someone, I know I need to call the principal to let her know what happened. Hopefully, she will tell Jetson he needs to slow down when he's near the school, even if there aren't normally kids in the teachers' parking lot. I get off the phone with her a few minutes later after she assures me that she will have a talk with him, and by the time I put my car in Drive, I'm not shaking like I was. I go directly to the drug store, and when I arrive, my cell phone beeps telling me I have an incoming message.

Dinner tonight?

I stare at the simple text from Gareth then look through my windshield at the drug store I'm parked in front of and close my eyes. Last night with Gareth and his boys was perfect, and waking up this morning in his arms was something I could seriously get used to. That said, I've been thinking all day about what Mitchell said, about wanting a sister or more specifically I've been thinking about Gareth's reaction to the statement.

Logically, I know it's way too early in our relationship—or whatever this is—to be thinking about children, but I can tell that, where my feelings toward him are concerned, I'm already falling. And after spending time with Max and Mitchell, I know I could easily fall in love with both boys. But at the end of the day, I do want kids, and if Gareth doesn't want more, I don't know if it makes even a little sense for us to keep seeing each other.

Busy tonight, another time? I stare at the text after I type it out, feeling my stomach turn as my fingers hover over the Send button. Pressing Delete until the words disappear, I know I'm totally screwed. **What time?**

Six. Bring stuff to sleep over.

My heart pounds. **I can't sleep over. I need to catch up on some work tonight.**

Bring it with you.

I let out a deep breath and try again. **I don't feel right leaving my cat alone so much.**

I stare at my phone, waiting for him to reply, and then jump when it suddenly rings and his name appears. Sliding my finger across the screen, I put it to my ear. "Hey."

"Do you really have a cat, or are you trying to get out of staying with me?" he asks, sounding like he's fighting back laughter.

"I really have a cat." I roll my eyes, wondering who would lie about having a cat.

"Where was he the other night?"

"I didn't say he likes me enough to be around me," I grumble.

He starts to laugh. "You could bring him with you tonight."

"I'm not bringing my cat to your house." I balk at the suggestion.

"Why not? The boys and I like animals."

"Melbourne doesn't like humans. He barely tolerates me, and I think the boys might wonder why I'm showing up to dinner with my cat and all the things he needs, if I'm just supposed to be there for a couple of hours before going back home."

"True."

"Wow, did you just agree with me?"

"I guess I did," he says, and I can't help but smile. "I'm sure he'll be okay without you for the night," he adds, and I sigh. I should have known he wasn't giving up.

"Gareth."

"Don't you want to stay over?"

I do. I want to stay over. I want to spend time with him and his boys. I want to get to know all of them. I just know I'm digging a deeper hole for myself by doing that. "I do. I just—"

"Where are you now?" he cuts me off before I can finish my sentence, not that I know what I was going to say.

"What?"

"Where are you right now?"

I look through the windshield and my muscles bunch. "Umm... at the store?"

"Are you asking me if you're at the store or telling me that's where you are?"

Seriously, why is he so annoying? "Why are you so annoying?"

"You only think I'm annoying because I can read you already. So, where are you?"

"The drug store," I tell him, and like a switch is flipped, he goes completely silent. I don't even hear him breathe. "Gareth?" It takes him so long to answer I almost pull my phone away to see if the call is still connected.

"I'm here."

"Are you okay?"

"Yeah." He clears his throat. "I'm heading now to pick up Max from school, and Mitchell has track until five, so we'll be home around 5:30 and eat a little after six. Does that work for you?"

"Yeah, that works," I say softly.

"See you then, babe."

He hangs up before I can say goodbye and I drop my phone to my lap, staring at the dark screen and trying to figure out what just happened. I don't get why he asked me where I was or why his mood seemed to change when I told him. "Men are so confusing." I sigh, grabbing my handbag before I get out of the car and go into the store, where I pick up what I need along with a few boxes of condoms.

I reach my apartment twenty minutes later, and as soon as I shut the door and start to slip off my coat, Melbourne, who is lounging on the couch, meows loudly, gaining my attention. "Oh, I'm sorry. Did I interrupt your nap?" I ask sarcastically, and I swear he rolls his eyes at me before he jumps down, swishing his tail.

I shake my head as he prances into my bedroom then start for the kitchen, only to stop when there is a knock on my front door. Not expecting anyone, I check the peephole and frown when I see no one is there. Figuring it's just the kids in the complex messing around, I start to turn from the door when there is suddenly another knock. Wanting to scare them a little, I swing the door open, only it's me who is taken by surprise, because not only is Gareth standing in my breezeway, but so is Max.

"Please tell me you have food. I'm starving, and Dad didn't bring me a snack," Max offers as a greeting, and I blink at his adorable pleading face.

"I… I have food," I stammer out.

"Thank God," he groans, walking past me into my apartment, and I turn to watch him take a seat on my couch then look at his father when his hand touches my hip.

"He's not actually starving. He had two granola bars on the way over here."

"You didn't tell me you were coming over."

He shrugs. "We have some time to kill before we have to pick up Mitchell, and your place is closer than mine to the school. I drove by, figuring if I saw your car we'd stop, and if not we'd go on home."

I start to tell him he still should have called to let me know he was coming over with Max, but before I can open my mouth, he leans down, gently touching his lips to mine. When he pulls back, I see he's smiling.

"Did you have a good day?"

"Yeah." I clear my throat, wishing he didn't have split personalities or turn me into a complete idiot with a simple kiss.

"You have a cat!" At that exclamation, I turn quickly to warn Max that Melbourne isn't exactly nice, but find my cat on his lap, rubbing his jaw along Max's chin, and can hear him purring loudly even from across the room.

"I thought you said your cat doesn't like people."

"He doesn't," I mutter, and Gareth laughs while shutting the door.

"He's so cool." Max smiles at me, scratching the head of the cat who has obviously been switched with mine.

"Let me find you something to eat." I smile back at him before stepping into the kitchen.

"What's his name?"

"Melbourne," I call out. "Or I think it is. My cat doesn't like people, so I don't know who you're holding." I hear him laugh from the other room and I smile.

"You don't have to feed him, babe. He can wait to eat until dinner," Gareth tells me, wrapping his arms around my waist from behind, and I lean back into his embrace then tip my head to the side until I catch his gaze.

"I don't really have anything nutritious to feed a growing boy, but I'm not going to let your son starve."

His eyes search mine for a moment then he shakes his head, kisses the tip of my nose, and lets me go to leave the kitchen. Not sure what that was about or why goose bumps are breaking out on my arms, I go back to searching for something to feed Max.

"Max, are chips and salsa okay?" I shout. When he calls out a yes, I dump a jar of salsa into a bowl then dig through the cabinets for corn chips. Carrying the bowl and the bag with me into the living room, I stop in my tracks when I see Gareth pick up Melbourne and flip him to his back to rub his stomach—a move that would for sure get my eyes scratched out.

Okay, so my cat is obviously sexist and only likes men. Good to know.

"What do you want to drink, honey?" I ask Max as I set down the chips and salsa in front of him.

"Water is okay."

"What do you say to December, kid?" Gareth asks, and Max pauses with a chip close to his lips.

"Thanks."

"No problem." I touch his hair and his eyes widen. Damn, why did I do that? I shouldn't have done that. "Um." I look at Gareth, balling my hand at my side. "Would you like something to drink?"

He looks at my hand then me. "Do you have tea?"

"Yeah."

"That'd be good, babe." My skin tingles.

Focusing on the task at hand and not everything I'm feeling, I go back to the kitchen and come back a minute later with their drinks and a Diet Coke for myself.

"How was school today?" I ask Max, taking a seat on the couch next to him as he digs into the salsa with a chip.

"It was okay."

"Just okay?"

"I had science, so that was cool." He shrugs.

"Is science your favorite class?" I ask, dipping a chip into the salsa.

"Yeah, our science teacher, Mr. Tonk, is awesome. He's always doing experiments and stuff, which makes class fun."

"What's your least favorite class?" I inquire, while Gareth takes a seat diagonally from us with Melbourne.

"Math. I hate math."

"I don't like math either," I admit, and he eyes me doubtfully. "You don't believe me?"

"You're a teacher."

"I am, but I still don't like math. It's not a subject I find easy to understand, and even to this day I have issues with a lot of math formulas."

"What was your favorite subject?"

I don't even have to think about it. "English. I love reading. I always have."

"Were you a nerd when you were in school?" he asks with a smile twitching his lips.

"Probably." I laugh. "I was friends with everyone, and I always had people to sit with at lunch and hang out with, but I mostly spent time alone reading."

"I have a friend like that. He's cool, but he would rather play video games at lunch and between classes."

"Video games are cool," I say, and he nods, dipping another chip and popping it in his mouth. "Do you like to bake?" I ask him, and he frowns at me. "What?"

"Baking is for girls."

"Really? Says who?" I quickly glare at Gareth when he chuckles.

"I don't know, but Grandma bakes, and so do my aunts and their girls."

"Your dad doesn't bake?" I question, and he looks at his dad and then back at me, shaking his head. "Do you like eating cookies and cakes and stuff?"

"Yes."

"Me too." I grin. "Baking is how my mom helped me understand math, but you know something else cool about it?" He gives me a half smile. "There is a lot of science involved. If you don't measure and add just the right amount of ingredients, whatever you're making won't turn out like it should."

"I guess you're right," he agrees, studying me.

"What's your favorite thing your grandma or aunts make for you?"

"Chocolate chip cookies."

I look at the clock and see we have enough time to mix up a batch of cookie dough. "Come on."

"What?"

"You're going to help me make some chocolate chip cookies. We will have to bake them at your house, but we can make the dough here."

"Really?"

"Really. Well… I mean…" I look at Gareth. "Is that okay with you?"

"Yeah," he agrees smoothly, but there is still an intensity in his expression that makes my legs feel weak.

I force myself to look away from him. "Come on, we don't have long before you have to go pick up your brother," I tell Max, and he gets up, following me into the kitchen. A few minutes later, Gareth comes in, taking a seat at the high table I use as a makeshift island. "The recipe we're going to use is in here." I hand Max one of my cookbooks. "Find the one for chocolate chip cookies while I get out the mixer." Once I have the mixer set up, I go back to where he's standing and look down at the recipe. "So we're going to double the recipe so we'll have plenty of cookies for everyone. Now, what do we need to do first?"

"It says you need to mix the eggs and butter together then add in sugar, vanilla, and salt."

"Perfect, here's the measuring cup." I hand it to him and he looks at it. "I'll grab the eggs while you measure out the butter."

"How much butter?"

"What does the recipe call for?" I stop at the fridge and look at him.

"One and a half cups."

"And since we're doubling the recipe, how much do we need?"

"Three."

"See? You got this down already," I say, and he smiles brightly. "How many eggs do I need?"

He looks at the recipe. "Four."

"Great." I grab four eggs while he dumps the butter into the metal mixer bowl, and then I hand them over for him to crack. By the time we have the first five ingredients in the mixer, he's a pro and completely at ease. "What's next?"

"Flour," he says, and I grab my flour canister from the counter and watch him measure out the first cup. I start to tell him that we have to shut off the machine before we add it, but he dumps it in, and flour hits the wire beater and flies everywhere. Gareth jumps from where he's been sitting and shuts off the machine before I can.

"Oh my." I look at Max and then down at myself. We are covered in flour, and there is still more falling to the floor like snow.

"I'm so sorry," Max whispers. I blink at him, seeing only his green eyes. The rest of him is covered in a thin layer of white dust.

"You…" I giggle then start to laugh so hard I double over. I stand and point at him. "You… You should see your face right now." I laugh harder and hear him start to laugh as well. "I should… I should have mentioned turning the machine off." I continue to laugh then attempt to swipe the flour off the front of me, which causes a plume of it to fly out, making me giggle once more. "I think…" I snort, looking around. "I think we need to take a picture. My sisters will get a kick out of this." I start to walk to the door so I can go get my cell, but Gareth grabs my hand and pulls me up short. "I need my phone," I tell him, tipping my head back to catch his eye.

"I'll get it for you. Where is it?"

"I can get it," I try again, and he shakes his head then looks behind me. I follow his gaze and see I'm leaving a trail of flour in my wake. "Oh, maybe you should get it. It's in my purse." His eyes warm, and I swear he's going to kiss me, but instead his fingers squeeze mine and he lets me go.

"Are the cookies ruined?"

I turn to face Max and find him looking into the mixing bowl.

"Nope." I walk toward him. "We just need to guess how much flour actually made it in the bowl then add in the rest."

"Cool." His eyes are dancing with laughter when he turns to look at me. "Baking is kind of awesome."

"Told you." I nudge his shoulder with mine then look behind us when I hear the click of a camera.

"Smile," Gareth says, and I strike a silly pose, which makes Max laugh. Gareth takes another picture then looks around. "Where's your broom?"

"I think we should wait until we are done to clean up, just in case we have any more accidents."

"That's probably smart," he agrees, and Max and I finish mixing in the flour and the rest of the ingredients, including the chocolate chips. Once we're done, we scoop the dough into a plastic Tupperware container then set it in the fridge.

"Now for the not so fun part." I look around at the mess then go to the pantry and grab my vacuum out of its charging dock.

"I think we should try to get as much flour off of us and the counters as we can before we use the vacuum," Max suggests while bending at the waist and shaking his head.

I laugh, watching flour fall to the floor, and then do the same while

Gareth starts to wipe the counters. It doesn't take us very long to clean up, but by the time we're finished and I look at the clock, I see they need to leave to go get Mitchell.

"Go start up the engine, kid. I'll be down in a minute," Gareth tells Max, tossing him his keys.

"Cool." He smiles at his dad then looks at me. "See you at the house."

"See you there," I agree right before he rushes from my apartment. "He knows not to try to drive, right?" I ask Gareth, and he laughs. "What's funny?"

"Nothing." He steps toward me, encircling my waist then trailing one hand up my back and into my hair. "Thank you for letting him help you with cookies."

"It was fun," I say breathlessly then moan as he claims my mouth, thrusting his tongue between my parted lips. Holding onto him, I melt into the kiss then feel completely drugged when he pulls away.

"We'll see you at the house in about forty-five."

"Okay," I agree.

He studies me for a moment, and then demands quietly, "Pack a bag. Your cat will be alright here alone for the night."

"Gareth."

He holds me tighter. "I want to go to sleep with you in my arms, and I want to wake up with you in my bed." Feeling weak, I nod, and when I do, he touches his lips to my forehead then lets me go. "See you soon."

"See you soon." I watch him walk out then go to my bedroom and into my bathroom to take a quick shower. When I'm done, I blow out my hair, get dressed in a pair of jeans and a plain long-sleeved shirt, and pack an overnight bag. Before I leave my place, I grab the cookie dough out of the fridge and my purse from the hook then head to my car. I make it to Gareth's at the same time he and the boys are getting out of his SUV, and I park next to them.

"Can I see your phone to show Mitchell the pictures Dad took?" Max asks, opening my car door before I have a chance to.

"Sure." I laugh, reaching into my large Coach tote that is covered with strawberries, pears, bananas, and apples. My stomach drops when my fingers brush across the plastic shopping bag holding my purchase from the drug store. Shit, I still haven't taken that damn pill. What the hell is wrong with me? With my hand suddenly shaking, I grasp my cell phone from the bottom of my bag then click on the Photos app before handing it to Max.

"I'm so mad I wasn't there," Mitchell says, smiling at me. "Can we bake cookies sometime?"

"Yes," I say, unsure if I'm lying or not. Tonight, I'm going to get myself together and have a very uncomfortable conversation with his dad, and if Gareth tells me he never wants more kids, I seriously don't know what I will do.

Okay, I do know I will be disappointed and will most likely cry. *A lot.*

"Right on." He looks from me to his dad. "What are we having for dinner? I'm starving."

"Chicken tacos," Gareth replies, and my stomach grumbles, only I'm not sure if it's from hunger or worry. "You boys go shower. Dinner will be ready when you get done."

Without a fight, they both take off toward the house then disappear inside. "What's with the look?" Gareth asks quietly, and I turn my head to face him, wondering how he knows something is wrong by just looking at me.

"Do you want more kids?" I blurt, and his eyes shutter, making me feel sick. I wrap my arms around my middle to keep myself together. "I.... God, I don't want to seem crazy bringing this up now, especially when we are just getting to know each other. But what you said to Mitchell the other day about him never having a sister has been replaying in my head. I feel like I need to know if you do or not before we continue seeing each other, or—"

"I saw the pill," he cuts me off.

I shake my head in confusion and feel my brows draw together. "What?"

"I saw that pill in your bag when I was getting your phone." He runs his fingers through his hair. "I wanted to toss it." He says and realize what he's talking about and pull one strap of my bag off my shoulder. I look inside and see the Plan B box is still in the shopping bag. "I didn't do it, I wanted to, but I didn't." My head flies up when he laughs without

140

humor. "I thought I knew what I wanted. Hell, the day of our first date, I told my sisters I didn't want more kids, and I meant it." He shakes his head then wraps his hand around the back of his neck. "Then the other night you told me about going to get that fucking pill, and I felt disappointed. And today, when I saw it, my only thought was to throw it away before you could take it."

I stare at him not sure what to feel. Elated that he's open to having more kids, pissed that he thought about tossing my pill without giving me a choice, without even talking to me. "I don't even know what to say right now."

He takes a step toward me and I hold my breath "You asked if I want more kids and the answer to that question is yes. If things between us work out, I want everything with you including children."

As relieved as that news makes me I shake my head and say softly. "If this is going to ever work between us Gareth, we both need to be honest about what we want and what we expect from each other. You need to talk to me."

"I want you," he says quietly, closing the distance between us. "I want time alone with you. Time for us to get to know each other. I want to watch you get to know my boys and experience them falling in love with you. Just like I seem to be." My entire body jolts from his admission, and my arms drop to my sides. "I'll try not to act on instinct, but truth be told I don't know what I'm doing. This is all new to me, I've never felt the way you make me feel."

"I've never felt like this either," I confess as he pulls me against him and I rest my hands against his chest. "I'm glad you talked to me."

"Yeah." He rests his lips against my forehead then his fingers curl around the underside of my jaw and he tips my head back so he can brush his lips across mine. "I'll try to get better about doing that."

"That would be good." I say sliding my hands up to the sharp edge of his jaw.

"Are we over our latest drama?"

I smile, "I think so."

"Good." He touches his lips to mine once more.

"We should probably go in and get started on dinner."

"Dinner is done." He gives my waist a squeeze. "Or most of it is. I just need to warm up the tortillas and a can of refried beans."

"Do you have magical powers that allow you to cook while you're not even home?"

"No, I have a Crock-pot that cooks when I'm not home," he says

"You have a Crock-pot?" I laugh.

"Are you laughing at me?"

"Of course not." I pat his chest. "I just didn't know guys use Crock-pots. I thought they were only for girls, kinda like baking."

"Smartass." He chuckles.

"I still can't believe you don't bake," I say as he turns us toward the house and holds the door open for me to enter before him.

"I've never had a reason to. My mom and sisters are constantly bringing over shit for the boys."

"Spoiled."

"Yep." He grins then kisses the top of my head while taking my purse from me. "Also, baby, you didn't need to buy condoms. I got us covered in that department," he tells me, taking the shopping bag out of my purse before hanging my bag near the door. My cheeks warm as I watch him take it to his room, and he grins at me when he comes back out.

Studying his handsome grin, I pull in a breath. One more crisis averted and even more proof I'm seriously falling for this guy and his boys.

Gareth

Chapter 11

"GRANDMA'S HERE," MAX shouts, and December's head flies up.

"Your mom is here?" She turns to look at me, and I want to laugh at the adorable nervous look on her face, but I don't.

"I'll be right back. It's all good." I reassure her, stopping to kiss the side of her head before I walk past the edge of the island where she's been working on her lesson plan for the upcoming week. It's Saturday, it's been almost a week since she and Max baked cookies, almost a week since we had our talk about one day having kids. Six days of having her at my house every evening for dinner with me and the boys, and in my bed every night.

"You're going to love Grandma," I hear Mitchell tell her right before I step out of the house to meet my mom on the walkway.

"It's only been days since I've seen you and it's like you've grown a foot," Mom says, hugging Max then letting him go asking. "Where is your brother?"

"Inside. He had to do dishes this morning," he replies smugly.

"You didn't?"

"Nope, me and December did them last night," he tells her, and a thoughtful smile curves her lips.

"Did you make her wash all the dishes?"

"Nah." He laughs, shaking his head. "She made it a game, so it was fun, and we got it done super fast."

"That's awesome."

"She's totally awesome," he tells her as they make their way toward me.

When they're close, I palm the top of Max's head, gaining his attention. "Go finish getting dressed and get your stuff together. We're leaving in thirty," I say, and he nods then leans up to kiss his grandmother's cheek before turning and doing a high jump over both stairs to the top porch.

"It seems like Max really likes this girl," Mom points out, turning to look at me once Max is inside and the door is closed.

"He does. Both the boys do," I agree. "What are you doing here?"

"Well, since you were obviously not going to invite me over to meet her—" She tosses out one hand toward the house. "—I invited myself."

"You know it's not like that. This week has been busy, and today we're taking the boys to Adventure Park in Nashville."

"I haven't seen my grandbabies in days, and I always pick them up from school at least a couple of times during the week."

I shrug. "I rearranged my schedule so I could be off in time to pick them up from school last week. I'll probably do the same next week, but after that, things will most likely go back to normal."

"Your aunt told me you've turned down a few jobs at the shop."

"Yeah," I agree, crossing my arms over my chest becoming aggravated with the direction this conversation is headed in.

"I'm worried, Gareth. The boys are getting close to this girl, and you're turning down work."

"Don't," I growl, keeping my voice low so the boys and December won't hear. "Do not go there. I want the boys tight with her. She's the kind of woman they should be close to, and I didn't quit my job, I just haven't been killing myself with overtime."

"Honey, I—"

"Jesus." I scrub my fingers through my hair. "You were the one who told me that I should find someone, Mom."

"You're right." She places her hand against her chest. "I... I think maybe I'm just a little jealous."

"You have nothing to be jealous of."

"When I talked to the boys the other evening, Max told me she baked cookies with him. I didn't even think Max would want to bake cookies. And Mitchell kept talking about how cool she is. And you. I haven't even seen you this week, or even talked to you."

"Mom." I sigh.

"I feel like I'm being replaced," she says with tears filling her eyes.

"You're not being replaced." I chuckle, closing my arms around her.

"Don't laugh at me."

"Mom, you're being crazy. We love you. That is never going to change."

"I know. I just…. I guess I liked the idea of you finding someone, but never really thought of where that would leave me."

I shake my head and rub her back. "The boys won't like seeing you upset like this."

"I'm almost done." She sniffles, and I smile. "I know I'm not acting like it, but I really am happy for you."

I tip my head down to look at her then tell her honestly, "She's making me happy. She's just as cool as both my boys think she is, and she fits in like she's always been here with us."

"You're falling in love with her."

Without a doubt. "She's special, and when you meet her, you'll see what I mean."

Her expression softens. "Can I meet her now?"

"Do you think I'm going to send you away?"

"I don't know. I did just show up here without letting you know I was coming over."

"You're always welcome in my home. And I know you don't know December yet, but she would probably be more upset than you if I sent you away without introducing you two."

"Really?"

"Yeah." I chuckle, and she laughs, wiping what was left of her tears from under her eyes. "Are you ready?"

She pulls in a big breath then lets it out. "I think so." She tips her head back. "Is my makeup a mess?"

"Nope."

"I know you're probably lying, but I'm going to pretend like you aren't," she mumbles, and I toss my arm over her shoulders and lead her up the steps to the porch. When I open the door, December and Mitchell, who are in the kitchen, turn toward us.

"Hey, Grandma." Mitchell waves.

"Child, you better get your not-too-old-for-a-whoopin' butt over here and hug your grandmother," Mom orders, and December giggles while Mitchell sighs, mumbling something I can't make out as he comes out of the kitchen to give her a reluctant hug.

"You okay?" I ask, tangling my fingers with December's when she's close. She gives me a nod, but I still notice her hand shaking slightly when my mom turns to face us.

"You must be December. I'm Lidia," Mom reaches out, taking her free hand, and then glances at me quickly. "I can see now why all my boys seem to be falling for you."

"I...." December's fingers convulse around mine. "It's nice to meet you. The boys talk about you all the time."

"They're good boys." Mom smiles.

"They really are," December agrees, and Mom lets her hand go as Max joins us.

"So you guys are going to Adventure Park today?"

"That's what I was told this morning." December glares at Max and Mitchell when they start to laugh. "But I've told these guys that I will be sitting at the picnic tables reading while they test the strength of nylon and polyester."

"My type of girl."

"You have to at least try zip lining. Even Grandma did that one time," Max says.

"That and the hanging log bridge," Mitchell chimes in.

"It will be fun, babe." I squeeze her hand.

"I'll take pictures of you guys having fun, with both my feet planted firmly on the ground."

"Chicken." Max flaps his arms.

"Yep," December confirms, looking amused.

"Stick to your guns, honey. I swear I don't know how these three convinced me to climb up a tree then jump off a platform. I thought I was going to wet myself when I was flying through the air, I was so scared," Mom says, and both boys start to laugh while December grins.

"You should come with us, Grandma," Max invites.

Mom shakes her head. "No way. One time was plenty for me. You four go have fun, but if it's okay with your dad, you and your brother could come stay the night with me. We can go see a movie tonight then get up early and go have breakfast at Pfunky Griddle in the morning," Mom offers, knowing she's going to get her way. To this day, I don't know why that place is one of the boys' favorite breakfast spots. It's kind of like cooking at home. Each table is centered around a griddle, and you order what you want then the ingredients are brought out to you for you to make your own breakfast.

"Can we, Dad?" Max asks, placing his hands together like he's praying.

"That's cool with me, but it's up to Mitchell if he wants to go." I look at my oldest.

"I'm down." He shrugs, trying to play it cool.

"Yes." Max throws his hands in the air. "I love Pfunky."

"We all know you do." Mitchell rolls his eyes at his little brother.

"I haven't been there in years," December says, and I see my mom lock onto that piece of news the moment it leaves her mouth.

"You two should meet us there in the morning."

"I'm sure December wants to sleep in tomorrow," I respond. December turns to look at me, and I try to tell her without words that I don't want to get up to go out to eat just to make my own damn breakfast. I'd much rather eat her in the morning and relax in bed afterward—something I haven't been able to do with her since we've started seeing each other.

"I don't mind getting up early," she says, and I sigh.

"Then it's set. You two can drop the boys off to me on your way back home from Nashville, and we'll meet you in the morning for breakfast."

"Great," I agree, and I know I sound as annoyed as I feel. "Boys, hug your grandma then go pack your overnight bags. We need to hit the road." They both do as ordered then hurry down the hall.

"Have fun today," Mom says, leaning up to kiss my cheek, and then she looks at December. "Don't let them talk you into anything, and I'll see you two for breakfast." She grins when December laughs.

Once she's gone, I tighten my fingers on the hand still held in mine. "We need to work on our silent communication skills."

"What?" she asks, and I turn her to face me.

"Agreeing to go to breakfast."

"It's not a big deal. I love Pfunky... or I did when I went there years ago."

"Yeah, and I would've loved to have you to myself tonight and in the morning without having to worry about waking you up in time to leave before the boys find you."

"Oh." Her eyes round. "I didn't think about that."

"Yeah, I kinda got that when you agreed to go to breakfast in the morning, which is gonna be early," I say, and she bites her lip, looking away. "You owe me huge for this, and just so you know, I'm looking forward to making you pay," I growl near her ear, and pink touches her cheeks, making me feel a little better.

"How in the world did I let you guys talk me into this?" December cries, tightening her arms around the log that is shooting up through the platform we're standing on.

"Babe, I got you. Just relax and take a breath."

"Don't tell me to relax and take a breath, Gareth," she pants, resting her forehead against the log and squeezing her eyes closed.

"You can do it, December!" Max shouts, and she opens her eyes and turns her head to look at where he and Mitchell are standing on the next platform.

"You totally got this," Mitchell calls, giving her a smile.

"See? The boys know you've got this. And I won't let anything happen to you," I say, rubbing her back.

"Promise?" She moves only her eyes to look at me, and my heart squeezes.

Christ, this woman has no idea. "I promise, baby. Just trust me." I lean back and hold out my hand. She studies it for a long moment before she puts her hand in mine, and when she does, I release the breath I was holding and look across to my boys.

"Max, move to the next platform. Mitchell, I'm gonna send December over to you," I call out, and Max quickly swings himself onto the next platform while I adjust her rope overhead so it's clear of mine. "Baby, you're gonna jump to Mitchell," I instruct, and she eyes me warily. "I'm not going to leave you here alone. It's better if you jump to him, he jumps to the next platform, and I come over next."

"Okay."

"Okay." I touch her cheek with my gloved hand then ask, "Ready?"

"Not really, but yes."

"You've got this. Get into position then I want you to jump. It's not far."

"You mean it's not far across," she grumbles, making my lips twitch.

"On three." I count her off, and she jumps across the open space then squeaks when she lands on the wide platform. Both boys cheer, and Mitchell hugs her, making her laugh. "All right, I'm coming over. Mitchell, go on ahead," I say, and he jumps to where his brother is, and Max moves on. We continue on like that through that part of the aerial obstacle course, and I listen to her let out a relieved breath when she jumps down to a large wooden deck.

"This is my favorite part," Mitchell says as I jump down and land next to her.

When she turns to see what he's talking about, I see her face pale.

"This just gets worse and worse," she hisses, taking a tentative step to the edge to look out at the floating log bridge, which is basically a long row of logs tied individually, making them completely unstable.

"I'm going first," Max says, attaching himself to the catch rope, and then he quickly makes his way across without stopping once. Mitchell is right behind him, and the boys high-five on the other side.

"You know how you said I owe you huge for agreeing to go to breakfast with your mom?" December asks as I attach her to the catch rope at the top of the bridge. "I think we are beyond even. Actually, I'm pretty sure you owe me now."

"You're probably right," I agree. "That said, you've got this."

"I don't have a choice but to have it, since I can't go backward, and I'm for sure not jumping from here."

"True." I kiss the tip of her nose that is scrunched in annoyance, leaving out that there is a ladder to get down. I can tell, even if this is freaking her out a bit, that she's starting to enjoy herself. And what is the point of life if you're not living it?

"Here goes nothing." She sighs then grabs hold of both side of the bridge. Stepping onto the first log that swings under her weight, she lets out a scream and the boys laugh. She lifts her head, and I'm sure she's glaring at them. "I don't know how I'm going to pay you guys back for this, but just know I will be plotting my revenge."

"Aw, just admit it's fun," Max says, still laughing.

"Whatever," she grumbles under her breath, carefully moving to the next log then the next. When she's safely to the other side, she starts to laugh, and the boys wrap their arms around her and start jumping up and down with her in excitement.

I stare at the three of them, feeling completely overwhelmed with a mixture of pride and happiness like I have never felt before.

"It's your turn, Dad," Max breaks the spell, and without a word, I attach my harness then walk across the bridge with the ease of practice.

"Now my favorite part," Max says.

"What now?" December asks gloomily. "Are we jumping over a pit filled with man-eating alligators?"

"Nope, just flying through the air."

"Oh joy," she groans, and we all laugh as we head to the last platform where there is a zip line set up.

"Who's first?" the kid running the line asks when we approach, and Max steps up. A moment later, he lets out a hoot as he jumps down and disappears out of sight.

Once Mitchell is gone, the kid looks between December and me, and I can tell by the way she's holding herself that this is making her more nervous than anything else she's done today.

"You've got this," I assure her once again, checking the lines even after she's hooked in and cleared to go. "Meet you on the other side." I kiss her quickly then wait for her to pull up the courage to jump. When she does, her scream fills the air, and then a moment later, her laughter is bouncing off the trees.

"Girls," the kid says, shaking his head, and then he looks at me and his eyes widen. "Sorry."

"It's not a lie." I smile then let him hook me up, and a second later, I jump off and watch the trees fly by. When I reach the other side, my eyes lock with December's happy ones. I don't even wait for the worker to unhook me; I do it myself then take three steps in her direction, pick her up off the ground, and kiss her without thinking, listening to both boys snicker.

"Gareth." She pulls back, sounding unsure, but I don't set her down.

"I'm proud of you."

At my statement, her eyes warm and her fingers touch my cheek in a silent thank you.

"Can we go eat now?" Max asks, and the woman in my arms smiles down at me then looks at my boys and shines that beauty on them.

Lying on my back in December's bed, I lift my head when she comes out of the bathroom. I watch her walk across the room her face clean of makeup, her hair down and a clingy night gown contouring to her body. As sexy as she looks, I don't know if I like it more than my tees she normally confiscates when she sleeps at my place. I expect her to walk around the bed and get in on the other side, so I'm surprised when she comes directly to me and puts one knee in the mattress then swings the other over to straddle my lap.

"Today was fun." She grins, resting her hands against my chest, and I'm momentarily stunned by the light of happiness in her eyes, a light I know I had a part in creating.

"It was." I slide my hands up her thighs then over her hips watching her pupils dilate.

"I love spending time with the boys."

"They like spending time with you too baby." I say and her face softens.

"And thanks for agreeing to sleep here." She shifts her hips as my hands glide up her waist under the silky material exposing her stomach and her nails dig into my flesh making my cock twitch as I push the material up further. When she lifts her arms, I take it the rest of the way up then drop it to the floor watching her hair fall around her shoulders, covering the tips of her breasts. Soaking her in, I wrap one hand around her hip, my eyes catching on her tattoo, and I trace the ship and waves made from words with my fingers.

I've lived a thousand lives and traveled to unknown lands on waves of italic print and ships made from printed paper.

I read those words tattooed into her flesh along her ribs and tighten my hold on her. "Why this?"

"Because it's true. I've always lived through books," she says quietly, looking down at her hand as it covers mine on her side, then lifting it and meeting my gaze. "Not anymore."

"Jesus." I lift my head from my pillow and place my mouth against hers. When her mouth opens and her tongue touches mine, I roll her to her back and feel her warmth brush against the tip of my cock as I settle between her thighs.

"Gareth," she breathes, latching onto my shoulders with her nails and lifting her feet from the bed, curling her legs around the back of my thighs.

With my name warm on her lips, I sink into her slowly, feeling her slick walls contract and each of her breaths as they mix with mine. This is nothing like the frenzied pace we normally share; this is something more, something I've never experienced with anyone else. Her desire and excitement fuels my own.

I grasp both her hands in mine, pulling them up over her head— holding her, controlling her, connecting with her. Her sensual scent and wet heat pull me deeper into the unknown. I drag my mouth from hers and our eyes lock, my own look of awe reflected back at me. I soak in the sounds of her needy cries and absorb the feel of her soft skin and body under me. Everything about her and this moment is my undoing.

I lose myself inside her, and we fall over the edge together as one.

Two pieces of a puzzle, fitting together perfectly. Breathing heavily, I roll to my side with her in my arms, holding her tightly and knowing in this moment that she's exactly what I've been missing.

"We didn't use a condom," she whispers, and I squeeze my eyes closed for a moment then pull back to look at her and my teeth grind together. "We can't—"

"Ember," I cut her off, capturing her face with my palm. "The chances of you getting pregnant are slim."

"The chance might be slim, but there is still a chance it could happen."

"Yeah." I agree, brushing her hair out of her face.

"Okay, but how would you react if I ended up pregnant?" she asks, studying me closely.

"I'd react like every other man on the planet who found out the woman they love is carrying their child. I'd be scared but excited."

"You don't love me," she says, placing her hands against my chest and putting pressure there.

"What?" I ask then I realize exactly what I said. And I know it's true. I'm in love with her.

"You're not—"

"I am," I interrupt. "I don't even know when it happened, but it's true."

"You... You...." She snaps her mouth closed when I grin.

"Yes, me."

"How?" She frowns.

"I don't know." I start to laugh. "Should I have started a list?"

"Don't be a jerk."

"I'm not being a jerk. You're asking me a question I have no answer to. I don't know how I fell in love with you; I just did. I mean, I didn't really stand a chance, did I? You're you—beautiful, kind, great in bed, great in the kitchen, great with my boys who adore you. You love reading more than TV, are a little bit of a nerd, and the only woman I know who would carry a purse covered with fruit." I rest my forehead against hers. "But most importantly, you make me happy, and I want to do everything to make you feel the same," I say, watching tears start to fill her eyes.

Meow.

155

"You have to be kidding me," she cries, shaking her head.

"You also have an awesome cat."

Meow.

"I hate him," she whispers, using the sheet to blot under her eyes. "He just ruined a perfect moment."

Meow.

"Babe." I chuckle then start to laugh hard when Melbourne meows loudly again and paws against the door. "I'm going to go let him in."

"Fine." She sighs, flopping to her back in defeat.

I lean over her, placing my face close to hers, and lower my voice. "If you end up pregnant, baby, we'll figure it out together, all right?"

"Yeah." She touches my cheek then leans up to press her lips to mine, groaning a second later when Melbourne makes his presence known with another loud meow.

With a smile, I get up, and as soon as I open the door, he comes in and circles my legs as he begins to purr. "I really do not know why he likes you so much. It's not like it was you who rescued him from the pound, buys him the best food money can buy, or gives him a warm place to sleep."

"Babe, you're sounding a little jealous." I smile, going back to the bed and scooping her up.

"I'm not jealous that my cat likes you. I'm *annoyed* that he likes you and the boys more than he likes me."

"Dudes gotta stick together."

"Whatever," she mutters then looks around. "What are we doing?"

"Taking a shower."

"I showered earlier."

"Yeah, but I want to eat you, so you're going to take another one."

"Oh... well then, I guess I can shower again."

"I figured you'd see things my way." I smirk then flip on the shower.

An hour later, I eat her until she comes, and after I finish inside her, I fall asleep with her in my arms, wondering how soon is too soon for her to move in with me, so I can have this with her every night.

December

Chapter 12

$\mathcal{I}$ HOLD BACK a giggle, watching Max place a banana between two oranges in the produce section, and then snort when Mitchell rolls his eyes at his little brother and dismantles his handy work.

"What's funny?" Gareth asks, placing his hand on my lower back, and I glance up at him.

"The boys."

"Do I even want to know?" He looks toward where they are now picking up cantaloupes.

"They're just being boys," I reply, and he shakes his head, used to me finding humor in most everything they do. "Anyway…" I grab a bag of salad and toss it in the shopping cart. "I talked to my mom when I got off work today."

"Is she good?"

"Yeah, she just wanted me to extend an invitation to you and the boys to her and Dad's annual Memorial Day barbeque," I say quietly, pulling my eyes off Mitchell and Max, who are now ahead of us. "I told her I wasn't sure you'd be cool with that but promised I'd still ask."

"I don't see why we can't make that work. The boys and I normally just do something at home. I'm sure they won't mind having dinner at your parents'."

"Okay, but my whole family will be there, so it won't just be my parents. Do you think that will be too much for them?"

"Babe, they aren't the kinda kids who mind being around people. They'll be fine," he assures me with a soft look.

"They haven't even met my parents yet," I remind him.

"So let's set something up. Memorial Day isn't for another week. Ask your mom and dad if they want to come to my place for dinner this Saturday, and they can meet the boys then."

"Are you sure?" I ask, and he stops the cart and turns fully toward me.

"Why do you keep asking if I'm sure, when I'm the one giving you a solution to a problem you're having an issue with?"

"I don't know." I let out a breath. I really don't know. I think I'm still in shock. I can't believe he loves me and how good things are between us. Honestly, I keep waiting for some kind of drama to happen, because everything seems too good to be true. That's one of the reasons I haven't told him that I love him. I don't want to jinx myself or us.

"Babe, relax. The boys will be all right whether they meet your parents now or then, but if it'll make you feel better, ask your parents to come over for dinner."

"I'll ask them over for dinner," I decide.

He laughs shaking his head. "Now that that's done what are we gonna do for dinner tonight?"

"I thought Max wanted meatloaf." I frown, pretty sure that's the reason we came to the store after we picked up Mitchell from practice.

"Mitchell doesn't want meatloaf."

"Yeah, but Mitchell got to pick dinner last night, so it's only fair that Max gets to pick tonight," I tell him, thinking that we sound like a married couple discussing their children and not a couple who have only been dating for a couple months.

"True, meatloaf it is then," he agrees, and I lean into his side as we continue down the aisle. "I'm having Mom pick up the boys the rest of this week."

His statement catches me off guard and I stop in my tracks. "Why?" I ask. I've gotten used to having him and Max show up at my apartment until it's time to pick up Mitchell, and then having dinner with him and the boys every night.

"Sorry, baby. I have a couple big projects at the shop I'm working on, and a few tattoo clients have been asking me to sketch some stuff up for them. I've put them off as long as I can, so after tonight, I probably won't be home until after six."

Work. How could I forget he works two jobs to take care of his boys? I can't be upset about that. "I can pick up the boys if you want," I say without thinking then wonder if that is too much. Yes, we have conversations like this thing between us is settled, but the truth is it's very new. And I don't even know if the boys would want me picking them up. "I mean, if your mom is busy, I don't mind picking them up. I'm sure they want to spend time with her."

"I'll talk to the boys."

"Talk to us about what?" Mitchell asks, appearing from behind us holding a box of cereal.

"I gotta do some overtime this week. I was just telling December that I won't be home until after six, and she said she could pick you two up from school if Grandma is busy," Gareth replies as Mitchell places the box he's holding in the cart.

"Can you pick me up even if Grandma isn't busy?" Max asks startling me, and I meet his gaze. "Grandma's always dragging me around to run errands. I'd rather just go home after school and hang with you."

"I'd rather hang with you too," Mitchell agrees, and I want to jump up and down but I control the urge.

"You sure you're cool with picking them both up and staying with them?" Gareth asks.

"I get off work at 3:30, so I have plenty of time to make it over to Max's school before he gets out, and we can either wait for Mitchell or go home until—" I shake my head. "I mean, go back to your place until he's ready to get off. Plus, I like spending time with the boys," I explain, looking between the two of them.

"Awesome," Max says, making me smile.

"Just don't act like you're so excited when your grandma finds out about this change of plans. She's going to be disappointed that she isn't getting to spend time with you two," Gareth tells them, and I start to feel guilty.

After breakfast with Gareth's mom last week, I learned quickly that her boys are *her* boys, and although she was very nice to me, I could still tell she considered me an intruder.

"Grandma will be cool. We'll just go to her place on the weekends. Plus, that will give you and December time alone," Mitchell says, and I feel warmth spread up my neck to my cheeks.

"Why would they need time alone? They're alone all night after we go to bed," Max tells him, and then he looks at me. "Why don't you ever stay to have breakfast with us in the morning?"

"Wh-what?" I sputter.

"You always leave super early, like… it's still totally dark out."

Oh my God. How long have they known I've been sleeping there?

"I'm just saying you could have breakfast with us, since you're sleeping over."

"I don't think we're supposed to know she's been staying over," Mitchell says dryly, and Max frowns at him.

"Are you two cool with her staying the night?" Gareth asks before Max can question his brother, and I look around, thinking the middle of the grocery store isn't exactly the best place to be having this conversation. Really, I don't know if I should be around for this conversation.

"It's cool with me." Mitchell shrugs like it's all the same to him.

"Totally," Max agrees, mimicking his brother's shrug, and then he looks at me. "Can Melbourne stay in my room with me?"

"I…. Umm, sure," I reply, and he grins.

"Well, now that we've settled all that, let's finish up here so we can get home. Mitchell, you go grab milk, eggs, and a couple of packs of bacon, and Max, you run down and grab a case of Coke while me and December get the stuff for dinner."

"On it." Max takes off, but Mitchell lingers behind like he has something to say. Once his brother is out of earshot, he turns to face his dad and me, and I reach out for Gareth's hand and hold my breath, unsure what to expect or how much more I can take.

"I know you have to work, but do you think we can keep having dinner together every night as a family, even if it's late?"

"Sure bud," Gareth answers gruffly, and I tighten my hand around his when his fingers squeeze mine.

"Cool." He says softly before he tucks his hands in his pockets. "I'll be back." He turns and walks away and I watch him go then look up at Gareth.

"So—" I clear my throat. "—is it me, or did a lot just happen?"

"A lot just happened."

I bite the inside of my cheek then shake my head, "I wonder how long they've known I've been sleeping over."

"No idea. Also know it really doesn't matter. I'm just happy they're cool with you stayin' the night."

I drag in a deep breath. "I guess you're right."

"They both adore you."

"I love them," I admit.

"Only them?" he asks quietly as his eyes search mine.

I look around. "I'm not going to tell you that I love you the first time in the middle of the grocery store."

"Why not? I don't give a fuck where you tell me, just as long as you mean it when you say it. Besides I already know you love me," he says smugly, letting my hand go to place his arm around my shoulders.

"What do you mean you know?"

"It's written on your face every time you look at me," he says, and I wonder if that's true. Actually, I'm sure it is. I probably look like one of those emojis with the big heart eyes.

"Whatever. Let's just focus on getting the stuff for dinner," I mutter.

He brushes his lips across mine then leans back, grinning. "You're even cute when you're annoyed."

"I'm not annoyed."

"You are," he returns, and I roll my eyes. "Are you happy though?"

At his quietly asked question, I rest my hand against his stomach, and tell him the truth. "I'm happier than I ever have been."

"Then I'm doing my job," he says, still talking gently. I don't know how we got to this point, especially after the way things between us started out, but I'm glad we're here now.

"You know, you're very mushy for a guy who looks so gruff," I say, and he laughs. "What? It's true."

"Babe, I'm not mushy."

"You kinda are."

"I'm not," he denies.

"You really are," I say just to tease, and he shakes his head then ignores me as I pick on him through the rest of the store.

"Aw, fuck," Gareth mutters from the driver seat, and I look up from my Kindle, wondering what has him annoyed, and notice his eyes are on a bright blue Mustang parked next to my car in his driveway.

"Shit," Mitchell growls from the back seat.

"Mom," Max whispers, and my heart starts to pound when I see a petite woman with shoulder-length dark blond hair and alabaster skin get out of her car then slam the door with her slim, denim-covered hip. Her eyes lock with mine and narrow to slits through the windshield as she turns when we pull in to park. But even with the ugly look on her face, she looks like she belongs on the arm of a rock star... or a cool mechanic and tattoo artist.

"This is not fucking happening," Gareth says on a low growl, sending a chill down my spine as he shuts down the engine. Then the back door opens, and Max runs around the hood to his mom. I hate her a little when she barely spares her son a glance, her attention now fully focused on Gareth. "Fuck," he mumbles under his breath, grasping my hand. "Baby." I turn my head toward him. "It will be okay."

Will it? This isn't zip lining or the boys meeting my parents. This is Beth, the boys' mom, his ex—a woman who he admitted messed him up—showing at his house looking beautiful and cool.

"Wait for me to come around to help you down," he orders, and I nod, unhooking my belt feeling sick to my stomach. When he gets out and shuts the door, fingers wrap around my shoulder from the back seat, and I turn to look at Mitchell.

"I've got your back." He gives my shoulder a squeeze then opens his door and hops out, slamming it closed before I can tell him he's a really fricking great kid but that I'm an adult and will find a way to deal.

As soon as my door is open, Gareth reaches in, taking hold of my waist. I lean into him, placing my hands on his shoulders, and then let gravity work as I fall safely into his hold to my flat feet.

"That's December, Dad's girlfriend," I hear Max say from behind the open door, and Gareth rumbles a quiet expletive as he hands me my purse then puts pressure on my hip in a silent demand to move so he can shut it.

"I got the groceries, Dad." Mitchell stops at our side then looks at me. "You wanna help me put them away?"

"Sure." I adjust my purse on my shoulder then reach out to take a couple of bags, since he's overloaded. But he steps back, shaking his head making me want to roll my eyes, because he's already just like his father.

"Is only my youngest going to greet me?"

At that question, I turn slightly and experience up close exactly why Gareth had two kids with her. She really is beautiful, even with the sneer she's trying to hide.

"Mom," Mitchell says, and I step closer to him without thinking, not liking the slight twinge of pain and anger I hear in his voice.

Her attention comes to me briefly when I move, and then she focuses on him once more and asks, "That's all I get? Mom?"

"I haven't seen you in months," he tells her, and my heart hurts. How can she stand to be away from her boys that long?

"I've been working; you know that."

"Yeah." He shakes his head. "I'm going to go put the groceries away and start on homework. Come on, Max. You should do the same."

"I…." Max looks around, starting to realize that everyone isn't as happy as he is that his mom's here.

Not liking the sudden unease I see in his frame, I plaster my best pretend smile on my face and hold out my hand. "I'm December."

Beth looks down at it like it's covered in toxic waste then sighs, placing her hand in mine. "Beth."

"It's nice to meet you." I let her hand go. "I think these guys are just hungry and tired after work and school today. I'm sure you get that," I say then look up at Gareth. "I'm going to get started on dinner."

"All right, babe. I'll be inside in a few minutes." He touches his fingers to my jaw then looks at Max. "Go on in, kid."

"But—"

"I need to talk to your mom. Go get started on your homework," Gareth tells him, and Max's shoulders slump as he turns away.

I want so badly to place my arm around him and tell him it's okay, but I don't. Instead, I stay behind him as we walk the path to the house and up the stairs to the porch, and then I cringe when I hear Beth snap, "Seriously, Gareth, what the fuck? Is she living here with you?"

"That's none of your business, Beth," Gareth replies, and then I don't hear more, because I shut the door to block them out.

When I turn around, neither of the boys are anywhere in sight. I hang up my purse and jacket then pick up Max's coat from where he draped it over the back of the couch, hanging it up. I then straighten the cushions, fold the blankets, put away the video games left out, and stack all the boys' sports equipment in the corner, thinking I need to get a basket for it all to go in. When I finally make it to the kitchen, I find the groceries still in the plastic bags from the store. I turn on the oven then unpack everything, trying to ignore the urge to go peek out the blinds to see what's happening in the driveway.

"Do you need help?" I turn my head toward Max standing at the edge of the island, and I notice his eyes are a little red like he's been crying.

"Definitely," I say, dumping the two packs of meatloaf seasoning into the bowl that I've already got the milk, eggs, and breadcrumbs in. "I don't like squishing all the stuff into the meat, so you'd be doing me a favor if you helped me out." He nods, not giving me even a small glimpse of his normal happy smile. "Wash your hands, honey."

He does, and then I softly tell him what to do, and while he mixes everything together, I fill a pot with water and add the already cleaned corn, putting it on the stove. Then I place a bag of ready-to-steam potatoes in the microwave and set it for ten minutes.

"My mom isn't bad," he says, catching me off guard as I pull out a baking dish from one of the lower cabinets, and I look at him as I stand from my squatted position.

"Pardon?"

"My mom… she isn't a bad person," he repeats without looking at me.

"I don't think anyone thinks that, honey," I tell him gently, setting the baking dish next to him on the counter.

"She's funny, and she tells cool stories, and she always brings me stuff." I don't say anything, because I honestly don't know what to say. "She's cool, like you, but different. I... I don't think she really wanted to be a mom, but she does the best she can."

"Max," I whisper, hating that he even thinks that, let alone believes that it's true.

"She's just her, and when she's around, I like spending time with her."

"She's your mom, honey. Of course you like spending time with her."

"I also like spending time with you," he says, and I can tell by his tone that he feels guilty about that.

Even though my throat is tight with emotion, I still manage to tell him, "I like spending time with you too." Then, not caring if I should or not, I wrap my arm around his shoulders then lean my head against the side of his. "It's okay to care about more than one person, Max."

"Okay," he mumbles, not sounding convinced.

I pull in a breath, releasing it slowly and wondering what I can say to make him feel better, but before I can find the words, Gareth comes back into the house. His eyes go between his son and me before they lock on mine in question. Unsure how to tell him what his son just said without using words, I give him a tight smile and he drops his eyes to Max. "Come here, kid. Your mom wants to say goodbye."

"She's leaving?" he asks worriedly, his body still against mine filling with tension once more.

"Just for now. You'll see her tomorrow. She's going to pick you up from school and hang with you for a while, if that's okay with you."

"It's okay," he says, hurrying to wash his hands before rushing out of the kitchen and house.

"Just a few more minutes, baby," Gareth tells me, and I nod then watch him walk back outside.

I look down at the bowl of mush in front of me, muttering, "You were the one who was waiting for drama. Well, here you go. Now you just gotta deal with it."

"Are you talking to yourself?"

I jump in place and turn to mock glare at Mitchell. "Don't sneak up on me."

"I didn't sneak. I walked in here like I always do." He grins.

I shake my head. "Well, don't walk so quietly."

"Do you want me to wear a bell like Melbourne?"

"That doesn't sound like such a bad idea. Maybe I'll sew some into your jeans," I say, listening to him laugh while I dump the meat mixture into the baking dish and shape it into a loaf before washing my hands and placing it in the oven.

"Are you okay?" he asks, grabbing a can of Coke from the fridge.

"I think I should be asking you that question," I say as he casually leans back against the counter.

"I'm used to my mom showing up out of the blue then disappearing again for a few months. It's been the same way my whole life. You're new to her games."

"That must have been hard to deal with growing up."

He shrugs then takes a sip from his Coke and looks toward the front door. "Just sucks for Max. He still buys into her bullshit when she's around and then is hurt when she takes off and doesn't call for weeks or months at a time," he says, and even though I don't agree with him cursing I curb the urge to say something about it.

"He loves his mom," I say, leaving out that he loves her too, otherwise, he wouldn't be hurt by her actions.

"Yeah." He lets out a long breath.

"He's lucky he has you. You're a good big brother."

"I guess," he concedes, pushing away from the counter. "Do you need help with dinner?"

"I'm good, honey."

He lifts his chin. "I'm gonna start on my homework."

"Sure," I tell him. He gives me a small smile that doesn't reach his eyes then leaves the kitchen, and I hear his bedroom door close. With a sigh, I go to my bag and grab my cell phone along with my Kindle then take a seat on the couch. I send my mom a text just to tell her that I love her, and tears fill my eyes when she texts back a moment later, **Beyond**

each and every galaxy.

I don't believe for one moment that Beth doesn't love her boys, but I do know she's hurting them with her actions, and that is something a mother shouldn't do to her children—especially not over and over again. I wish I knew how to fix things between them, not for her but for the boys.

I bite the inside of my cheek, wondering if she would even listen to me if I tried to explain things to her. I doubt she would. Actually, I'm sure she would be offended if I even tried. I'm also not sure it's my place. With a sigh, I turn on my Kindle, but as soon as the screen lights up and words appear, the door opens and Max and Gareth come inside.

"Go get started on your homework," Gareth orders, and without a word, Max disappears down the hall while Gareth takes off his coat.

I bite my lip when he tosses the jacket on the back of the couch and jerks his fingers through his hair. "Everything all right?" I ask softly, placing my Kindle and cell on the coffee table.

"No," he answers then moves past me to the kitchen, and I hear the fridge open and shut. I get up and walk around the edge of the island, finding him standing near the stove with a bottle of beer to his lips. When he sees me, he drops it and holds open his arms. I walk toward him slowly then wrap my arms around his waist and rest the side of my head against his chest. "She always does this," he says as his cheek rests against my hair and he pulls in a deep breath.

"Does what?" I ask, not moving.

"Shows when the boys and I have had enough time to forget she even exists." I cringe from the harshness in his voice. "It's like she can smell that we're happy and can't handle it, so she comes to fuck shit up."

"She can only mess things up if you let her, Gareth. And she didn't seem so bad."

"Babe, she was nice to you outside, probably because she was caught off guard by seeing you with us." Nice? That was her being nice? *Yikes.* "Just promise to stick this out with me and the boys. She's never around for very long."

I tip my head back, forcing him to move his head, and frown up at him. "Do you think she's going to scare me off?"

"I think she'll try," he replies gently, setting down his beer so he can capture my face with both his hands. "In her mind, me and the boys belong to her."

"I'm a Mayson, Gareth Black. I know I'm not adventurous or very outgoing, but I'm still a *Mayson*." His brows draw together, and I lift my hand to rub away the lines etched between them. "Family, love, devotion, and determination are what I grew up seeing all around me. I know what's important. I know why it's important. And I understand that sometimes, even when it's scary, you have to do everything within your power to protect it. I love you." I say and watch as his pupils dilate on the word love. "I'm not worried about me, or even you. I'm worried about what her being here will mean for the boys. Neither of them knows how to deal with her presence. Mitchell is angry with her, probably because he loves her and wishes that she loved him enough to stick around, and Max is torn, because he likes me and feels like he's betraying his mom by feeling that way."

"Seems you know my boys," he says tenderly.

I melt farther against him and slide my hands up to rest against his chest. "They're just like you. All you have to do is read between the lines to know what they're thinking or feeling." I tip my head to the side and ask, "She's picking Max up from school tomorrow?"

"Yeah." He leans back against the counter, keeping hold of my waist with one hand while using the other to pick his beer back up and take a swig.

"What about Mitchell?"

"I'll talk to him and see if he's down with her picking him up. If not then I can still have Mom grab him after practice, so you won't have to deal with Beth."

"What do you mean?"

"She's staying at one of the local hotels, so after she gets Max, she'll come back here with him."

"Oh." I chew the inside of my cheek, not sure how I feel about her being here in the house that has started to feel like a second home to me.

"I don't like it any more than you do, baby, but I don't want Max hanging out in a hotel room every day after school for however long she's here for."

"I get it." And I do get it logically. It's the illogic part of my brain, the part that contains irrational emotions like jealousy, that doesn't like it much at all.

"It won't be for very long."

"Are you trying to convince me or yourself?" I ask, only half joking.

"Probably both of us," he admits.

I smile and lean up on my tiptoes, touching my mouth to his. "Like you always say, it will be okay."

"Yeah." He squeezes my hip. "How much work do you have to do tonight?"

"Not much, I just have a few tests to grade, and they shouldn't take me more than an hour."

"I'll finish up dinner while you get started on them," he says, and I start to laugh. "What's funny?"

"Dinner's done—well, mostly anyway. The meatloaf has to finish cooking, and I need to mix up some ketchup and Worcestershire sauce to go on it before it comes out. But besides that, we should be able to eat in about fifteen minutes."

He raises a brow. "How long was I outside?"

"Not long."

"Long enough for you to make an entire meal."

"Max mixed the meatloaf. I just put it in a pan and placed it in the oven. The corn was already clean, and the potatoes just had to be steamed in the microwave. I didn't perform a miracle."

"That's where you're wrong," he says quietly, dipping his face closer to mine. "You're giving us normal. You're giving us exactly what you said you grew up seeing."

"It's just dinner, Gareth," I say, feeling a little off balance by his words and tone.

"Baby, you could have gotten pissed about Beth being here, but you didn't. You came in and started dinner, gave Max something to do when he sought you out, and sat on the couch with your Kindle like it was just another night. You don't even realize that the roots you've planted have become something to cling to in a storm, a safe place to go to when the

171

winds start to pick up."

"I—"

"You can add that to the list of reasons I love you," he says, and tears burn the back of my throat.

"Please don't make me cry," I croak.

"I never want that. I just want you to understand what you mean to the boys and me."

I nod and close my eyes while resting my forehead against his chest. When his arms wrap around me, I wonder if he's right—if maybe, just maybe, I'm stronger than I think I am.

Gareth

Chapter 13

$\mathcal{T}$HE MOMENT I pull up in front of my mom's house, Mitchell walks out carrying his gym bag over his shoulder, and Mom pokes her head out but doesn't move past the doorway like she normally would. She's pissed Beth's in town spending time with Max, she doesn't think I should allow her time alone with him, and even though I don't like it much either, I know it's something Max needs and wants. So I have to put my personal feelings aside for my boy's happiness.

"Can we talk about me getting my driving permit?" Mitchell asks, opening the back door and tossing his bag in the back before slamming it and getting in the front. "It's getting really annoying having to wait on other people to drive me around."

"You can't drive alone with a learner's permit, bud," I tell him as he buckles up.

"I know, but if I get my permit now, when I turn sixteen, I'll be able to drive without anyone with me. And just think—you won't have to worry about getting me and Max to school, 'cause I can drive us there and home."

"Jesus, weren't you just turning ten?" I ask, pulling out onto Main.

"Dad, please don't start reminiscing," he groans, making me smile. "I want my license, not a walk down memory lane."

"If you put in the time, I'll take you down to take the test."

"Yesss!" He shoots his fist into the air.

"That said—"

"Oh, man," he cuts me off. "Can't we just forget whatever you're going to say?"

"Not unless you got some money saved for wheels that I don't know about."

"Please continue," he murmurs, making me chuckle.

"As I was saying, if you get a job this summer and save what you earn for a car, I'll match you dollar for dollar."

"Seriously? Even if I make four thousand dollars?"

"Even if you make four thousand dollars," I agree.

"Thanks, Dad."

"Anything for you, bud." I glance at him as I turn onto our street.

"December is still going to be here for dinner, right?" he asks, and I see his eyes on his mom's rental car parked where December normally does.

"She should be here soon," I confirm, shutting down the engine. "I called to let her know I was on my way to pick you up when I got finished at the shop, and she said she'd be here after she stopped to get dinner."

"What are we having?"

"No fucking clue," I say, and he grins at me before he gets out.

After beeping the locks and rounding the hood, I expect to find him inside but notice instead he's stopped at the top of the porch. I start to ask him what's up then curse under my breath when I hear the sound of Max's favorite video game being played way too fucking loudly. With a deep breath, I push into the house and shout over the firing gun on the TV. "Turn that shit down."

Max looks at me then quickly fumbles to find the remote under the bags of junk food spread out before him, and as soon as he lays his hands on it, he shuts off the game.

Beth, who is lying on the couch, lifts her head and smiles asking. "How was work?" before she looks to where Mitchell is disappearing down the hall toward his room.

I ignore her and focus on Max. "I'm guessing, since you're playing video games, that your homework is done."

"Mom said—"

"Is your homework finished?" I repeat, cutting him off, and he looks to his mom and swallows before he shakes his head. "You know the rules. No video games during the school week unless your homework is done."

"I told him it was okay," Beth says, and I cut my eyes to her. "It's not a big deal, Gareth."

"You're wrong, Beth. It's after six, which means when he should be relaxing before going to bed tonight, he's going to be up doing the homework he should have gotten done when he came home from school."

"I told him it was okay, so if you're going to be mad at anyone, be mad at me," she argues, standing from the couch, and I fight the urge to roar or pick something up and toss it across the room.

Fuck me, she will never change. This is what she does best, makes it seem like I'm the asshole and she's the good guy before she disappears, leaving me to deal with the aftermath.

"Go get started on your homework. December is gonna be here soon with dinner," I tell Max.

"How sweet. Your girlfriend is bringing you dinner," Beth says, and I see Max's shoulders slump before he heads down the hall.

"Just go, Beth." I sigh. I don't have the energy to deal with her shit right now.

"I'm thinking about moving back to town for good."

"Great," I reply, not believing for one second that will happen, especially since she's been saying the same shit for years.

"I'm serious."

"Good." I look at her. "Max will like having you around more often."

"I'll want fifty/fifty custody after I get settled."

"No." My jaw clenches.

"Did you just say no?" she asks, placing her hands on her hips.

"I'm sorry. I meant hell fucking no," I grit out.

"If I go to a lawyer—"

I laugh without humor, interrupting her, and her expression gets tight. "Spend your money, Beth. Go to a lawyer, and while you're there, explain the last few years and exactly how much time you've had with our sons, how much money you've sent for their care," I tell her quietly, not wanting the boys just down the hall to hear. "Then tell your lawyer that you want a judge to grant you fifty percent custody because you're pissed and jealous that I've found someone solid and the boys like her."

"You won't be so smug if I go to a lawyer, Gareth."

"You might be right, Beth, but in a month, this conversation won't mean shit, because you'll be gone again. Now, please get out of my house."

"Whatever. Tell Max I'll be at the school tomorrow to pick him up. And tell Mitchell I want to spend time with him."

"Mom will be picking up Max tomorrow. You can come over and hang with them if you want. As for Mitchell, he's old enough to choose if he wants to spend time with you. And since every time you've been around he's disappeared into his room, I'm thinkin' he doesn't want that."

"I don't need to be supervised with my own son, and you've turned Mitchell against me," she hisses then turns to the door when there's a knock and stomps to it, swinging it open. "Give us a minute." She slams it closed, and I see fucking red but check the urge to bodily remove her from my house.

I move past her to the door, and the moment I open it, December gives me a wide-eyed, adorable look. "Sorry, babe." I take two bags from her, recognizing the scent of barbeque coming from them.

"We're not done talking," Beth informs me as December hangs up her purse and coat.

"We are." I keep the door open for her to leave. "The boys need to eat, finish their homework, and then get ready for bed."

"You're such a fucking asshole." She glares at me from her position in the middle of the living room then she shoots her eyes to December as she walks to my side.

"I don't want her—" She points at December. "—around our sons."

December's nose scrunches at the statement, but besides that, she doesn't react.

"Go to your hotel, Beth."

"I'm serious, Gareth. I don't want her around my boys."

"Guess what, Beth. In life, you don't always get what you want. Now, please leave before I call the cops and have you removed."

"You wouldn't."

"Try me." I hold her stare.

Reading my look, her face twists into a sneer and she points at me then December. "Fuck you and you." She stomps to her bag, grabs it, and continues to stomp past us. As soon as she clears the threshold, I shut the door and shake my head.

"Well, that was intense," December says quietly, and I focus on her as she places a hand against my stomach.

"I told you she was being nice yesterday."

"You did. I didn't believe you." She bites her lip. "Are you alright?"

"You're here. The boys are here. I'm good." I tip my head down and brush my mouth across hers. "Let's get the boys fed."

"Sure," she agrees. I go to the kitchen with the bags, and a moment later, she comes in with her arms full of the shit off the coffee table. Without a word, she puts the stuff away while I unload dinner from the two full bags she brought with her. "I got a little of everything," she says as I place a large container of coleslaw next to one just as big that's filled with mac and cheese.

"I see that."

"I figured if there were extra you could take it to work for lunch."

I grin. "Babe, when has there ever been leftovers when you've been around and the boys are present?"

"True." She returns my grin, and I lean over, kissing the top of her hair, and then notice Max standing on the opposite side of the island, looking nervous.

"I'm sorry, Dad."

"Come here, kid," I order, and he shifts his feet before coming around to me. Once he's close, I pull him into a hug. "I love you."

"I know," he mutters.

I tip my head down to look at him. "Are you filled up on junk food?"

"Mom just put a bunch of stuff on the coffee table for me. I didn't eat

179

much of it."

"All right." I let him go. "Get plates out then go tell your brother it's time to eat."

"I'm standing right here," Mitchell says, and then he looks at December. "Thanks for bringing dinner."

"Sure, honey." She smiles softly at him then looks at me, and I know she can feel the undercurrent of tension that seems to be filling the kitchen by the second.

"Dad," Max prompts, and I look to where he's standing and getting out plates. "I… I don't want to live with Mom, even if it's just part time."

"Max—"

"I heard her say she's going to get a lawyer. I just want…. Well, I just want to say I don't want to live with her, even if she moves here."

"Dude, Mom isn't moving back to town," Mitchell tells him, sounding annoyed. "She's never moving back here. She's just saying that, because she's mad that Dad and December are together, so she's trying to mess that up."

"But—"

"She doesn't care about us, Max." Mitchell turns on his brother. "When are you going to get that?"

"Mitchell," I growl, as December whispers, "Mitchell, honey—"

"It's true." He glances at December then faces me. "She doesn't care about us. She only cares about herself, and he needs to get that."

"I know that!" Max suddenly screams, and December, standing close, wraps her arms around him. "I know she doesn't, but she's still our mom."

"Shit, Max." Mitchell shakes his head. "I'm sorry, dude." The torment I see in his expression makes my gut twist. "I'm sorry. I shouldn't have said that. I—" He drops his eyes to the floor.

"I want both you boys to look at me," I order then wait for them to focus on me. "It's okay to be angry or disappointed with your mom, but it's not okay to take that out on each other. We're a family, and as a family, we stick together. We talk shit out and then we move on. Max, you're not going anywhere, even if your mom moves back here. You won't be living with her unless there comes a time when you're a little older and you make that decision for yourself," I assure him, and his chin wobbles. "Mitchell, I get why you're angry, and you deserve to feel that way, but your brother has a right to his feelings too, and you need to respect them."

"You're right, Dad," he says, and I lift my chin.

"I love you both, and I hate that you're hurting." I pull in a breath. "It fucking kills me that you're fighting about your mom." My jaw clenches and unclenches with frustration. I feel like my hands are tied when it comes to Beth and the role she has in the boys' lives. I never want them to resent me for not allowing them to have a relationship with their mother, but the relationship she has with them is not healthy in the slightest. "We need to figure out a way for both of you to get what you need to be happy."

"I just feel bad for Mom," Max says quietly then he looks at his brother. "She's all alone."

"She wants to be alone, Max," Mitchell says just as softly. "She didn't have to leave. She never had to leave us. She made that decision for herself."

"I guess you're right. I still feel bad for her," he mumbles.

I reach out, tagging them both behind the neck then pulling them close. "No more fighting. Got it?"

"Yeah, Dad," Mitchell says, and Max nods.

I give the two of them a hug then let them go and look at December when she calls them over. I'm momentarily taken aback by the love and concern in her expression as she hands the boys each a plate that she's already piled high with food. Christ, it's fucked up my boys have to deal with their mom when she decides to show up, but if things work out like I know they will, for the rest of their lives, they will have a woman in their corner who is solid and dependable.

I might have chosen completely wrong when I picked Beth, but at least I got it right this time around.

"Please don't stop," December whimpers against my mouth while I use the hold I have on her hips to bring her down hard each time I thrust up.

"I'm not gonna stop." Fuck, I couldn't even if I wanted to, not with the heat of her pussy suffocating my cock. Christ, I have never felt anything better than her.

"Gareth." Her walls clench, making my breath catch, and I urge her to go faster. I lift my head and slide my mouth down her neck and capture one tight nipple between my lips. "Yesss," she moans, tossing her head back, and I let go with one hand to cup her neglected breast then tug the nipple between two fingers, making her hips buck in response.

"Faster, Ember. Fuck me faster," I growl, and she starts to ride me harder as I slide my thumb closer to her center, listening to her breath turn choppy. When I circle her clit, she cries out and her pussy starts to spasm, pulling me deeper. I give into the urge that's been riding me hard since she climbed on top of me and roll her to her back to fuck her hard. Hooking my arms behind her knees, I keep her just like I want her, spread open for me. When my balls draw up, I drop my head and take her mouth, thrusting my tongue between her lips and kissing her deep as I come inside her.

Lightheaded and spent, I drop the hold I have on her legs and gather her against me so I can roll to the side and keep the connection. It takes a minute for my breathing to even out, and when it does, I notice she's snoring softly and shake my head. I've never known a woman who can fall asleep as quickly as she can. I swear, on more than one occasion, she's passed out when were in the middle of us having a conversation.

I kiss the top of her head then look at the clock and fight back a groan when I see it's time for her to get up and get ready for work and time for me to get the boys up for school. "Ember."

"Hmm." She snuggles closer and my cock, still half hard inside her, twitches.

"We gotta get up, baby."

"Can't I do homeschool?" she groans, making me laugh, and then I feel her lips press against my pec. "I can't wait until Saturday, when we get to sleep in."

"I know, baby. Just a couple more days." I hold my lips to the top of her hair then say, "Go shower while I get the boys up. I'll meet you in the kitchen."

"All right." She tips her head back, and when her sleepy eyes meet mine, I press a kiss to her lips then her nose. I slide out of her, push out of bed, and go to the bathroom to get rid of the condom and wash my hands and face. When I walk back into the bedroom, I see she's fallen back asleep, so I wake her again then pull her up to stand in front of me, ignoring her grumbling.

"I'll bring you coffee."

"Mm-hm," she mumbles, stumbling into the bathroom.

I tag my sweats from the floor, put them on, and then leave the room, heading across the house to open Max's door first before turning on the lights.

"Seriously, already?" he asks, lifting his head while Melbourne stands and does a stretch.

"Yep. Sorry, bud."

I leave his door open and go to Mitchell's room, expecting him to be asleep when I walk in. But surprisingly, he's up, sitting on the side of the bed. "I'm up."

"I see that," I say, and he grunts in response before rubbing his hands down his face and standing. I leave him and stop to look in Max's room just to make sure he's up and see him at his dresser, so I head to the kitchen and start a pot of coffee.

The minute there's enough in the carafe, I pour December a cup, add her creamer and sugar, and then take it back to my bathroom, where she's blow-drying her hair and wearing nothing but a short, baby pink robe. I set the cup on the counter next to her, and she shuts off the dryer and picks up the mug, looking at me in the mirror. I wrap my arms around her waist and press my nose to her neck, breathing in the scent of her body wash that smells like berries.

"Are the boys up?" she asks breathlessly, making my cock twitch.

"Yeah." I flick her earlobe with my nose. "They're both zombies, but they're up."

"Mornings suck." She takes a sip of coffee.

"My morning didn't suck." I smirk, and she blushes as she smiles at me in the mirror over the rim of the coffee cup. I turn my head and kiss her neck then meet her gaze once more. "You want breakfast?"

"Just toast please."

"Got it." I give her waist a squeeze and kiss her neck before letting her go. I scramble eggs for the boys and drop bread in the toaster for her and them, and as I'm stirring creamer into my second cup of coffee, I feel fur slide against my ankles. I look down at Melbourne as he circles my feet.

"Dad, is December still picking me up after practice?" Mitchell asks, coming into the kitchen as I go to the pantry to grab a container of Melbourne's food and dump it in his dish.

"Yeah, why? What's up?"

"I have a test in English coming up, and I'm going to ask her if she can help me study for it while we're at her place."

"I'll totally help you study," December says, appearing at the edge of the counter with her hair pulled back away from her face in a low ponytail. She's wearing dark slacks and a hot pink button-down shirt that has green dinosaurs on it that match her bright green flats. Fuck, she's the only woman I know who can wear shit that is completely ridiculous and still look fuckable.

"Thanks, I need all the help I can get. I barely passed the last test in that class."

"I've got your back. We'll go over the stuff you don't get tonight and make sure you're ready for the next test."

"Cool." He smiles at her, and she smiles back before walking her empty coffee mug to the dishwasher and putting it inside. When she comes back to the counter, I hand her a plate with a piece of toast then watch her pull off the crust before she starts to eat it.

I look at the clock, and when I see the time, I yell, "Max!"

"I'm coming!" he yells back, and I take a sip of coffee.

A minute later, he takes a seat next to his brother, then after a grumbled "Good morning," he starts to eat.

"I think this summer we should enter the boys in one of those hot dog eating contests. I bet we could make a killing," December says loud enough for the boys to hear. They both grin as they continue to shovel food into their mouths. "Seriously, you two are pros. It doesn't even seem like you need to breathe." She laughs as they eat even faster, and then she looks at the clock and places her last bite of toast in her mouth, chews, and swallows then reaches for my coffee, which I hand over.

"I'll see you tonight." She smiles, handing me the cup back after she takes a sip, and then she looks at the boys. "Mitchell, I'll see you after practice, and Max, I'll see you later."

"Later," Mitchell says, and Max says the same as she grabs her purse.

"I'm gonna walk December out to her car. I'll be back. You two finish eating then get packed up." Getting nods from both of them, I walk her outside and kiss her like I've wanted to since she walked into the kitchen wearing that ridiculous shirt. By the time I walk back into the house, the boys are in their rooms, so I pick up the kitchen then go back to my room. I jump in the shower quickly then get dressed before taking the boys to school and heading to work.

Hearing my cell ring, I roll out from under the car I'm working on and grab the towel out of my pocket to wipe the grease off my hands as I walk toward my toolbox. When I see Mom's name flashing on the screen, I pick up my phone and answer. "Yeah."

"Gareth Daniel Black, I swear to God I'm going to kill her," Mom hisses in my ear, and I roll my head on my shoulders.

"What happened now?" For the last two days, Mom's been hanging at the house with Beth and Max until I get home, while December's been picking up Mitchell from practice and taking him to her place to hang until Beth leaves. Needless to say, this has not been going well. Mom's never liked Beth, and with her leaving her children, her dislike of my ex has only grown. Having to spend time with her and be nice for Max's sake is taking its toll on her.

"What happened? What happened?" Mom shrieks.

"Mom, I'm in the middle of work. Can you please just tell me what's going on without the drama?"

"She showed up with a dog, Gareth."

"Pardon?"

"She showed up at your house with a dog for Max," she says. "It's not just a normal dog either. The thing is huge, and of course the moment

Max saw him, he fell in love. So now you have a giant dog who I don't even think is house broken."

Fuck me. "Where's Melbourne?"

"What?" she asks, sounding confused.

"December's cat, where is he?"

"I haven't seen a cat. I didn't even know December had a cat," she replies, and I shake my head.

"Let me talk to Max," I say, and the phone goes quiet for a second before I hear her yell Max's name and listen to her tell him I want to talk to him.

"Dad, I swear I didn't know."

"I know, bud, but you gotta do me a favor. Find Melbourne and put him in my room."

"Oh crap!" he yells, and then the phone goes silent for a moment before Mom comes back on the line.

"I didn't know you had a cat."

"It's December's cat."

"Then why is he here?" she asks. "Never mind, stupid question. So what are you going to do about the dog situation?"

"I've been thinking about getting the boys a dog for a while now. I just haven't had time to talk to them about it. So if he's friendly, we'll keep him."

"You'll keep him? She didn't even check with you before she showed up with a dog, Gareth. You don't even know what his story is."

"Mom, she wants a fight. She wants to feel like she can still get a reaction out of me. The thing she doesn't understand is I just don't give a fuck anymore. The boys are happy, I'm happy, and eventually she's going to see she doesn't factor into that. Hopefully when that happens, she will get her shit together and find a way to be in her kids' lives without the drama or disappear, and if we're lucky, stay gone."

"I guess you're right." She sighs. "I still think you'll feel differently when you see the dog she brought into your house."

"What kind of dog is it?" I ask, now curious.

"A werewolf."

"Always wanted one of those," I mutter.

"Let's see if you think this is funny when you get home," she says, and I sigh. "I have another hour at least until I'm done. Will you be good until then?"

"I'll be fine. I can't make any promises about the mother of your children though."

"Just remember she's never around for long, and a judge won't lessen your sentence just because you're old."

"Whatever. I'll see you when you get home."

"See you." I hang up and start to set my phone down but stop when it rings and December's name pops up. "Hey, babe."

"Tomorrow's Friday," she says as a greeting, and I feel my brows dart together.

"What?"

"Tomorrow is Friday, Gareth, which means tomorrow my parents are planning on coming to your house for dinner."

"Okay?"

"Okay," she whisper-hisses, and I realize she's been whispering this whole time.

"Why are you whispering?"

"Because my place isn't huge and Mitchell is in my living room and I don't want him to hear me."

"You don't want him to hear you tell me that tomorrow your parents are coming to dinner?"

"No. I don't want him to hear me freaking out about my parents coming to dinner with your ex—his mom—around."

"She's not going to be at dinner tomorrow, Ember. We'll take them out. I'll send Mack a text and see if he has a table at Flame available. If he doesn't, I'll make reservations somewhere else."

"Thank you," she breathes, and I know then she's been more worried than she should be about this.

"Babe, breathe. It's going to be all good."

"I just want dinner to go well."

"Then it's probably better that we don't have dinner at home," I say, and then add, "Beth got Max a dog."

"What?"

"Beth got Max a dog. Mom says it's a werewolf. I'm not sure those exist. Still, it would suck if they do and he transformed at dinner with your parents around."

She giggles then pulls in a sharp breath. "Melbourne's—"

"In our room," I cut her off. "I told Max to find him and put him in there. Do you know if he's ever been around a dog before?"

"I have no idea. Are you keeping the dog?" she asks, sounding curious.

"Yeah."

"Just like that?"

"Like I told Mom, I've been meaning to talk to the boys about getting a dog, so at the end of the day, Beth saved me listening to the boys fight about what kind of dog they each want. And I'm not giving her what she wants, which is for me to be the bad guy who tells Max he can't keep the dog, which I know would start another fight."

"I really don't like her very much," she murmurs then sighs. "I should let you get back to work, we can talk about this stuff later."

"I should be done in an hour."

"All right, I'll see you at the house then, and don't worry about stopping to pick up dinner. I got the stuff to make spaghetti, since it's easy."

"Sounds good baby. I'll see you at home."

"Yeah." Her voice is warm and soft. "See you at home. Love you."

Fuck, I love that. I love knowing that no matter what bullshit happens, what I have to deal with, at the end of the day, I get to go *home* to her and my boys.

Chapter 14

"Sloth, come here." Max pats his thigh, and the huge gray dog—who looks like his face is melting off and nothing like a werewolf—walks slowly to where he is standing just outside the open back door. "You can do it, not much farther," Max encourages him, but the big dog gives up and stops to rest, causing the loose skin covering his body to slide toward the floor.

"I don't think I've ever seen a lazier dog," Gareth mumbles, and I glance up at him briefly. He's right; the dog is lazy. He's also seriously overweight. Beth, not surprisingly, didn't tell Gareth much about where she got him, just that she adopted him from somewhere in Nashville. If I'm being honest, the ugly dog is actually very sweet, which is a surprise, since he was a gift from Beth. I just worry he has some kind of health issue that is making him as lazy as he is.

"I think I should see if I can get him an appointment at July's clinic, just to make sure there's nothing wrong with him," I say, watching Sloth get up, move out the door, and go to Max, who is now standing out in the middle of the yard shouting for him.

"That'd be good, babe. If she has time to see him today, I can take a break from work to run him over there."

"I'll send her a text before I finish getting ready for work." I turn toward him and rest my hands against his stomach then lean up on my tiptoes. "Will Melbourne be okay out here?"

"Babe—" His lips twitch. "—I think that dog is in more danger than the cat is."

"You're probably right." I lean up farther, touching my lips to his, and his hand slides down to my ass, making me laugh. "Stop."

"I can't."

"Try." I smile against his mouth then wiggle free from his hold and walk backward until I reach the hall for the bedroom, listening to him laugh. Grabbing my cell off the bedside table, I send July a text telling her to call me when she has time as I head into the bathroom to get dressed.

"Hey," I answer my phone when it rings with her name as I'm tucking my shirt into my slacks.

"I got your message. What's up?" she asks, and I look at my top in the mirror then smile. One of my favorite things about teaching younger kids is that I have a reason to purchase clothing that would otherwise look ridiculous on a woman my age. Like today's navy blue long-sleeved button down that has tiny colorful hot air balloons all over it. "Hello, are you there?" July calls.

"Sorry, yeah, I'm just in the middle of getting dressed for work," I reply, sliding a thin red belt through the loops of my navy slacks. "Anyway, Gareth's ex got the boys a dog, and I just wanted to see if you had time to check him out today."

"What kind of dog is it?"

"A big one," I say.

She laughs. "That's helpful."

I roll my eyes. "I honestly don't know what kind of dog it is. Beth didn't leave any paperwork or anything. All I know is he's big and looks like his skin is melting off."

"He could be a Shar Pei. Did she say what pound she got him from?"

"No, just somewhere in Nashville."

"All right, tell Gareth he can bring him in anytime today and I'll fit him in."

"Thanks, I owe you."

"You can pay me back by coming out to have a drink with me and the rest of the girls Saturday. We all want to know what's been going on," she says, making me feel guilty.

The last few weeks, I have been consumed with Gareth and the boys. Not that I'm complaining. I wouldn't want to be anywhere else but with them. Still, I've hardly talked to my sisters.

"I'm sorry. It's just been…"

"Crazy," she finishes for me.

"Exactly." I sigh. "What time Saturday are y'all meeting?"

"I think nine, unless we have dinner before; then it will be a little earlier."

"All right, I'll meet you guys. Just let me know when and where."

"Cool, and you should know Mom's beyond excited about tonight."

"I know. I'm just not sure if she's excited about meeting the boys or going to dinner at Flame."

"The boys," she assures, and then asks, "Can Gareth hook me up with a reservation for Flame?"

I laugh. "I'm not sure, but you can ask him when you see him today."

"All right, and I'll see you tomorrow. Have a good day at work, and tell Gareth I'll see him later."

"I will. Love you, and talk to you soon."

"Soon, love you."

I hang up then slip on my flats and grab my bag. When I walk into the kitchen, the boys are eating, and Sloth is lying on the floor next to the back door like he came back in and gave up moving any farther. "July said you can take Sloth in anytime today and she'll make time for you," I tell Gareth, going to his side and taking his cup of coffee to have a sip.

"Is July your sister who's a vet?" Max asks, and I nod. "Why is Sloth going to see her?"

"He's a dog. He has to go to the vet," Mitchell says, and Max looks over at him. "It's normal after you get an animal that you take him to get checked out. It's not a big deal." He shrugs then goes back to eating, and Max looks at me for confirmation.

"He's right. It's normal."

He nods then asks, "Is your sister going to be at dinner tonight?"

"No, tonight, you're just meeting my parents, but you'll meet my whole family on Memorial Day. My parents have a huge pool party and barbeque every year, and all the Maysons, along with tons of friends, show up. It's always a lot of fun."

"Awesome." He grins.

"It is awesome." I grin back then glance at the clock and take one more sip of Gareth's coffee before I hand it back to him. "I need to stop at my place to pick up some stuff before I go to work, so I need to run."

"I don't know why you don't just move in. It's weird that you're always here and still have an apartment," Mitchell tells me, and Max nods like he agrees.

My heart lodges in my throat, and I stare at the two of them, unsure about what to say.

"I'll walk you out," Gareth says, setting down his coffee and placing his hand against my lower back as he looks at the boys.

"We know—eat and get packed up," Max mumbles, making Mitchell laugh.

Still feeling overwhelmed, I look at the boys. "I'll see you both tonight. Have a great day at school." I pick up my bag from the end of the counter and make sure I have my lesson plan and the tests I graded last night before going to the door to put on my coat.

"Wait," Mitchell calls, and I stop to face him. "Are you still picking me up after school?"

"Yeah. I mean… if you still want me to?"

"I do. I just…" He looks away for a moment like he's suddenly uncomfortable. "It's just we're having a mock track meet, so you can come down to the field to watch if you want."

My chest gets warm and tight at the same time. "Of course I want to," I say without crying, which is a surprise. "What time does it start?"

"As soon as practice begins." He lifts one shoulder. "About 3:45."

"I'll be there with all the bells and whistles." Why did I say that? "I mean, I'll just be there like a normal person, not with bells or whistles. That would be weird."

He presses his lips together like he's fighting a smile, and I hear Max snort and I look at him. "You're such a dork."

"I'm not a dork," I deny.

"Babe, you're a little bit of a dork," Gareth says, and I tip my head back and find him grinning. "An adorable dork, but still a dork."

"Now you guys are just ganging up on me." I fake pout, and they all laugh. "Whatever, you're all lucky I love you, because if I didn't, I'd be offended," I say, and the room suddenly grows still. I feel Gareth's hand come to rest against my back, and I chance a look at both boys, who are now watching me with expressions I don't fully understand. Not sure what to do, I smile like I don't feel the weird energy beating against my skin. "Have a good day at school, guys." I finish putting on my coat then grab my bag as Gareth opens the door for me to step out before him. When we reach my car, I open the door and bite the inside of my cheek as I reach over, placing my bag on the passenger seat. "Did I just totally mess up in there?"

"No, baby." He turns me to face him and curves his fingers around one side of my neck. "Their mom tells them she loves them, but she never shows it, and I'm sure you understand that love is just a word without action behind it. They love you. It's just going to take time for them to trust that you love them too."

"I'll prove it to them."

"I know you will." He rests his forehead against mine. "You're doing it every day." He uses his thumb to tip my chin back then touches his lips to mine. "Have a good day at work."

"You too, and let me know what July says after she sees Sloth."

"I'll send you a text."

"Okay." I force myself to let him go and take a seat behind the wheel. Once he closes the door, I roll down the window, and he grins as I tap my finger to my lips.

"Love you, dork." He bends to kiss me one more time, and I smile as I start the engine and wave goodbye once I'm backed out of the driveway.

After stopping at my place to pick up the supplies I need for the project we're doing today in class and my outfit for dinner tonight, I reach the school forty minutes later. As I'm parking, I notice a tow truck pull into the lot and stop. Wondering who's having car trouble, I grab the handle of my bag, get out, and head into the school. I stop at the teachers' lounge and poke my head inside, seeing a few teachers drinking coffee and chatting.

"Hey, guys. A tow truck just pulled into the teachers' lot. I don't know if one of you called them, but they're here if you did," I say, and everyone looks to where I'm standing just outside the door. Then Jetson, who's sitting alone, pushes his chair back and rushes past me, almost knocking me over. I turn to watch him run down the hall and a moment later disappear outside.

"His wife left him a few months ago," Mrs. Travis says, as I step into the lounge to grab a cup of coffee. "He was cheating on her, and when she found out, she decided to clear out their bank account and freeze everything. I bet his car is getting towed for nonpayment."

Not feeling comfortable talking about a fellow teacher, even if he is a jerk, I don't respond, but that doesn't stop everyone else from continuing to talk about him. After I finish making my coffee, I take it with me to my classroom and sip it while I put my stuff away and get ready for my kids to show up.

When lunchtime rolls around, I grab my Kindle, my cell phone, and a cup of noodle soup from my desk. While I'm waiting to use the microwave in the teachers' lounge, I read through a group text between my sisters and cousins, confirming that I really did agree to go out with them tomorrow night. As I'm texting them back to let them know I will be there, Gareth texts, but instead of reading it, I just dial his number and wait for him to answer.

"I just sent you a text."

"I know, but I'm on lunch, so I'm calling instead. So how did the appointment go?"

"Sloth is healthy. He does have an infection between some of the folds on his face, and your sister thinks that, along with the fact that he can hardly see, is what's making him seem so lethargic," he explains.

"Did she give you medication for the infection?"

"She did. She also suggested he have surgery to remove some of the excess skin."

"Surgery? Is it necessary?"

"She thinks so. She says it's common for his breed to have surgery when they're young, but he just never did."

"Did she say when she can get him in for surgery?"

"Babe, it's close to two grand, and that's with a serious discount from your sister."

"Okay. And?"

"And... right now, I don't have that kind of dough to toss at a surgery that isn't a necessity."

I do some quick calculations. I've been saving for a new car for a while and have more than enough money saved. I just haven't had time to go look for a car. "I'll pay for it."

"You're not paying for Sloth to have surgery."

"Why not?"

"Because you're not."

"Why not? I have the money, and if it means he will have a better life, then I think it is a necessity."

"I can't even get into this with you right now. I need to get him back to my place and get to work," he says, sounding angry, which is something that seriously annoys me, because I know it's just his damn ego that won't let me pay for the surgery.

"Fine, we'll talk about it tonight."

"There's nothing to talk about. You're not paying for Sloth to have surgery. I'll work some overtime and take care of it."

"Do you mean overtime on top of the overtime you're already working? Because if that's the case, you might as well just move to the shop, since you spend so much time there anyway."

"I have to work to provide for my family," he growls, no longer sounding angry but pissed.

"Yeah, and you know what? I have a job and am offering to help," I hiss, becoming pissed myself.

"You have an apartment and your own bills to worry about, Ember."

"Fine! Then I'll just move in with you. That way you don't have any more excuses for why I can't help you out."

"Give your landlord notice today."

"I will!" I snap.

"Good," he snaps back, and then rumbles, "I gotta go."

"Whatever." I pull my phone from my ear and press End on the call.

197

"Ugh, that was the most I've ever heard you say, and also the weirdest conversation I have ever heard," Tasha says, and I feel myself turn ten shades of red as I look up at her. "Was that your boyfriend?"

"Yes."

"Did you just tell him that you were moving in with him?"

"I think so." I look at my phone. What the hell just happened?

"Girl, you've got balls. Good for you." She smiles then shakes her head. "I also think you might be a little crazy."

"He makes me crazy."

"He's a man; they do that. I've been with my guy for almost ten years, and most days I wake up thankful he's in my life. But from time to time, I wake up wondering if anyone would suspect me of taking him out if he suddenly disappeared," she says, moving forward to use the microwave after the person in front of her is finished with it. "How long have you two been together?"

"Probably not long enough to move in together," I mutter, wondering if he was serious about me moving in with him. I mean, I want to, but I don't know if he was just saying I should because I said it, or if he really wants me to.

"I hear you. Then again, I met my guy on a Friday and moved in with him on Sunday."

"Did you really?"

"Yep." She takes her stuff out of the microwave when it dings then turns to face me. "I know you normally have lunch alone, but you can join us if you're up to it. I promise we don't bite."

"Are you sure? I mean about joining you, not the biting," I clarify, and she laughs.

"I'm sure." She takes her container of food to a table, and I put my soup in the microwave. Once it's done, I join her and a few other teachers for lunch, and for the first time since I started working here, I spend the hour getting to know my co-workers instead of reading. And surprisingly, I have to say I actually enjoy it.

When I reach the track field, I head up the bleachers and take a seat then wave at Mitchell when he looks up at where I'm sitting. He lifts his chin and his lips tip up slightly before he focuses on the older gentleman when he stops to talk to him.

I know this is just a mock track meet, but all the kids look like they are taking this seriously, including him. My stomach starts to fill with nervous energy when the guy pats his back and signals for him to go line up with a few other boys. Once all the boys are in position a horn sounds, and Mitchell takes off so fast he looks like a blur as he passes three runners. When he reaches a curve in the track, he passes another, seeming to pick up even more speed. I stand from where I'm sitting on the bleachers and start to jump up and down when he passes the last runner, and I scream, "Go, Mitchell!" as loud as I can when he crosses the finish line in first place. His chest heaves as he accepts high-fives and back pats from his teammates, and then he rests his hands on his hips and looks to where I'm standing. I catch his grin and grin back then look around, noticing none of the other people in the bleachers are standing, so I take a seat.

"Is that your boy?" I look down at a woman sitting two seats below me and feel my heart melt a little, because Mitchell and his brother *have* become mine.

"Yeah, one of them."

"He's fast."

"He is," I agree.

She tips her head to the side. "I've never seen you here before."

"I work a lot," I lie, and she nods like she understands, and then she stands and comes up the bleachers to sit next to me.

"I'm Amanda." She holds out her hand for me to shake then lets it go and points down to the track at a kid who's doing stretches. "That one with the blond hair is mine." She waves when he looks, and he rolls his eyes at her. "He's obviously overwhelmed with joy that I'm here," she says sarcastically, and I giggle. "Will you be at the meet next weekend?"

I didn't even know there was a meet next weekend. Still, I will for sure be there. "Definitely."

"Awesome, me and a few of the other moms bring snacks and drinks to the meets. Would you want in on that?"

"Sure, is there a sign up or something?" I ask, wondering if I will be stepping on Lidia's toes. I'm sure Gareth's mom is the one who normally does this stuff.

"No, we're not that organized. It's just kind of a free for all. Bring whatever you want," she replies, and then she grabs my hand, startling me. "Except things with nuts, gluten, dairy, or sugar." I blink at her and she laughs. "I'm just kidding. Bring whatever you want. We also won't judge you if you bring wine."

"Got it." I smile, and she lets my hand go. Then for the next hour, we chat and watch the kids practice, and when it's time to leave, I get her number and tell her I'll see her at the meet before heading down to the track to meet Mitchell.

"I want to hug you, but I don't think that's cool. So can I get a high-five?" I ask, and he laughs then holds his hand so high above his head that I have to jump to reach it. "You're seriously fast. Do you want to run track in college?"

"I don't know. Maybe." He shrugs. "I used to want to play baseball, but last year the track coach asked me to try out for the team after he saw me doing some drills and I told him I would. I didn't think I would like it as much as I do. I just don't know if I like it more than baseball," he says as we leave the field and head for my car. "This summer, I'm going to join one of the summer baseball teams and then decide what I want to do next year."

"I bet you're just as great at baseball."

"I don't know. There are lots of great players on the high school team. But I like the game."

"I'd like to see you play sometime," I say as we get into my car. "And I hope you don't mind, but I kind of told one of the moms that I'd be at your meet next weekend."

"That's cool," he replies as I pull out of the parking lot and head for the house. "Are we going home?"

I glance over at him when I hear the anxiousness in his tone. "Yeah, I figured it'd be easier, since you need to shower and I need to get ready so we can leave in time for the reservation your dad made at Flame." I chew the inside of my cheek. "I'm sorry. If I had my stuff at my place, we could go there. It's just… I've been staying at your house, so everything is there."

"It's okay. I just…." His words trail off as he shifts in his seat. "Hopefully she'll just leave when we get there. If not, I'll stay in my room until it's time to go to dinner."

"Your dad said he'd be home early today. When he gets there—"

"She won't leave just because dad comes home," he cuts me off. "And dad won't tell her to leave. He doesn't want Max to get upset."

He's right about that. Gareth puts up with a lot of crap from her because he doesn't want Max upset, and although I understand him wanting his boys to have their mom, I also see that she takes advantage of that knowledge. I just don't think she understands that every time she does something to push the limits of his kindness, she's pushing him closer to his breaking point. And one day, that thread is going to snap, and I personally do not want to be around when that happens.

"What is your mom like?"

I come out of my thoughts at his question and glance at him. "My mom?"

"I just mean, is she like you?"

"No. Well… I don't know. Maybe. She's sweet, funny, and sometimes annoying and overbearing. She was always the parent cheering the loudest when I had a game or something in high school, and she's still one of the first people I call when I have something happen in my life."

"So… like you."

"I guess," I concede, understanding just then that I'm like my mom. "When you meet her, she's probably going to fawn all over you like you're five and not fifteen." I smile when he laughs. "She's going to love you and your brother. Both my parents will."

I turn onto the block and when I reach the house, I see Gareth's mom's car parked on the street, but Beth's car isn't in the driveway, so I pull in, park, and shut down the engine. Mitchell gets out as I turn to grab my bag, and then I open my door, hearing my name called. I look around and smile when I see my cousin Harmony coming across the street wearing a pair of gray scrubs.

"Every time I see your car parked over here, I want to come say hi, but it's always way too late or too early." She gives me a hug then looks at Mitchell, smiling. "Hey, kid."

"Hey." He lifts his chin then looks at me. "I'm going to go shower."

"I'll be in, in just a minute," I tell him, and he nods, placing the strap of his bag up onto his shoulder before he heads inside.

"Are you living with Gareth?" she asks, grabbing my attention, and I focus on her.

"Pretty much. I haven't officially moved in, but I'm here every night."

"That's the way it seems to happen." She leans back against my car. "I'm happy for you. He's a good guy, and his boys are sweet."

"They're the best," I agree. "How are you liking your new job?"

Awhile back, she had some drama happen and she quit her job at the hospital in town. None of us were sure she'd go back to nursing, but a couple months ago, she got a new job in Nashville at the children's hospital.

"I love it. I hate that I have to drive to Nashville four days a week, but I love what I do, so it's worth it." She turns, and I do the same. We watch Gareth pull into the driveway, and when his eyes come to me, I remember our conversation from earlier today and wonder if he's still mad.

Once he's parked, he gets out and comes around the back of his SUV, lifting his chin to Harmony. I tip my head back when he stops in front of me, and my heart starts to pound from the look in his eyes.

"Did you give your landlord notice yet?"

"No."

His lips twitch like he thinks something is funny. "Do you need me to call them for you?"

I narrow my eyes. "I think I can handle it."

"Call. I'm gonna go get in the shower."

"I will," I snap, staring into his eyes.

"I think that's my cue to go home," Harmony says, sounding like she's trying not to laugh, and I look at her breaking my stare down with Gareth.

"You don't have to leave."

"I think I do." She grins. "Anyway, I'll see you tomorrow night. We can talk then."

"Do you want to ride together?"

"Sure, just send me a message and let me know what time."

"I will, and tell Harlen I said hi."

"Will do." She smirks then calls out later as she walks across the street.

"What's tomorrow?" Gareth asks, and I turn to face him.

"Me and the girls are going out." I wait for him to protest, but surprisingly he doesn't. "Can we talk about this moving in business?"

"What do we need to talk about?"

"About the fact that I can't tell if you're being serious or not. About how the boys might react if we say I'm moving in."

"I'm being very serious." He takes a step closer, capturing my hip. "And you were there this morning when both boys agreed that it's stupid for you to have an apartment when you're staying here."

They did say that. I just don't know if they really get what that would mean. "I... I think we should still sit down and talk to them about it."

"Then when we get home from dinner tonight, we'll talk about it with them just to make sure they are good with it. If they are, you can give notice, and we can start moving you in."

"Okay." I lean into him. "Then me and you can talk about how we are going to divide up the bills and Sloth's surgery."

"Sure," he says with a shrug, and I narrow my eyes, because that was way too easy.

"I'm serious, Gareth. If I'm going to be living here with you and the boys, I'm going to do my part."

"Yeah, and we'll discuss all that after you move in."

"No, we'll talk about it before I move in."

"After," he says, and I start to see red.

"Before, Gareth," I snap.

"After, Ember," he growls.

"Aww, is all not well in paradise?" Beth asks, walking up the driveway toward us, and I spin to face her, hating the smug look on her face and the fact that she saw us arguing.

"I told you we have plans with the boys and not to show tonight, Beth. So why are you here?"

He did? I didn't know he told her not to come over tonight.

"I told Max I'd buy him the video game he was talking about. I'm just dropping it off to him." She waves the game she's holding in her hand out toward us. "And relax, I'm not staying. I have a date."

"Send whoever he is my condolences," Gareth says, and I press my lips together to keep from laughing.

"Whatever." She glares. "Are my boys inside?"

"Like I said, we have plans. Bring the game by tomorrow, or give it to me and I'll give it to him."

"And steal my thunder? No fucking way. He told me you refused to buy it for him."

"Did he? Did he also tell you that I refused to buy it, because I have to pay for other shit, like food and the roof over his head?"

"God, you're so fucking dramatic. Whatever. I'll just bring the game to him tomorrow." She spins on her heel and stomps to her car.

When she pulls off I turn to face Gareth and rest my hands against his waist and he tips his head down to look at me. "We'll talk about the bills and stuff when I move in," I give in hoping to ease some of the anger I can feel coming off him in waves. He closes his arms around me and I tip my head back. "Let's just go get ready and try to have a good night tonight."

"Yeah." He dips his head, touching his mouth to mine briefly before leading me into the house.

When we get inside, Lidia leaves after saying she will be over tomorrow afternoon, and Gareth goes to make sure the boys are getting ready. I go to the bedroom, taking my bag with me, and shower quickly. Gareth comes in to take a shower while I'm curling my hair and leaves before I start my makeup. With my hair finished and my makeup done, I leave the bathroom to get dressed.

Once I put my heels on, I go back into the bathroom to check myself out in the mirror over the sink. Since there isn't a full-length mirror in the house, I stand on my tiptoes trying to get the whole look. The black simple halter-top jumpsuit is a lot like the dress I wore on Gareth's and my first date. It doesn't show a lot of skin, but it's still sexy in a sophisticated kind of way especially with my makeup and red lipstick.

"Jesus," Gareth rumbles, and I find him standing in the doorway. I swallow as he walks toward me, devouring me with his eyes. "You look gorgeous." His arms wrap around my hips and he drags me against him.

"Thank you. You look handsome." I rest my hands against the smooth navy blue material of his dress shirt and his hands palm my ass.

"I know you said you want to go out with your girls tomorrow, and I'm cool with that, but you should know Mitchell is staying with a friend and Max is going to spend the night with his mom, so the house is ours."

"I'll make sure it's an early night," I say immediately.

"That'd be good." He slides his nose across mine then my cheek to my ear, where he nips softly. "I'm still fucking you tonight." His eyes drop to my feet briefly. "In nothing but those heels and that lipstick."

"I'm good with that." I move my hands to his shoulders panting and tingling in a few specific places. I lean deeper into him pressing my tits against his chest watching his eyes darken.

"We should go," he says but he doesn't move to let me go instead he lowers his head and kisses me so wet, and so deep that I'm breathless and weak-kneed when he drags his mouth from mine. "Meet you in the living room," he says gruffly, wiping his hand against his mouth as he leaves. It takes me a minute to get myself together and when I finally do fix my lipstick then leave the bedroom knowing one way or another tonight will end well for me.

"I just can't get over how handsome you both are. Aren't they both so handsome?" Mom looks at my dad, and he gives her a non-committal grunt, which makes Mitchell and Max laugh.

"Mom, can you not freak out my boys with your craziness please?"

"*Your* boys? Oh, I love that." She beams, and I fight the need to roll my eyes then feel a hand come to rest against my lower back.

I look over my shoulder at Gareth, and he nods toward the front door of the restaurant. "Our table is ready."

"Yay. I, for one, am starving," Mom says dramatically as we move through the crowd to get inside.

"Me too," Max tells her, and she smiles down at him like he's her new best friend.

"You are just like your mom," Mitchell whispers, and I turn and mock glare at him as the hostess signals for us to follow her to the same staircase we went up last time we were here.

"Take that back," I order.

"No way, it's true. You're both nuts," he keeps whispering, and I hear my dad chuckle and Gareth make a noise like he's trying not to.

"Just wait. You already said I could come to your next meet, and because of that comment, I'm going to totally embarrass you by screaming and acting a fool every time it's your turn to run," I threaten, and he grins then shrugs like he doesn't care.

"This really is beautiful," Mom says, looking around when we reach the top of the stairs and are led to a large round table. Just like before, the space is empty except for us, and I wonder if anyone ever really eats up here.

"Good evening. My name is Simon, and I will be your server this evening," Simon says, coming forward grinning at Gareth the moment we're seated. I barely cover the giggle that escapes with my napkin. When he walks away after taking our drink orders, Gareth places his hand on my thigh and squeezes, and I look at him.

"Any regrets now?" I ask just loud enough for him to hear.

His eyes stay locked on mine, and I watch a million emotions filter through his gaze before he captures my hand in his and brings it to his lips. "Not even one."

I hear my dad make a sound and my mom pull in a sharp breath, and when I look at the boys, I notice they look content, happy, and relaxed. It's right then I know I found the impossible, a real life happily ever after, and I promise myself that I will do everything within my power to take care of it.

Gareth

Chapter 15

I STEP INTO the bar December asked me to pick her up from and scan the packed space, spotting Sage standing at the bar. I head his way, and the moment he sees me, he grins. "What's up, man? You here to pick up December?" he asks, patting my shoulder.

"Yeah." I do another scan, not seeing her from where I'm standing.

"Back left corner." He lifts his chin, and I finally see her sitting at a high-top table, laughing along with her sister April. "Do you know my brothers Bax and Talon?"

I force my eyes off December and turn to face both men, noticing they look just like their dad, Nico. It's something I probably should have realized about Talon when I saw December out at dinner with him, Sage, and Kim if I hadn't been dealing with the jealousy I was feeling at the time.

"What's up?" I shake both men's hands, and then a moment later, Wes, Harlen, and Evan walk in, joining us at the bar, soon followed by Jax and Cobi as well.

"So who's going to put a stop to that?" Wes asks, lifting his chin toward the table where the girls are seated, and I note a group of men have moved in. One of them is standing way too fucking close to December, smiling down at her like she's as cute as she fucking is.

I push away from the group and hear Evan mumble behind me,

"Swear to Christ, I could put a rock on June's finger big enough to be seen from Mars, and some dick would still think it's okay to get up in her space."

Fuck, December doesn't even have a ring on her finger to let men who might hit on her know she belongs to someone, and that's something I'm going to have to change… and fast. As soon as I reach the table, I glare at the guy who is still smiling like an idiot then lean down to kiss December's cheek. "Hey, baby." She turns to look at me and her eyes light up. Fuck, she's beautiful.

"You're here." She stands, swaying slightly in the heels she has on, so I reach out to steady her with my hand on her waist. "I was just telling this nice guy—" She points at the guy, who is now looking at me with wide eyes. "—that my boyfriend would be here soon, and then *poof*! Here you are."

"Here I am," I confirm.

"You should know—" She rests her hands against my stomach. "—I'm a little drunk." She lifts one hand between us and holds her fingers an inch apart.

"I can see that." I smile, touching my fingers to her cheeks that are tinged with pink from the alcohol she's drunk.

"You should also know—" She lifts up on her tiptoes so our faces are close. "—I've never had drunk sex before."

Jesus, my hold on her automatically tightens, and I look around the table at the girls, along with Wes, Harlen, Jax, Cobi, Sage, and his brothers. "We're out of here," I announce, listening to her giggle as I lift her off her feet, and laughter erupts behind us as I carry her away from the table and out of the bar.

When we reach my SUV, I open the passenger side door and place her inside then run around the hood. "Can we stop by McDonald's?" she asks, putting on her seat belt as I get in behind the wheel.

I turn to look at her. "Pardon?"

"Can we stop at McDonald's? I really want a hamburger."

"Babe, you just told me you've never had drunk sex. I'm not taking you to McDonald's. I'm taking you home and fucking you."

"Oh." She licks her lips, dropping her eyes to my mouth. "I like your plan better." Shaking my head, I capture her behind the neck and pull her forward to kiss her quickly.

"Glad you approve." I release her and back out of my parking space. The drive home only takes a few minutes, and the moment I pull into the driveway, I shut down the engine and get out, meeting her at her door just as she's opening it. I lift her from her seat, and her legs wrap around my hips as I carry her inside. When I get the front door closed, I cover her mouth with mine, not bothering with the lights as I walk her through the house to the bedroom before stopping just inside to press her against the wall.

"Where is Sloth?" she asks, and it takes a second for me to remember we now have a dog.

"With Max."

"Oh," she says, and then her fingers push through my hair. "Why are you stopping?"

"I'm not." I smile tearing her dress off over her head. I slide her panties to the side, finding her soaking wet, and thrust two fingers inside her.

"Oh, God." Her head falls back and she moans my name while her pussy clamps down around my fingers. Wanting inside her more than I want my next breath, I drag my fingers from her slick heat and lick them off before I free myself from my jeans.

"This is going to be fast," I warn, wrapping one hand around my cock and hooking her knee up over my elbow, and I thrust into her in one smooth stroke. "Fuck there is nothing better than being inside you," I groan, resting my forehead against hers, waiting for the urge to come to pass before sliding out and back in again. Her nails dig into my shoulders and her heels dig into my ass as I fuck her hard. "Touch your clit, baby." Her hand slides between us, and I watch her fingers roll her clit, feeling her walls clamp down around me.

"Gareth."

I pull her away from the wall and carry her to the bed, placing her on the edge. "Lose the bra and panties," I demand while lifting my shirt over my head and dropping it to the floor. I turn on the light then kick off my boots along with my jeans and place myself back between her legs, holding her open with my hands on her inner thighs. I slide into her, watching myself disappear, and then groan when she cups her breast with one hand. She slowly moves her fingers down her stomach and rubs her clit.

Breathing heavy and lightheaded from the orgasm building, I thrust into her hard and hiss her name as she starts to come, forcing me to follow. With the little strength I have left, I lift her in my arms, putting one knee in the bed then the other, before I fall to my side, settling her against me. When our breaths even out, I trail my fingers down her cheek and ask quietly, "Are you asleep?"

"No," she whispers then lifts her head and grins down at me. "Drunk sex is awesome." Laughing, I slide my hand up into her hair and pull her head down so I can kiss her then tuck her face against my neck. "I love you," she whispers against my skin, and those three words seep into my soul, filling me up in ways I never imagined.

"I love you too." I tip my head down to kiss her hair then curl her deeper into my side. When her weight settles into me and her quiet snores fill my ears, I carefully get up and adjust her in the bed, dragging the covers over her before I go to the bathroom. Once again, I didn't use a condom, and although I know I shouldn't want her to get pregnant before she has my ring on her finger and my last name, I'd secretly be thrilled if it happened, which goes to show just how far gone I am.

I clean myself up then take a rag to the bed and do the same for her before tossing the cloth toward the bathroom and getting back into bed. Once I'm settled, she seeks me out, burrowing into my side, and I curve my arm around her back then reach up to shut out the light and follow her off to sleep.

"It's Sunday. I'm not going! I'm hanging at home with Dad and December," I hear Mitchell shout, and I stop the treadmill and hop off, grabbing a towel to wipe the sweat off my face.

"You can't keep avoiding me!" Beth shouts back as I step around the corner into the living room, where she and Mitchell are facing off. Max is sitting on the couch, with Sloth at his feet and December is standing at the edge of the hall that leads to our bedroom.

"Beth, maybe—" December starts, and Beth turns on her, holding her hand up and cutting her off.

"You are not in this, bitch."

"Mom!" Max cries as Mitchell growls, "Don't talk to December like that."

"I can talk to her however I want!"

"No, you absolutely can-fucking-not," I say and she turns, narrowing her eyes on me.

"Mitchell is my son, Gareth. Your girlfriend is not involved in my relationship with him."

"When you're in her house, it's most definitely her business, and when it comes to the boys, she has the right to share how she feels. And—" I lean forward to emphasize my point. "—if I ever hear something like that come out your mouth toward her again, you and I are going to have issues."

"Is she living here with you and my kids?"

"*Your* kids?" Mitchell's voice is full of disgust, and Beth turns away to look at him. "We aren't yours."

She plants her hands on her hips. "I gave birth to you, Mitchell, so as much as you might not like it, you're still my kid."

"Being a mom is more than giving birth to a child." He shakes his head. "You'd get that if you ever stuck around for more than a few weeks at a time."

"I have a career that keeps me on the road, Mitchell," she says defensively.

"You're a glorified bartender for washed up rock stars. You're not working for the government trying to accomplish world peace," he fires at her.

Shit, I know it's wrong, but I still feel my lips twitch.

"I can't believe—" She turns, pointing at me. "—you are allowing him to speak to me like this."

"He has a right to tell you how he feels, Beth. And sometimes, the truth is a hard pill to swallow."

213

"You've brainwashed him." She glares at me then points at December. "You and her have turned him against me!"

"No they haven't." Max shoots up from the couch, and Sloth stands with him, barking once. "Dad wouldn't do that, and neither would December."

"Max." She points at him. "You need to stay out of this."

"Why?" he asks, moving to stand next to his brother. "Mitchell is right. You're not around; you're never around."

"Are you going to tell me she has been? You don't even know her."

"This isn't about December," Mitchell states, crossing his arms over his chest and looking much older than he is. "This is about you and the fact that you have been out of our lives more than you've been in them."

"I'm trying to change that. Why do you think I'm moving back to town? I want to work on my relationship with you boys."

"I heard you," Max whispers sadly, and my muscles seize from the pain I hear in his voice. "I heard you last night, when you thought I was sleeping. You said that you were leaving here soon and that you couldn't wait to get back out on the road."

"I…." She steps toward him, and he steps back. "You misheard me. I'm just leaving for a few weeks, and then I'll be back."

"I know," he agrees. "You always come back. I also know you always leave again. It's okay; I get it. It's who you are."

"What is that supposed to mean?" she snaps, and I see his bottom lip start to tremble right before he turns and takes off down the hall to his room, slamming the door before Sloth can get in with him.

Fuck.

"Oh no," December whispers, going to follow him, but Beth lunges to block her path. I move forward quick, but not quick enough. December spins around and places her hand in Beth's chest, shoving her back. "Do *not* try to get between me and my boy," she hisses, looking like a pissed off mama bear. "Get out of this house." She looks at me. "She needs to leave."

"You… You can't tell me to leave!" Beth yells as December moves around her and heads down the hall toward Max's room with Mitchell on her heels.

"You need to go," I tell Beth, and as she turns on me and steps forward, placing her finger an inch from my face, I drop my eyes to it.

"This is bullshit. You know this is total bullshit."

"It's not, Beth, and if you actually paid attention during any of that conversation, you'd understand that all your kids ever wanted from you was time and attention. You can't blame them for being pissed at you for not giving them that."

"It's your fault."

"My fault." I cross my arms over my chest. "How's this my fault?"

"You've turned them against me." She tosses her hands in the air. "You've made them hate me."

"I've done nothing but make it easy for you to see them when you've felt like it, and I have never, not fucking once, made you jump through hoops to spend time with them. You can try to make this out like it's my fault, but I'm not the bad guy, Beth. You've had years to build a relationship with your boys, but you didn't, and that's on you. Now you have to deal with the consequences."

"I love them."

"Then prove it." I sigh.

"I shouldn't have to prove anything."

Completely over her manipulative bullshit, I walk to the door and hold it open for her, and she glares at me then the door before she stomps past me. The moment she steps outside, I call her name, and she turns to look at me over her shoulder. "You should know I will never force them to spend time with you, so if you want a relationship with them, you need to find a way to earn their trust and build one."

"Whatever," she mutters before storming away.

I don't watch her go; I shut the door and lock it then head down the hall to Max's room, knocking once before I turn the handle. I find him sitting on his bed with December beside him, her hand on his back. His brother sits on the floor at his feet, Sloth lying next to him. "You okay, bud?"

"Is Mom gone?" he asks.

"Yeah."

He nods and drops his eyes to his lap. I look at Mitchell, and he gives me a shrug and a sad smile.

"You know your mom loves you," I say.

He lifts his head and locks eyes with me. "You always say that, and she always says she loves me, but Mitchell was right. She never shows it. And you should show it if you love someone."

Feeling like I've been kicked in the gut, I swallow then order, "Come here," over the lump in my throat.

"Dad—"

"Please come here." He gets up and walks toward me slowly, and once he's close, I wrap my hand around the side of his neck and dip my chin so we're face-to-face. "You're right. You should show the people you love that you love them, but sometimes people don't know how to do that, and your mom is one of those people."

"You don't have to make excuses for her," he says quietly, and I rest my forehead against his. "I know how she is, and I love her, even if she isn't good at being a mom. I just wish she were different sometimes."

I close my eyes to hide the pain his words cause and whisper, "Max."

"It's okay."

"It's not okay, not even a little bit."

"It is, because I have you and Mitchell, December, Grandma, and Aunt Selma and Sejla, along with a whole bunch of other people who love me. I guess—" He licks his lips. "—I guess I just feel bad, because she doesn't have that."

"She could," Mitchell inserts, and Max looks at him. "She could have a whole bunch of people who love her too, Max."

He stares at his brother for a long time before whispering, "I guess you're right."

"Max," I call again, and his eyes come back to me. "You can't be responsible for her happiness. It's not your job. Your job is to be a kid."

"Okay." He licks his lips.

"I love you, son."

"I know." He nods, and I touch my forehead to his one more time then squeeze his neck. "You good now?"

"Yeah, Dad."

"Good." I let him go, and he goes back to sit next to December, who wraps her arm around his shoulders and leans her head against the side of his.

"I'm hungry," she says after a moment, and we all focus on her. "Who wants ice cream? I'm really craving vanilla ice cream and french fries."

"You're so crazy," Mitchell mutters with a smile, and Max laughs while I chuckle.

"Why am I crazy? Have you ever had vanilla ice cream and fries?"

"No," the boys reply at the same time.

"Then you can't say I'm crazy." She stands and walks toward me then stops to look over her shoulder. "Well, are you two coming?"

"Sure, why not?" Mitchell gets up off the floor and holds out his hand for Max. Figuring they need a minute, I take December's hand and lead her from the room.

"I need to get a clean shirt," I tell her and she nods. "You all right?"

"Yeah." She gives me a sad smile.

"He's gonna be okay." I kiss her forehead and she nods. "Be right back." I leave her in the living room and go to the bedroom, seeing her school shit scattered across the bed where she was working when I went to go work out. I grab a sweatshirt off the top shelf in the closet and I tug it on, thinking I need to set her up a space in the bedroom where she can work when she's home. I also need to get some people together to help me move her out of her place sooner rather than later.

With that thought in my head, I leave the bedroom and usher my family out to my SUV. I drive them into town for hamburgers, fries, and frozen custard. By the time we get home, the boys and December are laughing and teasing each other, the drama from earlier a distant memory.

I drop the wrench in my hand and exchange it for a screwdriver, trying to work through the anger I'm feeling. This morning as soon as I got to work Beth called to tell me she was leaving town and that I needed to let the boys know. Even though I know they'll be okay, I'm still pissed she didn't even have the balls to tell them herself, especially after what went down yesterday. I guess I shouldn't be surprised, still it kills me that she doesn't give a fuck. The only silver lining is they now have December who will help ease the blow.

"Gareth." I come out of my thoughts hearing my name shouted and roll out from under the car I've been working on.

Once I'm standing, my mom's eyes lock on me. "Mom, what are you doing here?" I ask, wiping my grease-covered hands on a rag as she hurries through the shop toward me. As she gets closer, I see the worry etched around her eyes and the tears still wet on her cheeks. "What happened?"

"I've been trying to call you." She stops close, holding up her shaking hand that is closed around her cell phone. I look to where my phone is across the building, sitting on top of my toolbox too far away to hear with the noise in the shop.

"What's going on? Are the boys okay?"

"I think so."

"You think so?" I repeat as a heaviness starts to settle in the pit of my stomach.

"I can't get a hold of them. All the schools went on lockdown. There was a shooting at the elementary school." She lifts her shaking hand to hold up her phone once more. "I've been trying to call you."

"I…." Fuck, my knees get weak. "When?"

"I found out about thirty minutes ago. Anna, who works at the police station, called me, because I told her that you were seeing a first grade teacher when we spoke the other day. She wanted to make sure I knew so I could tell you."

"Fuck." I prowl toward my toolbox, stripping out of my coveralls as I go.

"You can't go there. The cops have the school surrounded. They're telling parents and family members to meet in the field at the high school," she says from behind me as I grab my cell phone and keys.

"Go to the high school."

"Gareth, you can't go to that school!" she yells.

"I know." I turn to face her when I reach my SUV. "December's uncle and cousin are both cops. I'm going to see if I can track them down and find out what they know." I hold her gaze. "Please, go to the high school." I catch her nod as I swing up behind the wheel then put the key in the ignition and head toward the school. Dialing December first, I listen to it ring until the voicemail cuts on.

"I love you, baby. Fuck…." I try to pull in a breath. "I love you. Call me and let me know you're okay." I hang up and dial Cobi, and when he doesn't answer, I dial Sage.

"Fuck!" I hit the steering wheel when my call is sent to voicemail then curse once more when I reach the intersection for the school, which is blocked off with a line of police cruisers. Even knowing they won't let me pass, I drive forward, and an officer steps out into the road, holding his hand up for me to stop. I roll down my window when he comes to my door. "Sir, you need to turn around. This road's closed."

"My girlfriend's a teacher at the school. I can't get a hold of her."

"I'm sorry, sir. They are telling all family members to wait at the high school. That's where everyone will be bussed to once they clear the school."

"Can you call Nico Mayson or Cobi Mayson on your radio and tell them that Gareth Black is trying to find out about December?"

"I'm sorry, sir, I can't do that." He shakes his head, and I want to get out and force him to make the call, but I know if I do, I'll be spending the night in jail.

"At least tell me that no one was hurt." I know I sound desperate. I *feel* desperate.

"Officers are still clearing the building. Right now, we don't know what's going on."

"Fuck." I shove my fingers through my hair then look down at my cell when it starts to ring. When I see December's name on the screen, my throat gets tight. I don't bother saying a word to the officer. I pull away from him and put my cell to my ear. "Baby."

"I'm okay." Her voice sounds tight, like she's trying to keep it together.

I stop and put the truck in Park not wanting to wreck. "Where are you?"

"I'm with my kids. We're waiting for a bus to take us to the high school to meet their parents."

"I'll meet you there." I squeeze my eyes closed.

"Okay."

"Keep it together, baby," I order, and I listen to her pull in a shaky breath. "I'll be with you soon."

"I have to go. The bus is pulling up now."

"Love you."

"I love you." She hangs up, and I drop my phone to my lap and scrub my hands down my face pulling in a few deep breaths to get myself under control then put the engine in Drive.

When I reach the high school, I don't even bother searching for a parking spot. I park on the grass near the front of the school and then jog toward the fields, where a large crowd of people is gathered. I search through the sea of faces, looking for December, and almost fall to my knees when I find her standing with my mom, and her parents. I rush toward them, and like she senses I'm close, she turns and locks eyes with me as I eat up the distance between us.

"We're okay. Everyone is okay." She falls into my arms then looks up at me. "I... I need to make sure my kids all find their parents."

I nod, and she takes my hand and leads me over to a group of young children who all look nervous.

"Okay, you guys. I want you all to hold hands and follow me. We're going to move away from the crowd so it's easier for your moms and dads to find you." She smiles reassuringly then leads the kids to a section of grass. She has them all sit down in a circle, and my mom and hers sits with them as her dad and I help December direct parents to their children. When the last little boy is walking away, held tight in his mom's arms, she turns to me and I wrap my arms around her, holding her close as she sobs.

"What happened?" I ask, still not sure of what took place. Really, I don't know if I have the stomach to handle knowing what happened.

"One of the teachers, Mr. Jetson...." She hiccups. "I guess he was fired last Friday at the end of day. The.... the principal saw him walk into the school today and went to talk to him and ask him why he was there. He... he pulled out a gun on her and tried to shoot her, but she managed to get out of the way. The… the janitor saved her. He heard the shot and was able to sneak up on Jetson and take him down before he was able to hurt anyone."

Jesus, I hold her tighter and bury my face in her hair. Having seen this same thing play out on the news way too fucking often, I know exactly how lucky each and every person in that school was today. "Until the police came to clear my room, I didn't know what was going on. All I knew was there were shots being fired in the school and it was my job to protect those kids. I was so scared."

"I know, baby." I run my hand down her back. "I know, but you're safe. They're all safe."

"Yeah," she whispers, leaning back to wipe the tears off her cheeks. "Can… can we get the boys and go home now?"

"Yeah, baby." I tuck some hair behind her ear then kiss her forehead, nose, and lips before turning her and tucking her under my arm. I look at my mom and her parents. "We're going to find the boys and get them home. If you're up to it, you can join us for dinner."

My mom looks at December and her face softens. "I think you and your family need some time alone, honey. I'll be over—"

"You are our family," December cuts in, reaching out her hand toward my mom, who looks at it for a moment before taking it and pulling her away from me for a hug.

When she leans back, she takes a hold of December's face. "Have some time with your boys, I'll be over later. Okay?"

"Okay." December whispers and mom nods before letting her go so her parents, who are standing close, can hug her. When they release her, I tuck her back against my side.

"We'll meet you guys at the house in a bit," Asher says placing his arm around his wife who's crying.

I lift my chin and let out the breath I feel like I've been holding forever then take my woman to go get our boys and take them home.

"I'm glad you're okay." I hear Mitchell say later that evening as I'm dumping pasta into the pot of boiling water on the stove.

"Me too," Max says, and even though I can't see them from where I'm standing, I still know the three of them are sitting side by side on the couch, exactly where they all ended up as soon as we got home.

"Do you guys know I love you?" December asks, and my jaw clenches so tight I think I might crack teeth.

"Yeah," Mitchell replies at the same time as Max.

"Good, don't ever forget it," she murmurs, and I squeeze my eyes closed.

Stepping away from the stove, I wrap my fingers around the edge of the counter, drop my head forward, and close my eyes. Like my boys, December has become vital to me, a living, breathing extension of my heart, a part of me that I know I wouldn't be able to live without. Until her, I never believed in happily ever afters, but I know she was brought into my boys' and my life to prove they really do exist.

Epilogue

"YOU DID OKAY for yourself, baby girl." I look up as my dad comes to stand next to me then lean into him when he wraps his arm around my shoulders.

"I did, didn't I?" I reply quietly, turning to watch my boys mingle with my family like they have always belonged.

"They love you."

"I love them," I say, then add, "I always knew I wanted to find a guy who loved me as much as you do. I just never thought I would." His arm gets tighter. "I'm glad I was wrong about that."

"Me too." He kisses my hair and my eyes close.

"Thank you for being the best Dad in the world." I wrap my arms around his waist and rest my head against his chest.

"I think your guys are waiting for you," Dad tells me, and I open my eyes and see Gareth, Mitchell, and Max standing together under a string of lights set up around the pergola. Wondering what they're up to, I walk toward them, and my heart lodges in my throat when Gareth drops to one knee.

"What are you doing?"

"Asking you to spend the rest of your life with me."

"And me," Mitchell says.

"And me," Max adds.

I look around at my family then at my boys, and tears spill from my eyes.

"What do you say, baby? Are you gonna run or jump?"

"Jump. Definitely jump!" I rush toward him and throw myself into his arms, laughing as I pepper kisses on his face. I lean back when he takes my hand and watch, holding my breath, as he slides a gorgeous yellow gold ring with one large diamond and two smaller ones up against it onto my finger. I stare at the ring then look at my boys and know wherever Beth is, she's an idiot for not appreciating what she had. I also know I will never make the same mistake.

One year later . . .

"Open them," I say, and both Mitchell and Max tear into their boxes wrapped in white paper then toss the tissue paper out onto the floor. I see the looks of confusion then realization fill their eyes and laugh when they both look between their father and me.

"Seriously?" Max asks.

"No way," Mitchell says, holding up his shirt that says **Big Brother #1** the exact same shirt as his brother's, except Max's says **Big Brother #2**.

"Way." I laugh, and then start to cry when they rush forward to hug me. "I love you boys. I hope you know that."

"We know. You tell us all the time," Max says, letting me go so he can hug his dad while Mitchell sits next to me.

I do tell them I love them all the time. Fearing that you will never be able to tell the people you love how you feel will do that to you. Now, not a day goes by where I don't show them exactly what they mean to me. And I'm sure sometimes I sound like a broken record telling them that I love them all the time, but oh well. Some things are worth repeating.

"Hey, December," Max calls out, sounding shy and I look to where he's still wrapped in his dad's arms.

"Yeah honey?"

"Umm, do you think that maybe since the baby will call you mom, that maybe we could call you mom too? You know just so he or she isn't confused?"

My heart lodges in my throat and I look at Mitchell and he nods then at Gareth who smiles softly. "I would love that," I barely get out over the lump in my throat.

"Awesome," he says softly, and I sob.

Eight months later . . .

"Let me have her," I hear Mitchell say, and even though I'm completely exhausted after almost fifteen hours of labor, I still find the strength to smile.

"It's my turn to hold her. You had her for-like-*ever*," Max hisses quietly, and I force my eyes open. It takes a minute for them to focus in the dim lighting, but when they do, I see my boys sitting on the small couch next to my bed, fussing over their sister.

"How about you both stop fighting over your sister?" Gareth suggests, stepping into view, and then I watch with amazement as he gently picks up our daughter and holds her against his wide chest making him look even more perfect. "Your grandma will be here in just a few minutes to take you two home."

"Do we have to leave?"

"You boys need to rest," I say, and both of them look to the bed where I'm lying, and I give them a tired smile. "Soon, Molly will be home keeping us all up, and you'll wish you could sleep."

"She hasn't cried once, Mom," Mitchell says as he stands and walks toward me.

"Yeah Mom, even when the nurse had to do some tests on her, she was quiet," Max adds, walking around to the other side of the bed.

I smile at them, look at Gareth holding Molly, and shake my head. "I'm sure she knew you guys would all protect her," I say softly. "She's lucky and I'm lucky to have you guys."

"We're lucky to have you too, baby," Gareth says, and my throat gets tight. It's hard to remember my life before them, before I took a chance and jumped. Now I can't imagine anything better than what I have, because I truly have it all.

USA TODAY AND NYT BESTSELLER
AURORA ROSE REYNOLDS

Aurora Rose Reynolds is a *New York Times* and *USA Today* bestselling author whose wildly popular series include Until, Until Him, Until Her, and Underground Kings.

Her writing career started in an attempt to get the outrageously alpha men who resided in her head to leave her alone and has blossomed into an opportunity to share her stories with readers all over the world.

For more information on Reynolds's latest books or to connect with her, contact her at auroraroser@gmail.com

Made in the USA
Columbia, SC
21 February 2025

54198588R00148